THE UNION OF SMOKERS

PADDY SCOTT

Invisible Publishing
Halifax & Prince Edward County

Library and Archives Canada Cataloguing in Publication

Title: The union of smokers / Paddy Scott.
Names: Scott, Paddy, 1957- author.

Identifiers:
Canadiana (print) 20200165771 | Canadiana (ebook) 20200166263
ISBN 9781988784458 (softcover) | ISBN 9781988784489 (HTML)

Classification: LCC PS8637.C687 U55 2020 | DDC C813/.6—dc23

Edited by Leigh Nash
Cover and interior design by Megan Fildes
With thanks to type designer Rod McDonald

Invisible Publishing is committed to protecting our natural environ-ment. As part of our efforts, both the cover and interior of this book are printed on acid-free 100% post-consumer recycled fibres.

Printed and bound in Canada

Invisible Publishing | Halifax & Prince Edward County
www.invisiblepublishing.com

We acknowledge for their financial support of our publishing program the Canada Council for the Arts, the Ontario Arts Council, and the Government of Canada.

For amazing friend, mentor, Ruth Zuchter.

I have learned to smoke because I need something to hold on to.

—Elizabeth Smart, *By Grand Central Station I Sat Down and Wept*

I'm a Pine.

Or I used to be a Pine. It's kind of a grey area at the moment. Sliver Pine was my dad, but he's been dead for six years. And there's a chance my mother might be dead; she was a Pine too. I should be able to call myself anything I want, in that case, but if Mom ever comes back I'd like her to be able to find where they've put me. Earlier today my best friend in the world called me an orphan, but I wouldn't say that about myself either. Mary Lynn is a pretty smart cookie for someone from Quinton, but she doesn't know everything about me. Not yet. I'm going to try and fix that before the end, by which I mean my end, which could be any minute now, so I'm going to have to hurry.

Having Mary Lynn and her mom screaming orders at the useless ambulance attendant isn't helping my focus any, let me tell you. Nobody is going to hear a word of this if they don't clam up. Donna Mae is keeping cool and calm, though. I know she's listening. Maybe she can give her mother and sister the highlights later. One nice thing about living a short life: it's gonna be pretty much all highlight.

Pines don't last very long, is my first point, the ones related to Sliver at least. Kind of an occupational hazard of being too close to him, I guess. People don't like to talk about occupational hazards around here, especially if they're dependent on the source of the hazard for survival. If you worked at Quinton's creosote plant you'd know what I mean. Its hazards leaked all over the place, up to the moment earlier today when it closed for good because of all that leaking.

Nobody in Quinton talked about the creosote hazards either, because that's the sort of conversation that got you fired, even if the creosote made you sick. And maybe there's times when you can do nothing about the danger, like if you're a kid forced to muck around in it whether you wanted to or not, or the guy with a huge mortgage or debt and he can't see past his own payday to notice what's happening downstream. People can get trapped by their own need to survive, even if it kills them.

So, lucky for my audience here that I'm a hell of a theme essay writer. Not that anybody in Quinton knows it yet—all my great ideas, especially the ones I've pitched at school, have gone underappreciated so far. The cold hard fact is, I could present the most killer theme essay in the world about life and death matters and some people would still come away with the same *what the fuck* look on their faces they woke up with this morning. For example, just because I've used the word *smokers* in the title here, you're probably thinking, *great, another cancer story*, and you won't bother to pay attention at all because you believe you already know where this is going: cigarettes are bad, or the creosote plant is a terrible polluter, and people catch cancer from either. *Tell me something I don't know*, you'll shrug. Well, guess what? This story has hardly anything to do with cancer, although there is that one guy who might have it, but he's not too important so I don't know why I even bring him up, except as an example of how a victim of an occupational hazard might feel betrayed and do things out of anger and/or a need for revenge.

I do have a fair bit to say about smoking, though, and why unions are important, and an exorbitant amount of information about certain dumb-assed canaries who won't stay alive that I'd like to share. Those birds start out as kind of a big deal, so maybe I'll begin with them, bring everybody up to speed on warning signs, before I get to all the really interesting and informative business about love, family, farming, hazardous materials, Saskatchewan, and how people should be treated no matter what's wrong with them, where they're from, or what kind of shit happens to them—all the stuff a killer theme essay should have. That way, when I do get to the end, by which I mean my end, everybody won't be too weepy—they'll accept that all things die eventually, canaries and Pines included, and see how it's possible to live a rich, full, and well-informed life, even if it ends in your twelfth year, and more specifically, today.

I'll start with the canaries because they are small, fragile, and depend on a lot of outside help, just like certain people I know:

One of the first things I learned when I moved to my grandparents' farm was that animals drop off all the time. That's what they're born to do. Sometimes there's an obvious reason, like an axe to the head. And sometimes death is more mysterious, like the one my pet canary Bill experienced just this morning. When I got moved here after my dad, Sliver, exploded in a ball of lightning, I was only around six and therefore pretty empty-headed when it came to taking care of anything. But during the two weeks after Sliver went up in smoke, before I got found out, I did get a little first-hand experience in what it took to look after something helpless—namely, me. Waking up in a deadly quiet house every one of those mornings was a less great experience than you might believe. Bill made sure that wouldn't happen here, and I'd come to appreciate his singing his little throat off to let me know that life, in the farm part of the world at least, was dandy. When I walked out of my bedroom bright and early this time, I was a little concerned with how quiet things were in the Bill department. Standing on my toes to see inside the cage (I'm not very tall for a twelve-year-old), I saw Bill on the newspaper liner at the bottom, his beak open and his little chest going *thip–thip–thip*. Then nothing. He didn't even close his eyes. I hollered, "Bird's dead, Gram!" Not out of shock, mind you, but because Gram could've been anywhere in our very large house.

"What?" she shouted from the back porch. Everybody screamed "what" at everybody around here a lot. Most of our conversations began that way.

"I said the damn bird's dead."

"Tongue, please," Gram called as she bustled in through the mud room and set down a cucumber-and-beet-filled basket on the kitchen table. Today was pickling day. She wore a flowery print number, and a black-and-red plaid shirt over that, her typical look for pickle work. Swaddling her hands in the grey dishtowel she'd plucked off the hand pump beside the basin, she made a beeline for the cage.

"Sorry, Gram." Gram took a fit whenever I swore. On the other hand, Grumps didn't give a shit how I talked. I poked at the bird through the wires.

"Stop that… Is it cold?" Gram leaned in for a better look.

"How the hell should I know?" I mean, Bill was covered in feathers.

"Tongue, mister," she scolded softly, so close now that her breath bounced against the back of my head. When you have a brush cut, you notice things like Gram's warm breath.

Where I came from, beating a kid was as natural as lightning. Maybe if Gram'd been firmer with me, took a swing at my head once in a while, I'd have been less of a curse machine around her. Except she'd already told me that nobody hit anybody here, which actually turned out to be the case, so I knew I was in the clear as far as beatings went. Oh, don't get me wrong, I did feel bad whenever I made her cross, and tried to limit my swearing to out of her earshot. Problem was, thanks to Grumps, I knew so damn many great words, and sometimes they just slipped out. "Sorry, Gram. Yeah, it's cold, I guess."

She stared at the little body and, like Bill, didn't blink an eye. That's how farmers are. Staring and not blinking—at the fields or the sky, or the fields first and then the sky. Whatever the attraction is—crops, animals, weather—their expressions don't say much. Whenever Gram looked at me with a frown, though, I could read that crystal clear. It usually meant one thing—worry. I don't know why. I hardly ever worried about me since I got to the farm, because except for swearing, I hardly ever stepped out of line with Gram or Grumps.

"Okay then," she said, after giving Bill a ten-count to snap out of it. "I'll get you five dollars. You'd better go get yourself another one."

I looked at her like she'd gone simple. I really didn't want to make that long hump into town just to get a bird, even if it was dead quiet without Bill. "How am I supposed to get a canary home on my bike?" I had an ancient one-speed that used to belong to their daughter—my mother, apparently—and I didn't think we lived close enough to downtown for me to transport livestock with it.

"I don't know." Gram shrugged. "Can't you stick it in your pants?"

Grumps, having just ambled into the living room to catch the CHEX farm report, tossed in his two cents—"Jesus Christ, the boy can't stick a goddamn canary in his pants. Give him the goddamn cage or something"—right before he flipped on the TV.

Big help. Now I'm supposed to haul the goddamn cage around too?

"Hush," Gram scolded as she lifted the cage from its stand. She raised the tiny latch that kept the door closed and shook the deceased bird into a trash can nearly full of crushed cage linings and bird crap. Bill perched there on top like the yellow king of Crap Hill. She handed me the vacant cage. "Same thing. Same as Billy."

"Okay."

"Couch-Newton's."

"I know."

Don't get the wrong idea about me not wanting to do what I was told. I'd have been perfectly happy humping into town if it was to buy myself a horse or a goat and drag that home on my bike. A real animal I could raise from scratch without anybody's help. I thought I'd done a pretty good job with Bill, up until today at least, and kind of hoped for bigger challenges, where I could be of more use to Grumps around the barn. A horse or a goat couldn't live in the house, of course, so wouldn't be much company in any "pet" regard, and I'm one hundred percent sure neither one can sing, so I'd miss hearing *that* first thing when I woke up. And, because keeping my farmhouse life as worry-free as possible was Gram's department, buying another canary as soon as possible made some sense to her, I guess.

After the canary introductions, I'll make one more, very important intro:

What I really, *really* mean is, I didn't want to walk into Couch-Newton's swinging that big-ass cage in case one particular clerk, a gal by the name of Mary Lynn, was working. I was funny-enough looking as it was, at least if those pinheaded insults I got at school were to be believed. Toss a birdcage shaped like a giant ace of spades into the mix of my knee-high rubber boots, checkerboard hunter's jacket, and brush cut, and I could forget about getting Mary Lynn to pick up where we left off six years ago. At least I was wearing my blue corduroy bell-bottoms.

Couch-Newton's had men's clothing, farm supplies, canaries, goldfish, and all the black dust you could ever want when it blew in from the creosote plant on the other side of the river. I usually went with Grumps. While he bought his farm supplies or clothes, I'd hang around the birds and the fish in back and sneak peeks at Mary Lynn, who acted like she didn't know me at all, which was to be expected now that she was in high school and I wasn't yet.

Today, without Grumps to peek around, I was flying solo. I'd need the nerve-calming effect of a smoke before bursting into Couch-Newton's, just in case she was on duty. Setting the cage aside, I reached into my jacket for the baggie I used to store my collection of cigarette butts. After selecting and lighting a medium-length one, I took a few task-focusing puffs, checked my look in the reflection of the store window, made sure my bell-bottoms were fully engaged around the base of my boots, then sauntered in, cage in one hand, butt in the other.

The store only ever has, like, one clerk working at one time, and Couch-Newton's is a pretty big store, with hardwood floors that creak wherever you walk. It occurred to me, as I headed for the birds, that a kid could shoplift here no problem. I'm thinking this particular crime popped into my head so I wouldn't have to explain to a certain clerk why a cool cat needed a canary.

There must've been fifty birds in that one pen, all screaming like they were on the downhill run of a roller coaster, their beady, twitchy black eyes showing lowdown panic.

The goldfish were cool, though. They knew it'd be hard as hell to shoplift one of them. I grabbed a canary out of the coop and, since I couldn't walk out the door with it in the cage, squawking mad and yellow as the sun, I did exactly what Gram told me to do—I stuffed it in my pants. Then I beetled for the front of the store, cigarette in my mug and swinging my cage back and forth all light and carefree, to prove to everybody on duty how innocent I was. I was almost in the clear when I felt a tap on my shoulder.

"Whaddaya got there, kid?"

The question shocked my butt clean out of my mouth. It fluttered to the floor and smouldered next to my boot, and because I'd preferred that everybody believe I'd spit it out on purpose, I extinguished it with my toe instead of sticking it back in my mouth like I wanted. That's when I got hit with the most ignorant slag Quinton had ever invented: "Jesus, were you born in a barn?" Sounding especially bad since it came from Mary Lynn.

I spun around with both barrels at my lip, ready to unload some education about why snuffing out cigarettes in a barn is a terrible idea, and how our barn is ten times cleaner than this dump, but couldn't stop staring at Mary Lynn long enough to say anything informative. Also, it'd been so long since our last meeting, I didn't want my first words to sound like a reciting of the theme song to *Green Acres*. With my outrage momentarily knocked on its ass therefore, all I could muster was a weak apology as I continued grinding the ashes into the wood.

She didn't buy it and, in fact, had become a little suspicious. "Stop that. What's with the cage?"

"Nothing, toots."

Kids my age don't call a dame "toots" normally, but I watch a lot of movies with Grumps once Gram goes to bed.

Even if we had a colour TV, we're black-and-white movie types, me and Grumps. Mary Lynn sure didn't expect to hear Humphrey Bogart lingo come from a short farm kid, so she shot me a first-class scowl. Maybe I deserved it. The right to call anybody "toots" has to be earned—even though in this case I might argue that I already had.

She scoured the spaces between the wire bars. "It's empty."

"Good eye."

"Do you want something to put in it?"

"Nah, your birds are all yellow. I wanted a green one."

"Then you want a budgie. We don't have budgies—just canaries."

I knew the difference; I just needed some kind of excuse for why I was trying to leave with an empty cage. Also, I couldn't help getting back at her for the "born in a barn" insult, which, by the way, if we were standing in our barn instead of dusty Couch-Newton's, I'd have taken as a compliment, since I know, more than most here, how a clean barn can make for happy cows and sweet milk.

I made a face like the thought of a canary was too disgusting to consider, pet-wise.

"Forget it. What kind of store only sells canaries?"

"I don't know, kid. I don't know why we sell them at all. I just work here." She tapped her chest, where a company name tag was pinned to her plain white blouse. The three top buttons were undone, the first two probably by design. I'd bet a million bucks she didn't know about the third one.

"You sure have an exorbitant amount of birds..." I leaned in as if to get a better look at her name "...Mary Lynn. Expecting a big run from miners?"

"You don't have to be twenty-one to buy one, kid. If you want one, I can sell it to you."

I let the misunderstanding slide. Even I hadn't begun connecting canaries to things around Quinton yet, except for the one squirming in my pants the whole time I stood there. I don't know how Mary Lynn missed it. Instead she tossed an abrupt "have a nice day" approximately in my direction and sashayed back to the counter, where a customer of the non-shoplifting variety waited.

Hell, this wasn't the first time she'd turned her back on me with barely a second thought. Though, to remind her about the first time, I'd have to take her back about six years and plop her on a pony for an hour or two, with only the back of my fuzzy six-year-old head to stare at through most of the adventure. While she'd absolutely remember the crime, it was clear she couldn't pick me out of a lineup today, had one been assembled. Which is saying something, considering the crime was horse theft. That doesn't happen much anymore. To be fair, I get reminded every day about the first time we met because I have a photograph, propped up on my dresser thanks to Gram's annoying habit of trying to keep me well-adjusted.

In the picture, I'm sitting on Bruce the pony, who looks none the wiser for the theft I'm about to commit either. I'm wearing a checkered cotton cowboy shirt with fringes across the chest. It's a little tight around the middle. Slung down my back is the telltale white cowboy hat all finer hero cowboys wear, made adjustable by a red-and-white plastic whistle attached to a drawstring. My cowboy look sort of fell apart at my short pants and black leather shoes. From the waist on up, though, my getup was pretty convincing. Del the cop thought so too, when he delivered the picture to me personally a couple of weeks after it was taken.

The scabby photographer came to town once a year, hauling Bruce by a rope behind him. I moseyed up the street to the vacant lot where he set up shop every year. I must have been the only kid in town without a picture yet because the lineup so far was just me and one girl there already, her blond whips of uncombed hair hanging across her big blue eyes. She wore a plain-as-day yellow T-shirt, not nearly the whole production number I was dressed in, and because she had a two-cent pop bottle in each hand, when I asked her if she was here to ride or to have her picture taken, she simply clacked them together for her answer. (Like me, Mary Lynn has never been a fan of idle chit-chat. She'd probably be a good theme essay writer. I hope she's paying attention now.)

"Two bottles is four pennies. Y'needs another penny." The bottles were Orange Crush, but even for the funny shape compared to most bottles, they weren't worth an extra penny. Counting off the numbers on her fingers, one–two–three–four, her bottom lip started to quiver on completing her calculations. I can't say if that was the first time my heart broke, but in recalling that day now, I'm kind of getting the feeling that maybe it was. When we heard the pony's hooves clopping on the road, I tugged on the brim of my hat and told her I'd be good for the extra.

The photographer loped up beside us; he had very long legs, much longer than the pony, who was struggling to keep up.

"Howdy," the man said, smiling. "I'm Larry. This is Bruce." He slapped Bruce on the ass. "You're here for a picture, I'll bet, cowboy." He looked straight at me.

"Yep, I'm Gene Autry." I felt around in my pocket for the money I'd brought—a wrinkled, bloodstained two-dollar bill. The photographer wasn't paying attention to me anymore, though; he'd moved on to Mary Lynn, scrubbing his chin.

"Well, hello there, little darlin'. Who might you be?"

"Mary Lynn," she whispered.

He talked loud, in some kind of made-up Western accent, but not as good as the one I'd been using. Photographers weren't known for having accents, not like cowboys. He sounded like he'd stolen his sound from *My Darling Clementine*, that movie with Henry Fonda. That's where I got mine. Plenty of *y'alls* and *howdys* and *little missys* in that one.

"So whadda we after today, little missy? A nice picture or a ride?"

She stared at her two pop bottles and then at me.

"She wants a picture. I want a ride," I drawled.

Larry's eyes had narrowed onto a place hiding somewhere in the near distance, down a path where the shadows and shapes in the trees all wrapped around the trail and buried it. My accent snapped his focus back on us.

"Howdy again," he said. "Thought I lost you."

"Nope. This is supposed to be for us both."

The photographer snatched the two bucks flapping in my hand. He pressed the money flat against his pants, then held it up to the sun. "What's that?" (He meant the bloodstains.)

"Dunno." I shrugged. "Horse prob'ly. Maybe cow."

He gave me a look like I might be jerking him, but if he knew how Sliver made his living, then he'd know bloodstained money made perfect sense. He tucked the bill into his jacket pocket and fished out a little change. I had no idea if it was the right amount or not. "Okey-dokey then. A picture for you and a ride for your sister. Is that right?"

I'd taken a little too long at getting around to correcting Larry about my relationship to Mary Lynn, at least for Mary Lynn's liking, because she piped up almost immediately, "He's not my brother!"

If all Larry had to go on were our appearances, then we were pretty obviously not related. Still, she didn't have to sound so offended. I mean, I knew she wasn't my sister. I'd seen plenty of families walk past our house when me and Sliver lived in town. Complete sets: mother, father, sisters, brothers. They had a way of behaving with each other that told everybody they were a package deal, scooting in and out of each other's space. I had lots of empty space around me, nobody cutting in and out. So I couldn't help feeling a little jolt in my heart when Larry got confused by us together, because even being mistaken for someone's brother is not such a bad thing to hear, especially when you come from a crummy two-man family. I stared blind at the coins Larry placed in my hand and kept my mouth shut, then felt a second jolt when Mary Lynn decided to clear up how we should be viewed.

Larry reached down and had his hand on my ass before I knew what hit me and, quick as a snap, was dropping me onto Bruce.

"You'll want your hat on for your picture, eh, sunshine?" Everybody who didn't know me called me sunshine, due to my head's reddish glow. Larry gave it a rub before jogging to the camera stand. A few seconds later he was out from under his black cloth and loping toward us again. "There. Now that the dirty work's done, who's ready for a ride?"

"Me! Me!" squealed Mary Lynn.

And up she went, getting tucked in behind me instead of going solo. Bruce didn't have a proper saddle, just a blanket, so our legs dangled straight down like four strands of cooked noodles.

"You guys hang tight till I get back." The photographer rubbed Mary Lynn's back goodbye, then carted his equipment back to his truck, one normal step followed by one big step, like at every other step was a mud puddle. I ran like that too sometimes, whenever something had me so excited I could hardly keep it in. On his return trip he was wearing a smaller camera around his neck, hanging from a leather strap that was much skinnier than Bruce's reins, which had shiny, jangly bells attached to them.

Larry whistled. "Giddy-up, Bruce," and the pony shuddered. Mary Lynn let out a tiny squeak and grabbed my ears, which caused me to grab Bruce's ears. Nobody let go of anybody no matter how much me and Bruce swayed our big heads as we moseyed down the path. I'd taken this one plenty by myself, and I knew the stand of scrub and Manitoba maples it led to. When we got to the trees, Larry handed the reins to me, standing back to light a smoke. Hard to believe Bruce could walk any slower, but he did.

"You scared?" Mary Lynn whimpered into the back of my head. Even for being on a pony we were pretty high up.

"Nah. My ears hurt, though."

"I got nothing else to hang on to. You got them ropes."

"They ain't ropes; they's reins. And we ain't going hardly fast... You can grab my shirt if you gotta grab somethin'."

I shook my head again and she let go, taking hold of the hunks of flesh hiding beneath my cowboy shirt. A few easy clip-clops further along and she even eased off on that. The pony was actually a smooth ride once you got used to him. We could have been gliding along on a carousel Bruce. Still, when the photographer caught up again, a little winded, he was amazed at how far we'd gotten without him. He told me I could keep steering, I'd done such a great job, and he'd stay at Bruce's rear to keep Mary Lynn company. He curled his arm around her middle to instruct her on how to restart Bruce whenever he stopped to eat from the bushes, which was every ten feet or so.

"You gotta give him a little kick in the rear end, like this." Larry pulled her ankle back then bunted it against Bruce's flank. "You see? That didn't hurt him a bit."

The photographer's hand crawled like a tanned and hairless spider up Mary Lynn's leg. Bruce, that old warhorse, sent a tremor right through me. Even as an apprentice in the cowboy trade, I could sense the pony's concern. Like I said, we'd both been down this path before.

In a voice all a singsong the photographer piped up next with "Say, I've an idea, if you guys want. Why don't we take more pictures—you two together?"

"And Bruce?"

"And Bruce."

I have to give the young version of Mary Lynn credit here, for picking up on the opening lines from the world of boys and men. She released my shirt and wrapped her arms around my middle. I redoubled the reins around my hands.

"Whaddaya want us to do?" I called to Larry.

"Just sit there," he said.

"Do you want us to make faces?"

He shook his head. "No. Just sit there, quiet. I'll take a couple with you two the way you are."

"Kay," I said. "Hey, mister, make sure Bruce is in the picture."

"What? Yeah, whatever."

"Hey, do you ever have to beat him?"

"Yeah, I guess. When I can't get him to do what I tell him."

"Should I keep my hat on?"

"For Chri— I don't care, kid. Just let me load my camera."

"What about my whistle. Should I blow it?"

"No, don't blow your goddamn whistle."

"Why not?"

"Because it won't turn up in the fucking picture, that's why... I mean, it'll spook the pony."

"I'm gonna put it in my mouth."

"Knock yourself out... Look, let's all stay nice and quiet for a piece. Let's keep everything nice and relaxed, so no whistles, no more questions. Can you do that?"

I went to tip my hat but it had slipped between me and Mary Lynn. I tugged it free and punched it back into cowboy shape.

"Three–two–one, cheese," Larry called. A second later he was staring at the bottom of his camera, waiting.

Sliver had the same type, an automatic, which people liked because you didn't have a developer looking at your lifestyle. Sliver kept his masterpieces in a shoebox in the bottom of his closet—naked pictures of his girlfriends, animals he'd knackered for farmers. We didn't have a regular family album.

Larry shook the picture to get it to develop faster. I'd seen Sliver do that too, right before he tossed it in the box. Mary Lynn went *tap–tap–tap* on my shoulder, which I found annoying. "Quit it. What?"

"I don't wanna picture."

I wondered if her family had the same kind of camera. Bruce bobbed his big old head up and down, like he was ready for anything I decided. "Why not?"

Mary Lynn took a breath and held it. "Because I don't like him," she rasped into my ear.

I could feel Bruce's flesh quiver all the way through the blanket. He even spit the sumac bunch he'd been munching on and took a few steps down the path, slow, like he needed to stretch a little before doing anything too strenuous. If he was a canary, I think he'd have flopped over and died right then. Fortunately, he was a perfectly capable pony. I tugged my cowboy hat down tight and shouted over my shoulder, "Are ya sure?" then stuck the whistle in my mouth.

"Yes, please."

"Kay. Kick the pony's ass, will ya!" I leaned forward so my whistle was next to Bruce's head and blew every ounce of my breath, causing Bruce to rear up for probably the first time in years. With a mighty shake, he bolted down the path faster than he'd likely ever bolted before.

"Where we goin'?" Mary Lynn screamed over my whistle and Bruce's thundering hooves.

"Thataway!" I shouted, tossing our next stop into the wind over Larry's fading screams.

"Thatawhat?"

In fact, I had an idea that the path we were on ran in a westerly direction. I couldn't say for sure if that was the wild west, or the safe west I liked to believe my mother was holed up in, thanks to Sliver's occasional whisky-soaked ramblings on the subject of where she got to, on the days when she wasn't dead. He was kind of fifty-fifty on the topic of Mom.

We crashed between the bushes at a full Bruce-style gallop, so not too fast relative to a real horse. Still, we had the roads, our neighbourhood, and cameras all in our rear view in no time. I spit my whistle from my mouth. The sweaty, gasping pony didn't slow.

"Hey!" I shouted behind me. "We're clear! Stop kickin' the goddamn horse, will ya?"

Mary Lynn looked over her shoulder, then eased up on Bruce's ass, which he seemed to appreciate, rumbling to a trot and, a few yards later, stumbling to a stop above a sumac's berry bunch. The break gave Mary Lynn a chance to unclench her fingers from my sides.

"How far'd we get?" she sniffled, brushing the sweatiest strands of darkened hair from her face.

"Dunno. Five miles?"

"What? I don't think so. Do you know how far a mile is?"

"Ya-huh. A fair piece."

"Well, we didn't go five pieces, that's for sure. Are we stopped for good?"

"Nah. We'll keep going soon as the horse is done his snack."

"Won't he get sick on that?" She meant the sumac berries.

"Nope." I crushed one between my fingers to show her the stain. I even popped a couple in my mouth, pinching my face immediately because they are pretty sour. How Bruce could eat so many was amazing. If he did get sick, it'd be from being a pig. "People make lemonade outta this kind. Sliver told me so."

"Who's Sliver?"

I took the reins in hand again and gave them a flick, pretending not to hear the question. Son of a bitch if I didn't get the pony's attention. He started a lazy trot without even having to be encouraged more. Larry the photographer had likely gone back to his truck to try and head us off at the pass, because that's what varmints did. I tapped the reins against one of Bruce's cheeks just in case, and he turned down a side path. Good luck finding us now, pard.

As we chugged beyond the last sumac border, I gave the reins some slack again. Bruce bowed his head to nuzzle the grass at his feet. Mary Lynn used the break to jab me in the ribs. "Hey, I asked you: who's Sliver?"

"He used to be my dad. Sliver Pine."

"Ha, that's a tree name."

"Yes, ma'am."

"I'm not a ma'am. I'm a girl."

"Ye—yeah I know."

Before I got into any gory Sliver details, Bruce whipped his nose upright, then to a direction, just before breaking into a casually determined saunter. I worried that maybe he'd picked up Larry's scent, but after about ten yards I could smell the canal too. Bruce's needing water hadn't occurred to me, and we'd been running him pretty good—for a photographer's pony, that is. I let him do the driving because he seemed to know the way. He paused here and there to pluck green shoots growing where the sun splashed in—it felt like high noon to me.

Mary Lynn flicked the back of my head with a finger. "Isn't he your dad anymore? Did he quit?"

"Quit it. Nah, I don't think so. He just ain't no more, is all."

"Well, that's dumb. What happened to him?"

"He died, I guess."

"Oh. That's too bad. How?"

"There was a storm."

"What, did he blow over?" She giggled. "Get it? Because he's a pine?"

"Yep. Nope. Lightning." I shrugged.

She took a second so the *how* could sink in, then, having decided it was full of shit, called me a liar and raised her hand like she meant to smack me. I lowered my head, just a little, and waited. When her hand barely lit on my shoulder, it might as well have been a bird perching there.

"Aw, I'm not gonna hit you," she said.

"Mighty obliged." I meant it too. According to Sliver, I deserved the smacks I got from him. He told me I forced him to do things he didn't want to. He was like those dust devils I'd see on the street sometimes, before the town began dumping creosote on the roads, sweeping in all hell-bent and then, just as quick as they'd arrived, *poof*! No explanation or nothing. Those were the days I'd comfort myself with the thought that my mom must have been a disappointment to him too. Disappointing people bonded us, made us mother and son, made being a disappointment to Sliver not the terrible thing he liked to tell me it was.

I've always been fine with Mom taking off (if that's what happened to her) and am generally pleased with her contribution to how I turned out, even if she had no physical hand in rearing me. I take what I can where I can, like how because she never got to smack me I'm free to believe she never would. And she had obviously stood up to Sliver, once at least, so I can take from that how standing up for yourself around jerks is possible, maybe even necessary. When I'm done with this theme essay for good and I've fled the scene, that last is something people are free to take from me.

The fact that Mary Lynn held back on smacking my head did have me curious, I have to admit, because I didn't know stopping was even possible, especially for someone not related to me. "How come you didn't smack me?"

"Dunno. Because you ducked, I guess. Our dog does that. I don't smack my dog neither."

"Yeah, well, I ducked because I thought you were gonna smack me."

"So does our dog. That's why I changed my mind. He's nervous enough without me smacking him. You too, I think."

"Do you still wanna smack me?"

"Nah, I guess I don't. Not anymore."

"Cuz it's okay, if you think you feel like it. I won't duck this time."

"Nah... Why would you let me smack you?"

Good question. I knew if I ducked when Sliver swung at me, when he finally did land one it came twice as hard. "Well, I guess I wouldn't really want you to. I dunno. Would you feel better if you did?"

After a second or two to reconsider the offer, she announced, "Nah, probably not."

I'll bet it never occurred to her that somebody'd just sit there and take it. Mary Lynn didn't know half the shit I knew. Then again, I had no clue the kind of stuff she knew, where her folks were, how they treated her, if they were still alive. Maybe she knew just as much as me. Or worse.

"Hey!" Mary Lynn poked me in my ribs again. "Who's Gene Autry?"

"Quit it. A cowboy."

"Never heard of him. Is he some kinda superhero?"

"Superhero?" I'd never heard that word before. I only knew cowboys.

"Yeah, you know. Like in the cartoons, with special powers."

"Oh, then nah. He's just a cowboy."

I watched TV all the time, mostly the crap shows Sliver liked, or soap operas with the barflies he brought home, but on Sunday mornings Sliver would be hungover until noon, so I had the box to myself. Maybe Mary Lynn meant Hercules and *Underdog*. To me those were just guys who liked to step up a weight class once in a while. On this particular day I was, at best, a horse thief, a fact that didn't escape Mary Lynn's need to bring it to my attention.

"You stole his horse. Why? I didn't tell you to steal his horse."

"I know. Just seemed best."

"Did you think that guy meant to do somethin'?"

"I dunno." I shrugged. "I prob'ly thought the same as you. He just looked funny. And you didn't tell me not to."

"Didn't think I had to. Who steals horses?"

"Cowboys, if they need to."

Mary Lynn tapped her chin but let the matter drop. She didn't seem all that interested in cowboys anyway. Instead she began to sway to Bruce's rhythm, her sunlit hair—much finer against the light than Bruce's whippy tail could ever be—sashaying against her shoulders. She didn't notice me staring, her and Bruce both busy with flies. I knew, roughly, what the word *sister* meant, like I knew roughly what the words *father* and *mother* meant. I'd had experience with all of one, some of one, and although technically she was still none of one, I thought it'd be fun to give Mary Lynn the sister a shot, if only for pretend and she knew nothing about what I was up to.

Our route took us into a clearing within the stand of Manitoba maples. I called it "the room" for how walled-in the trees made everything. I'd come here sometimes after Sliver got done wailing on me, tucking myself in among the tall weeds, take a seat on the one tree stump here, and stare up at the sky, rain or shine. (I'd usually bring two inches of saltines and some raisins with me, so I preferred shine, because my crackers got soggy in the rain.) I cried a little bit the first few times, until it occurred to me that nobody was around to hear, making the effort kind of pointless. So instead of crying I started hatching plots for revenge, escape. I'd sit on the stump and speak my plans out loud, like the room was full of imaginary kids like me—those were my first tries at delivering theme essays, I guess. Never mind as well that my teacher thought my theme essays stretched the boundaries of good taste. The reason I'm even so awesome at them has a lot to do with this room. I know most kids don't hatch shit. They'd flop around, wailing until their tonsils fall out, because they knew somebody'd come along to scoop them up with a "there, there." Whaddaya gonna learn from behaviour like that? Nothing useful, is what.

The path back to westerly was about a hundred yards straight ahead. By following the canal we'd be shed of Quinton in no time. I wouldn't hear the words *Spring Valley* and

Saskatchewan in the same sentence as the word *west* until after I moved in with Gram and Grumps. For all six-year-old me knew about how big and how far away west was, it might have been right next door.

"The main road's just up there a piece," I drawled.

"Thank God," she said.

Bruce nodded his agreement with Mary Lynn. White foam flew everywhere, clearing his flaring nostrils enough to decide that now was as good a time as any to sample the canal's blend of dead fish and diesel. Since no amount of rein-tugging prevented him from heading for a drink, I decided that an old-fashioned toe-dangle in the canal might be a good idea for me and Mary Lynn too. I'd give her the good news there, that I'd decided she could come west with me and Bruce.

I reefed on the reins; Bruce obliged us long enough for Mary Lynn to skid off and boost me down before he made a beeline for the water. I followed the pony while Mary Lynn stayed behind to mutter to herself. We tiptoed around the rocks to the shore, and while Bruce dove his nose straight in, I removed my shoes and pulled up a slab of rock beside him. As luck would have it, a coal barge—a long, wide, flat-bottomed boat loaded with a mountain of shiny black nuggets—plowed a great wall of water as it chugged up the canal. Bulrushes whipped back and forth, some brown heads breaking clean off with the whiplash. A second round of waves pounded against the boulders and lapped all the way up my legs, which felt great as far as I was concerned. On the other hand, poor ol' Bruce got a gallon of canal water up his snout, so he called it a day and headed back for the field.

Planted on the boat's nose was a wheelhouse barely bigger than a two-seater outhouse, a man and a woman standing side by side inside. He had his hands on the steering wheel, his eyes glued to the canal walls. The woman had just handed him a cigarette when she spotted me on the rocks, so she flapped her arms like she was signalling for help. I must have been quite the pleasant surprise, a cowboy cooling his heels at a watering hole. Maybe she knew Autry too, because she acted like we had something between us related. When I waved back, she grinned super-wide and held out her hand. We could've shaken hands, if the guy hadn't started elbowing her that she needed to pay attention to the approaching locks.

"Bruce is gone."

Mary Lynn, having finally decided to join me, waited until the barge had disappeared before making her announcement. She tested the water with a bare heel, squealed, then pulled up a rock beside me.

"Bruce is gone?"

"Yep, right after that wave nearly drowned you." She flicked water with her toes, clearly not bothered in the least.

"Why didn't you stop him?"

"Are you nuts? He's huge. Besides, by the time I got done laughing at you, he was already halfway across the field."

"Shit. What are we gonna do now?" Plan B could have been to hitch a ride on the barge, had she said something earlier.

"Do? Well, I'm going home. Mom's gonna kill me enough already."

Oh, right. In all the excitement of our escape I'd forgotten she could do that. I tucked what I had planned for us in my back pocket. Maybe another time. "Yeah. I reckon the coast is clear enough."

"Yep. I reckon too," she said, mocking my drawl. She pulled her feet from the canal and shook them dry. "What are you gonna do?"

"Me?" I tilted my cowboy hat so it could perch on the back of my head. I stared upstream. "First thing, I'm gonna catch up to Bruce. Then I'm goin' west."

"Blech." She winced as I slipped my feet into my shoes. She reached down and tied them for me.

"Thanks."

"Yep. Lookit, I better go or I'm gonna get killed. Thanks for the ride money... and stuff."

We both knew what "stuff" meant, so maybe there wasn't anything else to say in the matter. I couldn't help feeling a little broken-hearted though, if that's what this feeling was. When I began tugging on my whistle's rope to snug my hat over my eyes, Mary Lynn, having mistaken my hiding my face for something else, suggested I could come home with her. Maybe her mom could drive me west. She gestured somewhere, probably to her house.

"Nah, that's goin the wrong way. There's west." I pointed at the sun, which had moved from high noon.

She clambered to her feet and made her toodle-oos. "Wherever. I guess bye-bye, in that case."

"Adios."

I squinted at the canal's sparkle, dipping my hand one last time to wet my lips. I couldn't carry a tune worth shit, so as Mary Lynn scrambled up the slope of the bank I put my whistle to my mouth and tootled something for her, soft and low and simple. I mean, a plastic whistle only has one note going for it; even Gene Autry couldn't coax a campfire melody out of that instrument. "Too...twee...too-too...twee-eee-eee," was what I mustered. A real cowboy would've made up a terrific song about the people he let get away. Then again, a real cowboy would've had a git box or a harmonica, or a Jew's harp. Or wouldn't have let the gal get away in the first place.

My tune faded into air. I climbed to the top of the bank and spotted good ol' Bruce, standing out like a sore thumb in the field. He'd gotten about halfway to the road before another meal had presented itself. I caught up to him easy.

"Come on, boy," I said, snatching up the reins. "We gotta hightail it."

I found a fat rock and hoisted myself up. If you don't count the brief period about ten minutes later, when our paths crossed at the cop car, I wouldn't see Mary Lynn again until I discovered her working at Couch-Newton's. That was six years later, when she'd developed ways of staring right through people who didn't interest her, which is probably why she didn't recognize me from Gene Autry.

A good theme essay writer will recognize any shortcomings in his subject lesson, and introduce supporting structures where necessary:

Going from horse thief to canary thief might actually be an improvement in Mary Lynn's eyes. It was this new and improved version of me in Couch-Newton's who hung back to adjust his pants, and also because her new customer, a man with a weepy son in tow, was waving a balled-up handkerchief, the unwrapping of which revealed another dead canary. He shoved it under Mary Lynn's nose like she was to blame.

Town folk see so much less of death than us farm folks, so not too surprisingly, Mary Lynn went "ugh" at the sight and turned sharply, her shoulder accidently knocking the yellow puffball from the man's hand. The floor made a squeak when it landed, causing the poor kid to screech with horror. A hilarious scene; too bad I couldn't stay. I had my own problems pecking at me.

Outside, after checking Main Street to make sure there were no witnesses, I reached into my pants and pulled out the bird. It didn't look pleased. I hucked it into the cage and latched the spindly little door, then hopped on my bike. I thought about going across the river and grabbing a plate of fries at the drugstore with some of the five bucks I'd saved, but before I'd pedalled five feet, the bell started clanging, meaning the bridge was about to swing. Since the bird was hardly dressed for a delay this late in autumn, I decided to skip a town lunch and hump the nearly two hours back to the farm on an empty stomach.

The reception I received was typical for a farm of two hundred acres populated by three people. We spread ourselves pretty thin sometimes.

"Here's your stupid bird," I yelled into the dark house, slamming the cage down on the kitchen table. Nobody answered, Gram probably in the outhouse and Grumps likely watching the livestock report. I flicked my rubber boots against the mud room wall, went to the icebox, and grabbed a chicken leg, then stomped into the living room to announce again that I'd made it back alive. I found Grumps nodded-off in the grey wash of black-and-white TV light. I don't know why he watched the farm reports. Our farm hardly had any livestock left. I helped him kill one of the last milk cows; we whacked it on the skull with the blunt end of the axe head. Too bad. If there's one thing I learned from Sliver, it's that the sharp end is always way more interesting.

The screen door went *smack* and his eyelids fluttered, and when Gram cried, "Jumpin' blue Jesus!" Grumps woke enough to holler, "What's the matter?" because Gram only swore when it was absolutely necessary.

"Doris is dead!" she cried.

I blinked down at Grumps. "Who the hell is Doris?"

"That's what she's callin' the new five-dollar bird you bought," he grumbled, then tilted his grey head back to its normal TV viewing position. "Better go see," he said, meaning me. A second later his stare disappeared into the grim report on hog prices—and maybe thinking about warming up the axe.

"Jumpin' blue Jesus," I repeated, equal parts inconvenienced and guilty, as I went back into the kitchen.

"Doris is dead?" I asked. Using a semi-mournful tone was the least I could do for the late "Doris," even though we'd never gotten to know each other all that well. Except for shoving her down my pants, I mean, which, if I'd known I'd picked out a girl bird I probably wouldn't have done.

I found Gram slouched, both hands on the table, over the second bird corpse of the day. Another five bucks was already parked between two fingers in that V-shape bills get from being folded for about a year.

"Here. Go try again, I guess," she sighed.

"What? Why the...?" I bit my tongue before the rest spilled out.

Gram didn't flat out admit that she still had little confidence in my ability to handle living, breathing things, let alone get them home in one piece, but at least she also didn't blame me directly for Doris's death. I would've mentioned the fin I had in my pocket if I wasn't positive it'd cause a re-evaluation of how successful her project of adjusting me to farm life had really been over these six years. I took the money and tucked it in my pocket with the other bill and left Gram jamming kindling into the firebox. As far as I knew, we were the last people on the planet who used a wood-burning stove to cook. Gram tossed Doris in there for good measure, sparing me the embarrassment of hauling a dead bird back to Couch-Newton's.

I finished my chicken leg while standing next to the manure pile, then carted a few wheelbarrows' worth over to Gram's garden, to get me back into her good books. We'd been putting it to bed ahead of winter, which means, if you don't know, coating it with cow shit. After that chore was done I shouted to the house that I'd be going now—Gram's face appeared in the kitchen window, followed by a wave. I straddled my bike, cage back in hand, and turned to watch the Doris smoke flying from the chimney. I'll bet she never felt so free as right then, finally shed of a cage and all.

Once safely out of view from any farmhouse windows, I removed my baggie and fired up a smoke, a smallish one because I couldn't smoke and haul the stinking cage at the same time I was biking a hump into town. What a pain in the ass humping is, the Victoria Road portion at least, all gravel, with potholes about a yard deep and a yard wide. Plus there aren't any shoulders to speak of, just ditches, so if a car comes at me I inhale and hope for the best. The highway at the end of Victoria is paved, though, making the rest of the ride into Quinton slightly better. And since I was going back to Couch-Newton's, I wouldn't be dealing with the swing bridge that spanned the Quint River. It took more than luck to sail right on through to the east side without stopping for some tub to chug toward the locks or out into the bay. It's mostly coal barges this late in the year and they don't stop on a dime exactly.

I parked my bike against Couch-Newton's and pressed my face against the glass. A little bit of light from inside the store had started to spill onto the sidewalk. I'd be hard to miss, in case she wanted to look. Unfortunately, yet another miserable canary mourner had all of Mary Lynn's attention at the moment, so I grabbed my cage and waded into the dusty background to wait my turn.

As a theme essay expert I should note here how useful fearless observing is. For example, I got to watch Mary Lynn go through a whole range of mesmerizing expressions, some of which I'd remembered from a long time ago: the thoughtful one she used when weighing information, in this case whatever her present customer was shouting at her; the sympathetic one when she had to reach out her hand, this time for the obviously dead bird her customer was shoving at her. I don't think I stared for the familiar things about her. I was more interested in how her face had developed fine bones and smoky eyes, and what a pleasant contrast it was to the red-as-a-beet face coated with sweat and rage opposite it, the lady clearly not hearing anything Mary Lynn had to offer on the subject of dead canaries, which, not surprisingly, wasn't much.

"No, ma'am, I don't know why it would do that." Every cashier in town used that tone when fending off the complainers.

"What do I tell the kids?" the beet moaned. She wore a black shawl over her head as if to drive home some stupid point about mourning, even while the store's furnace was roaring.

"I'm sorry about all that, ma'am, but the manager says once an animal leaves the door it's the customer's problem. Did a cat get at it or something?"

"A cat? A cat? Jesus Christ, we don't own a cat. What do you think, we buy canaries to let cats play with them?"

"No, ma'am. I guess not."

Too bad. What a hoot that'd be, watching a canary take on a cat. Mary Lynn gave the bird a final eyeball. "Come back tomorrow; the manager's back then. I'll explain it to him. Meanwhile, hang on to your bird."

I had to stifle the snot before it shot out my nose, because that's a pretty funny line at the school I attend. Mary Lynn, free now to turn her impatience to the next poor sap in line, heard my snort and practically choked when she saw me step out of the shadows.

"Howdy."

"Whaddaya want now, kid?"

She sounded hoarse. If I had to guess, I'd say it was from the mix of store dust and creosote plant dust. People had to take a shower after shopping at Couch-Newton's. I whipped out my five bucks, ready to make her day. "Fill'er up," I said, rattling my empty cage.

I'm not sure what *crestfallen* means exactly; I think Mary Lynn was it, though. She might even have told me to piss off had four more people not stomped into the store at that exact moment, each waving a tiny yellow ball. This was turning into that scene in *It's a Wonderful Life* when all the deadbeats screamed at poor George Bailey to get their money the hell out of Bailey Building and Loan—only these schnooks were flapping dead canaries rather than bank books.

"Self-serve," she declared, and turned to face the mob.

The live canaries huddled in silent, glum rows on their long, wooden perches, more resigned to their fates than ever. I grabbed whatever our next bird was going to be called from his line of doom, flipped him into my cage, and, as I headed out the door, tossed Gram's first fiver onto the counter. When Mary Lynn gave me a wink, I almost died.

Maybe that's what was killing the birds—too much affection all at once. Birds are frail on a good day. A guy can barely stroke one across the head without breaking its neck. Maybe Bill had had enough of me petting him. Maybe my pants were a little too tight for Doris. It's probably for the best that I'm not too affectionate around Gram and Grumps. I have to say, though, despite all the warning signs, I liked how things were going with Mary Lynn, even if I didn't know why I should feel that way. For my next visit maybe I'd toss a few "charming" logs onto the fire and see what I could stoke.

Back outside again I heard the bridge's warning bell sound, meaning a boat was approaching. Boat traffic was light this time of year, barges mainly, when towns and factories to the north and west along the system needed to stock up on coal for the winter. Not quite ready to make my second return farm hump of the day, and more importantly, sensing an opportunity, me and my nameless new pal pedalled hard to get to the river before the bridge's steel grate swung from the pavement.

I couldn't see the troll—the creepy guy who lived in a little hut on top of the bridge, whose job it was to watch for boats, then start the whole bridge-swing procedure. Cars and pedestrians—and kids on bikes—didn't concern him in the least. I believe he liked screwing with me especially. It couldn't be a coincidence how every time I pedalled for the bridge, he'd already got the gate half-lowered. Time was on my side today, though. With the troll occupied with whatever he had to do to make that happen, I dropped my bike, and me and the canary ducked under the gate. I felt the shudder under my feet that signalled our ride was about to begin, and once the metal platform was free of the highway, I sat down to dangle my feet and watch the water pass underneath the bridge as it pivoted to parallel with the river. I caught a view of a line of cars stretching from the creosote plant to the east-side bridge gate, about two hundred yards.

Forgetting my illegal place, I yelled up at the troll's hut, "What's the deal with the plant?" He stuck his head through his window, which reminded me a little of the doorman in *The Wizard of Oz*, before he yelled down, very undoorman-like, "What the fuck are you doing on the bridge?"

If all the signs posted around here are to be believed, you're not allowed to be on the bridge when it's in motion. As a theme writer, I tend to ignore signs that tell people how to behave. I'd miss too much of the vital stuff in life. Then how would people learn anything. I hollered back some bullshit about how I'd been here the whole time and it was his fault for trapping me. With that cleared up I asked again, "What's up with the plant?" and this time he obliged enough to shout, "They shut down her down," just before flipping the bayside light from red to green to let the barge know it was safe to proceed upriver.

"For good?"

The troll had begun a full-body coughing conniption, bobbing his whole upper half like one of those yellow plastic drinking birds. When whatever had been vexing his innards passed, he managed to hack "yeah" at me, in case I'd missed the gist of his jig.

Too bad for Quinton, in that case. The plant ran twenty-four hours a day, three shifts of cars coming and going, meaning as many cars were usually heading to the plant as leaving. While that's a lot of cars at any one shift change, they were split equally, the comers to the parking lot and the goers dispersing east, west, north, south, depending. The plant made and applied the preservative for telephone poles and railroad ties. But telephone poles were going the way of the dodo, and railroad tracks were being dug up more than they were being laid down. Only the usual by-products of the plant's process—dust, scabby fish, water nobody wanted to swim in, cancer victims—persisted full scale, a downstream problem almost exclusively until today, flushed by the Quint

River out into the bay. But now that nobody was going to be making creosote anymore, suddenly everybody in Quinton was forced to have an opinion about what they had done and what they were going to do. Some Quintonians might take a big-picture, it's not such a bad thing, view, but I'll bet ninety-nine percent of the town was wondering why get out of bed tomorrow. Or why get up at all. Of the cars lined up now, some were waiting to get to the unemployment line, but maybe a few were working up the nerve to drive into the river before the bridge swung back.

A bonus to sitting on the edge of a swinging bridge is I got to watch the barge plow through the algae and the oil from inches away. I pulled Doris's compatriot from the birdcage—he'd keeled over around the time the troll let me know the plant had closed. I bounced the bird in my hand once or twice for the old time's sake we never got to have, then hucked it onto the coal mound passing below. He'd be joining Doris as a puff of smoke shortly, but perched against the black he looked like a shiny gold nugget.

I could have humped back to the farm after that. I could have dumped my empty cage on the table and shouted throughout our house that canaries nowadays weren't cut from the same cloth Bill was, that it was impossible to trans-port canaries out of Quinton anymore, that I had outgrown them anyway. Instead, with that extra five bucks still in my pocket, I wasn't concerned about my lack of canaries at all, hadn't even pieced together why they were suddenly so hard to keep alive. A small part of me entertained the idea of carrying on across the river to Big Doug's smoke shop and buying a pack of Exports—to buy my very own pack of smokes!—but a bigger part of my head was muddled by Mary Lynn, enough to even overcome a smoker's desires. Another call on dusty Couch-Newton's and its yellow-haired clerk was called for. First things first, I reached into my checkerboard hunter's jacket pocket for my baggie. The ass-end of the barge was clear of the bridge, and traffic would be moving soon, so I selected one of my shorter butts to enjoy. I spent about a dozen matches trying to fire my smoke, but eventually I got a flame to stick long enough.

A personal lesson I'll bring up from time to time, because it can be applied to people as well as smokes: I hardly ever got anything to stick to me on my first few tries.

Why "The Union of Smokers" will always be a better title for a theme essay than something like "Disgusting Habits and Where to Find the Best Ones" or "Pick on Somebody Your Own Size," which might be two halves of my point below, just not the whole:

I hope nobody is too appalled by my smoking habit. Fact is, I've been smoking my whole life, although in the beginning I was just inhaling Sliver's smoke second-hand. And even for the first few months after I got moved to the farm, I sucked on Grumps's exhales exclusively. With Sliver I got Export exhaust in my lungs, but at the farm I enjoyed Lucky Strikes, when Grumps wasn't rolling his own. At the breakfast table, at the supper table, while watching TV, lying in bed as it crept under the door. That I'd start first-hand smoking was perfectly natural therefore. I kept my smoking to late at night in the beginning, after Gram and Grumps had gone to sleep, when I'd grab a good-sized butt from Grumps's ashtray and take a few minutes to lean out my bedroom window and ponder general life crap. Plus, on a farm there are tons of stars—much more than when I lived in town. Nothing added to the pleasure of figuring things out like a borrowed two-inch butt, my ass on the windowsill, my back against the window frame, and my head tilted up to blow smoke at the universe. I'll be forever grateful to Sliver and Grumps for what I see is a gift, even if they'll never know about it.

Gram deserves some credit for my habit too. She gave me white candles. I kept one in a silver candleholder on the dresser near the window because, as everybody knows, a candle's flame kills the smell of smoke. I lit that candle at night when I had my butts, because a twelve-year-old's bedroom shouldn't smell like Big Doug's place. Her candles all had tiny wax crosses melted into the sides. We call them holy candles at school because they've been blessed by a priest. Most kids I know have maybe one, tops, given to them at First Communion. I never earned one that way, even though I'm well past the usual age for the sacrament. Gram gave them to me without all the hassle of lessons. I think she thought I must already be pretty holy, based on how many candles I went through.

Some adults, if they're superstitious about certain things, like births and death and bad storms, like to fire up a holy candle. Gram has a bushel basket's worth in the bottom drawer beside the icebox. She'd tell you how she's more religious than superstitious, but either one worked on me just fine back then. Grumps, God bless him, nailed up lightning rods. That's more practical, to my mind. He has about seven on the roof of the house, quite fancy ones he built out back in his tool shed: weather vanes with roosters, boats with billowy sails, manure-spreaders pulled by tractors. Every one with a centre pole shaped like an arrow, every arrowhead aimed straight up to heaven, daring it to hit. He's pretty talented at showing his anger without saying much.

The barns and the chicken coop, like the house, are smothered in lightning rods too. I don't think Grumps put much stock in Gram's candle beliefs. He can be pretty cold-hearted when it comes to other people's superstitions. Farmers have to be realistic about life, even for all their looking for signs in clouds and bird flocks and almanacs.

Gram will light candles if an animal is about to give birth— cows, pigs, sheep, and every kind they own, except chickens. Personally, I think it's because chickens have what Gram calls a pecking order, where everybody gets to bully somebody below them. Not candle-worthy behaviour, in her mind.

Once, when I was new to them, Gram took me to the coop so we could watch the chickens. She showed me how to tell who went where by watching how they ate. Nobody wanted to be in with the low chickens, that's for sure. Those low chickens got pecked nearly to death just for trying to grab a snack—which might as well have been their actual death, because when a bird got to looking rough enough, Grumps plucked its raggedy ass from the coop and killed it for supper, before the other chickens could. Whack it with an axe, he would. And when the lowest hen became our supper, big deal. Those stupid chickens just aimed their beady little eyes at the next lowest sap in line.

I never got told what it was about one chicken specifically that pissed the other chickens off so much, although Grumps did offer up a general theory once: "You have the obviously weak and the not-so-obviously weak," he said. "Just like with people. Only, chickens have a sense about who is what. If a chicken is deformed in some way—inside or out—everybody knows, and that'll get the low ones pecked."

"Whaddabout people?"

"People aren't cooped up. They can run."

I guess. But what I believe now is that all chickens are all born low chickens, all humble and afraid, and the ones who didn't stick up for themselves early on got the business end of the bullies. Thanks to Sliver, I was familiar with bullies, so I decided that my first order of farm business once I got settled would be to reorganize the chickens. I hung around the pen, studying their goings-on until, after determining who went where, I gathered up some stones and hucked them at the bossiest one in the flock, every time it went after a weak sister. My plan was to huck stones at the bullies until they learned to behave themselves. *Poof!* went the feathers when I beaned one. *Poof!* went their smug looks and their uppityness as they ran for cover in the coop or up the plum tree. The weakling henpecked would scuttle helter-skelter a little at first and wonder where all the beaks-from-hell had gotten to, but eventually, when they saw the coast was clear, they'd cozy up to what they likely hadn't had in six months, which was a meal in peace.

The first few times after they got beaned, the pushy chickens would creep back down the wooden wheelchair ramp that chicken coops have for some reason or hop down from the lowest branch of the tree, twitching their heads here and there, not settled into my new arrangement just yet. They'd poke around the feed trough, a little suspicious over what the frig had just happened, until spotting a lesser chicken eating free and easy, and take a bite out of it. So *whoosh!* here comes another stone, and *poof!* there go a few more feathers, and up the ramp everybody would scuttle again, on the world's ugliest feet. (Grumps swore by chicken's feet, though—a delicacy, he said. You're supposed to peel them like shrimp after they're cooked. Well, I didn't know much about shrimp at the time, but I knew a lot about what chickens stepped in all day long, so I let Grumps help himself to my plate.) Finally, after a few days of retraining, the chickens were so beaten up by stoning that everybody was pretty well converted into equally humble chickens. At least until the once humblest chickens saw an opening and promoted themselves to top chickens, meaning I had to huck my stones at *them* now.

Pecking orders are very complicated and time-consuming, and need a sharp, continuous eye to keep everybody sorted. Also, the result I'd hoped for, some kind of pleasant community full of happy, equal chickens, never happened. The stupid birds just kept shuffling their positions back and forth. Worst of all, every chicken became so skittish that they forgot to lay eggs, which on a farm is their whole point for being around, apparently. Poor egg production became a topic of conversation at the breakfast table after Gram tried feeding us porridge instead of scrambled eggs. Then, one morning after a particularly poor oatmeal breakfast, Grumps invited me to join him on a walk. He had an axe in his hand, so naturally I was excited all to pieces, until our walk concluded at the chicken coop.

"What are we doin' here?" I asked.

"Well," he answered, "I gotta thin the herd."

"Thin the herd? The chicken herd?"

"Yep."

I felt a rush of panic like I hadn't felt since I'd moved to the farm.

"We raise chickens so we can sell their eggs. If they don't lay eggs, then all they do is eat food. And that job's taken." He rubbed me on the head, I guess in case I mistakenly thought he meant me.

Against a wall of the coop sat the stump of wood I used as a stool when I hucked my chicken rocks. Its other purpose was as a chopping block—I could tell by all the red on the end with the bent nail. Grumps would slip a chicken's neck under the bent nail, its head sticking out one side, her feet in his hand on the other. He'd pull the body to stretch the neck, then *whack*! Clean as a whistle, and pretty spectacular to watch about a second later.

"Come on." He waved me toward the pen. "Chase a chicken to me."

That's why Grumps needed me, I figured, for my chicken-herding skill. He didn't know about that other thing, my rock-throwing skill.

Boy, the chickens remembered, though. As soon as I stepped inside the pen, they hightailed it for the plum trees they'd normally use for shade. This day it was a last resort.

"Hmm," Grumps growled at the treed chickens. "Like they'd seen a fox."

"Yeah," I assented quickly, my eyes fixed on the trees and the restless hens, anywhere but at him staring down at me. "Maybe we got foxes."

"Throw some rocks at them trees, will ya? See if you can flush 'em down."

I didn't want to tell Grumps they were here in the first place because of the rocks, and hucking more wasn't going to help. Nevertheless, I lobbed a couple half-hearted stones.

"What's the matter? You got more arm than that." Grumps stood by the coop door—the people one, not the chicken hatch—tapping the head of the axe against the palm of his hand.

"I know," I muttered before whipping a rock overhand and, totally by accident, plunking one. The poor brown hen cackled like crazy, wobbled, then made the mistake of jumping to the ground. She immediately trotted toward Grumps. Maybe she didn't see the axe, but likely she was more worried about me.

Lopping off a head was regular business on a farm, nothing personal, therefore Grumps never made a big production out of it by taking the opportunity to force some larger life lesson down my throat while the axe was coming down. My dad, Sliver, loved life lessons, only they came at the end of a broom handle. And as the low chicken at Sliver's coop, I was always on the receiving end. From my experience it was best to let the lessons land, heal up, then move on, make your plans in peace. If these stupid chickens had done that with me back when I was stoning them they wouldn't be in this mess. I mean, nobody told them to stop laying eggs.

Grumps snared the hen by her feet. She flapped and squawked, but all she shook free was feathers. The other chickens, rightly alarmed, began screaming for the coop like it was church at the end of times.

"While I'm dealing with this one, crawl in through the hatch so nobody gets out, and grab me another."

I'll bet anything the expression *whole world upside down* came from farmers swinging chickens around by their lizardy feet, their pea-sized brains not understanding what had changed, and for the first few feet of wiggling myself inside the coop, I was kind of on board with that thinking, now pretty much eye to eye with the chickens. If I had been a low chicken, they could've pecked the hell out of me. Except I think they recognized me, because they all backed off, jamming themselves into a corner. I stood up and, while scraping the chicken shit off my hands, heard the sound an axe made when it hit wood.

"Goddammit," I muttered, suddenly pretty tired of the whole chicken-whacking business. Then I spotted an egg in one of the boxes.

"Hey, Grumps. Wait! I found an egg." Don't know why I said wait, knowing it was already too late for the one chicken. I hoped it wasn't the egg-layer.

"An egg? No kiddin'?" He didn't sound guilty for the news, even after offing a chicken.

"For real. I guess we don't hafta kill 'em, eh?"

"One egg ain't much. You got another yet."

"Nope."

"Are you gonna get one?"

I prepared myself for a life lesson like Sliver used to apply and told him, "No, sir."

"Good. Come on out then," he said.

I assumed he meant how I went in, so I got back down on my knees and crawled through the hatch, and down the ramp. When I picked my head up I saw the upside-down chicken pecking at grubs around the pen, her head on and everything. Grumps was sitting on the chopping block, having a smoke.

"Hi!" I shouted to the hen, galloping toward her like she was a long-lost sister. But when the bird took off for the plum trees I changed directions and skipped toward Grumps with a stupid-wide grin.

"The eggs will come back," he said. "The chickens just gotta be allowed to be chickens. So we'll leave them be for a little while, to get themselves grounded again."

"Yessir." I nodded, even if I didn't know how "grounded" applied to chickens—as far as I knew, it only applied to lightning rods.

I think he meant what he said to be one of those useful lessons we farmers—and we essay writers—should pass on to the simpletons in town, for those who don't know chickens from canned tuna, on how to treat small animals in general. Me and the chickens got along pretty good after that, even if one or two might've pissed me off a little, behaviour-wise. I let them be.

My other essay point is how, after he'd finished most of his current cigarette, Grumps snuffed it into the ground and went back to the house. I plucked the butt out of the mud and hid it in my pocket. I didn't know what I was going to do with it yet, but it was decent-sized enough that if I wanted to, I could have fired it up after everybody went to bed. I've been smoking butts almost exclusively since then, like the one I finished two seconds before the bridge bell began chiming, announcing that everybody could start doing whatever they had left of the rest of their lives. I flicked the stub of that crusty smoke into the river, scooped up my bike, and aimed it at Couch-Newton's.

A tiny meteorite whizzed past my ear before I could mount my bike, ash and sparks exploding on the ground right in front of me, coming to rest among a hundred other spent butts. I looked back to find the troll leaning out past his hut's railing, two brown-stained fingers aimed at me. "Read the goddamn sign next time, kid," right before wiping the tar from his last coughing fit. I don't know what kind of chicken the troll would be. He was pushy *and* weak. At first I'd have told you he was a top one, for how he controlled the flow of cars and boats and, whenever the opportunity presented itself, peck at me a little. My opinion of his place would change later today, but for the time being if he clucked anything else my way I didn't hear it. I was too busy scrambling after his butt, which had to be snuffed out before it burned down any less. While I was in the neighbourhood, I gave the other butts in the pile the old once-over, the keepers going in my baggie.

Troll butts, is what I call these. All my butts got personalized brand names, like gutter butts or Grumps butts, names mostly source-based, the way tobacco can be from Tillsonburg or Virginia. The difference is mine have been enhanced by the elements after the fact—rain, gravel, creosote. The environment adds to their flavour. Most of the troll butts looked to have been here from before the last rain, making that "nigh on a month of Sundays ago," according to Grumps. Naturally we in the butt-collecting biz prefer butts with at least an inch of smokeable left. Around town lately I'd been lucky to find anything half as long as this one. Quinton's cheapskates would smoke the filter if they thought there was a flake of tobacco left, and judging by the pile here, the troll was pretty typical. Today's flare was pure gold—a solid two-incher.

A guy can tell a lot about a town's viability by the quality of cigarette butts on the ground—the town's fortunes a reflection of what its citizens are willing to flick away. It's one thing to barely be able to buy your smokes, and a whole other kind of wealth if you can toss out a half-smoked cigarette. I've found the best butts were at bustling job sites, all the union lads barely half through one before the break whistle blew and they were back to work, happy as clams, never mind the butts left behind. Brand names too, king-size, two inches plus before the filter. They'd just fire up a fresh one for the drive home, to a house made complete by a fat yellow canary singing all the livelong day. Nobody getting whacked. Nobody running away on a horse. Nobody jumping into the canal with their kid while tied to a rock. (I'll get to that.)

The troll said the plant was closing for good. I guess that means even I won't be able to escape the hardships coming Quinton's way, the quantity and quality of a day's normal offerings, butt-wise and otherwise, severely limited as I go forward. As for those people who might be confused by the word *union* in my working title, and who can't wait to point out that, so far at least, there's just been one butt smoker humping to and fro, and might ask, "Who the hell has he got around him to form a union with?" Or, more insultingly, "Who the hell would want to join a union with that guy in it?" It's true that there aren't too many solo experiences I don't enjoy, like puffing on a butt in the living room when Gram and Grumps step out on bridge night, or puffing on a butt while fishing at the canal for mudcat. Or being the last guy left on the bus for the ride home from school, sliding down the window and sneaking a drag or two. To be fair, I said I was a collector of butts, not friends, so you'll have to sit tight and see what happens with this union business before you judge the success of this theme essay, even if you've already made up your mind about the smoking.

I tapped the black end of the troll butt on my tongue to test for heat—nobody wants a flare-up costing him his whole crop—then dropped it in with the rest and choked the baggie's neck off with the twist tie. It's important to choke the neck good, otherwise your clothes'll smell like a pool hall. Gram has a sniffer, and she does the laundry.

After a quick sniff of the result, I was on my merry way again. I had one whole smoke in there, courtesy of Grumps's sound napping yesterday afternoon. If I could figure out some way of getting Mary Lynn to stick around long enough, she might see how I have potential in some capacity. Giving Mary Lynn my whole cigarette would buy me about twenty minutes of convincing time. Hopefully I wouldn't need any more than that, since I already had my foot in the door—even if she didn't really remember me yet.

The bridge is the highest point at this part of Main Street, making for a peppy downhill ride when biking east or west. Ideally you'd want to be pointed west, because on that side of town, along with Couch-Newton's, there's the bakery, the health clinic that used to be a whole hospital, a ten-pin bowling alley, the jewellery store, a meat market, the other Catholic school, the Catholic church (and just about every other kind of church), the road to my grandparents' farm, and, eventually, the graveyard. In short, everything anybody'd need for a full, happy, and well-fed life. Point yourself east if you want—the speed will be the same—but that way's the now-closed-down creosote plant, Sliver's old pool hall, my Catholic school, and the neighbourhood where we used to live. My bus takes me to school nowadays, so even I don't go through my old neighbourhood anymore, unless I'm walking the shortcut to the canal on the days I'm asked to leave class for being a handful.

I was whistling full-steam down to western Quinton, toward Couch-Newton's and Mary Lynn, until some butt-hole opened his car door and sent me and all my potential topics of conversation flying. Lucky his window was down. I was free to go ass-over-apple cart clear to the next parked car while my bike stayed put, jammed into the driver side door. I hadn't even stopped skidding before the guy was out and screaming, "Are you fucking crazy, kid?"

"What?" I sputtered through a swelling lip. Wouldn't you know, that lousy ace-of-spades birdcage was sitting in the middle of the road without a scratch. A second or two later, when a passing tow truck sucked it underneath, I wasn't upset at the sight of the chalk-white line it etched into the road.

"Look what you done to my car!" he cried, both arms gesturing at his door.

"Fuck your car," I spat as I tugged myself up onto the curb and out of traffic. I took a gander anyway while brushing stones from my head. My bike stood straight up, bicycle-rack style, the front tire's rim clenched to dickhead's armrest, which was now punched clean through to the sheet metal.

"Fuck my car? Fuck you, ugly," the driver steamed between grunts as he reefed on my bike to free it. Pedestrians circled like a brownish-orange puddle behind his car. Everybody, including the driver of the car, was identically stained, especially around the upper thighs of their blue jeans, likely from wiping the creosote from their hands right before lunch. They wouldn't have much sympathy for me. The driver tossed my bike to the curb. A couple of people clapped in support of the chuck.

The westbound traffic, having been released by the bridge troll, crept bumper to bumper like a funeral procession. Most cars had their headlights on, and the ones that didn't turned them on when they got to the scene for a better look in the growing dusk. Every car's lower third was permanently caked with backsplash and grit. The plant donated a creosote by-product to the town to pour on the roads as a dust suppressant after the Ministry of the Environment told them they could no longer dump it in the river, on account of it was killing the fish. Watching the cars from slightly lower than eye level, I was reminded of a thing Grumps told me about how Gram and him and just about everybody else in Spring Valley, Saskatchewan, when leaving for fertile Ontario, made their own long procession on the Trans-Canada Highway: all they brought with them of their home province was the dust caked to their cars, he said.

With one eye on the driver's boots, twitching inches from mine, I reached into my pocket for my baggie. His boots were coated to the same black as my rubber ones, but lacked the cool red rubber stripe mine had around the top and down the back. I rooted around for a reasonably lengthy nerve-calmer, something to get me through a personal accounting of my various bruises, then sparked a match plucked from one of the six packs of matches kept in the baggie as well, edging the flame toward the butt. Usually my stupid nose puffed out about a dozen before a butt got lit, which is why I carry so many matchbooks. I might've been sucking on the one the troll flicked at me. It tasted that fresh. I hardly coughed at all.

My assailant growled when some poor slob called out, "You okay, Tab?"

Jesus, somebody'd named this knucklehead Tab!

Tab scoured the jumble of pumpkin-stained gawkers for the voice, then dipped his head. I wanted to shout, "He was in the goddamn car. How fucking hurt could he be?" but plugged my mouth with my butt instead. The creosote plant has (had?) a union. You have to be careful to not step on union toes. I think Tab knew what I was thinking, though, because he spat a gob of chaw between my legs to get my focus back to him.

Another creosote victim offered to call Tab a tow truck, which prompted a second brown gob to erupt from Tab's pursed lips and land very nearly on top of the first one. I'll say this for the guy: he could spit like a sonofabitch. "You're payin' for the goddamn tow truck."

"Screw you, Tab."

A couple of snorts arrived on my behalf out of the ever-growing crowd. A street lamp had Tab and I spotlit, making us a happy little sideshow in an otherwise grim day. Tab shifted in his boots, the spotlight probably an uncomfortable place for him. Me, I've been under them plenty. Reading theme essays to my class and getting heckled for trying to introduce farm-fresh ways of looking at things, public speaking contests, and getting the bum's rush by ancient legionnaires who resented my take on the good old days, you name it. I was one well-rehearsed asshole, compared to Tab.

"What'd you say?" he huffed, struggling to hike his forty-thirty union pants up past his crack (forty waist/thirty

48

inseam, Grump explained to me once during a visit to Couch-Newton's for thirty-thirty farmer pants). Wranglers these were, worn by every guy who worked at the plant, with a faded circle on the back pocket from cans of chew. Nobody could smoke in or near the plant, for all the oil or tar or whatever it is that stuck to the floors, the walls, the ceilings, and, obviously by accident, the logs. The whole place was one big inferno waiting to happen. Tab's teeth, displayed each time he sneered at me, were yellower than canaries, but no yellower than nearly every other unemployed adult in this town. Hardly anybody in town ever smiled at me, and if they did, I knew they meant it as a caution light: You're entering dangerous territory.

Tab pulled his forward-most boot a half-step back, as if meaning to kick a field goal with my head. He might've attempted one if so many people weren't standing around. I took a long, slow drag and blew smoke all over his toe, just to test how much of me he could stand before he combusted. Nobody ever gave me enough credit for the size of jerk I could be, which I would only be in town anyway; never on the farm. I liked that place and its people, and would especially hate to have Gram and Grumps's last direct descendant (depending on Mom's whereabouts) be some disrespectful kid they took in out of the goodness of their hearts. My so-called classmates, on the other hand, have obviously never had the benefit of farm living as a behaviour modifier, and were always quick to bust my chops about things like brown sugar sandwiches made with homemade bread, milk in a mason jar wrapped in a damp towel...chicken feet Gram snuck into my lunch bag. I would have preferred conversing with them—outside of this essay format, I mean—about how lunches on a farm are prepared, but those dumb jerks never gave me a chance. They'd immediately flap their arms and go *buck–buck–buck*, or whatever they think a chicken says, the second I peeled back a chicken foot skin. Dummies.

If I could hand out superpowers to kids, I'd give them an immunity to being ganged up on. In my limited experience, that's when the most damage happens. Not with belts or fly swatters or fists, but at the hands of the crummy group behaviour of so-called peers. Since I can't hand out superpowers, I hand out theme essays, like this one. Not that this one will do any more good for my classmates, though I know for sure Donna Mae is still listening.

Tab leaned his face as close to mine as his forty-thirty frame would allow and rasped, "Lookit, you little shit. Somebody's gonna pay for the tow truck and somebody's gonna pay for my door. So why don't you tell me your goddamn name and where you live, so I can wring the money out of the poor excuse for a parent that gave birth to you?"

Incredibly, I started feeling sorry for the guy. Gram and Grumps weren't flush enough to pay for their own car repairs, let alone his. I kept my yap shut this time. I had two, maybe three, drags left in my smoke and I needed focus before scraping myself off the road and going on to Couch-Newton's. Anyway, Johnny Law was going to be doing all my talking for me in three…two…one.

The cop pulled up in his black-and-white, its flashing light pumping red up and down Main Street. He bulled his cruiser right next to Tab's car and hopped out.

"Hey, Tab. Kid… Everybody okay?"

The cop's name was Del. We'd met a couple of times already, by which I mean on every important occasion in my life. Not that I saw his arrival this time as a sign or anything, which I should have, except my brain had gotten muddled by gravel and asphalt. He remembered me about as much as Mary Lynn did, and I wasn't going to remind him either.

"Hell no, everybody is not okay." That came from me, taking Tab and Del both by surprise.

Del shot a grin in my direction, then just as quick dragged his hand over his mouth to hide it from Tab, who blubbered, "You see, Del? The kid's a jerk. And a menace. He dove right through my window...and look at my goddamn door." He flapped his arms again, some at the sight of the door and some at the sight of me.

Officer Del, long and lean, towered over the damage like a weathered telephone pole that'd seen too much sun and not enough preservative. He shone a flashlight at the broken door and whistled. Del could whistle like a son of a bitch. He even knew "Bald-Headed End of the Broom," which I never held against him, even with my history.

"So what happened exactly?" asked after his tootle.

I believe the "exactly" was meant for Tab more than me, so I let him go first.

"He hit my door."

"Yeah, I got that. Why?"

"Because he went too fast...Fast!" Tab swooshed his hand through an imaginary window in case Del was the only cop in the world who couldn't wrap his head around the notion of speeding.

Del swung his light at my crumpled one-speed, lying where Tab had tossed it.

"Whaddaya get on that puppy? I mean, before." He walked up to the bike and rapped a tire with his knuckles.

I shrugged. "Depends on the wind direction. Two...three." The stupid bike didn't have a light, let alone a speedometer, so how should I know. I was missing Del's point too.

Del crouched down and gave the pedal a whack to make it spin. "How's the brakes?"

"Brakes're okay," I muttered.

"I'd say," he agreed. Pointing to the streak of black rubber dust on the pavement, he looked up at Tab. "How long you figure that is?"

"Dunno. Ten feet?" Tab overestimated.

"Really? Looks closer to four to me." Again with the flashlight.

Actually, the streak probably measured less than three, but I'd wised up and had no complaint with the line of questioning now. Poor dumb Tab still didn't see where Del was going at all.

"What's your point?" he asked.

"His point is," I said, "if I had ten feet's notice before you swung your goddamn car door open, I wouldn't've plowed into it."

Del told me, "Shush." He removed his hat to ask me what would turn out to be a life-changing question. "What's your name, kid?"

I looked at my shoes. We were entering shaky waters. I should've told him that: "Shaky Waters." In my next life that's what I want people to call me. This time, when he asked again, I told him a half-truth. "Pine."

Del repeated the name, after which time came my turn to catch the full bore of his eye.

My dad wasn't too famous around town. Oh, he had his followers, I suppose. Mostly the women he brought home from bars, and the sports figures at the pool hall. I knew what Del was searching the sky for, though. One of those highlight moments we shared together, rumbling for old time's sake again. I think the black cloud he settled his eye on today was the one where I had escorted him through my empty, rancid house six years ago.

Boom!

"Shit, you're Sliver Pine's son, aren't you?"

I gestured in the affirmative.

"Well, I'll be. You got big, kid."

"Thanks."

I might've started blushing, because my face felt warm. Thank God it was dark out. Anybody else and I'd have heard that as a slam, since I had no height to speak of. Not with Del. He'd been pretty supportive each time we've met. Also, he could just as likely have meant wide. I was very broad-beamed for a kid my height, thanks to all the hay bale lifting I'd been doing on the farm.

"How's your grandparents?"

"Fine. They're fine."

Del scratched his scalp under his cap. He looked at Tab, who had finally got the gist of Del's chat with me. We were compatriots, was what he rightly read.

"Jesus Christ," Tab started pleading. "What about my car?"

"Well shit, Tab. The effing accident's your fault to begin with. I mean, Jesus. You can't swing your goddamn door into traffic without a gander at your mirror. I mean, if he wanted to, the kid could have me charge you."

Del brought a sincere amount of arm action to his observations. Enough that Tab and Del both winded up staring, nearly sympathetically, at me. I snuffed my filter out on the ground with my boot and shook my head to mean that I'd let Tab's poor math slide this time. Bad timing. The sound of scraping metal arrived—I shit everybody here not—at that exact moment. The tow truck had returned, its strobe catching clouds of future dust devils, its undercarriage dragging the birdcage I'd forgotten all about. Which had to be foil paper by now.

"What about my birdcage?"

"Your *what*?" they asked together.

"My cage. He knocked it clean outta my hand."

Gram and Grumps shouldn't be on the hook for a cage, let alone a car door.

Tab tossed a sneer at the cop, then shut it down when he saw Del scrubbing his chin. Sometimes the most basic and obvious math is actually as easy as it looks.

"What about the cage, Tab?"

"Are you freaking serious?"

"Well, either get Harry to chip in or fork over the dough yourself. I don't care. All I know is, there's Couch-Newton's. I don't want them seeing a nickel from the kid."

Harry, the tow truck operator, laughed. He was rich. He had his name plastered on the side of his truck, in case there were any doubts who owned the company. The whole independent-operator side of town acted like they didn't have a care in the world. That's because they named their "thing" after themselves: Harry's Towing, Cal's Cleaners, Al's Tires, to let people know they weren't beholden to outside forces. Maybe the creosote plant should have named itself after something local. It'd still be in business if it had, I'll bet.

I will point out a less obvious positive about unions, the one where, if you consider the number of people walking around Quinton looking as if they've got the weight of the world on their shoulders, all those shoulders should make the world less of a burden:

Tab cast a broken glance over what was left of his creosote union crowd. I'd seen that *Jesus H. Christ, can this get any worse?* look on Grumps sometimes. Farmers get the look when we think we have an agreement with nature and nature isn't holding up its end. But that's farms and nature for you.

We try to not insult the earth too much. On the other hand, the creosote plant carried on night and day insulting the earth, killing fish, killing people, and even trying to play God a little by making wood last longer than it's meant to. On his worst days, Grumps's shoulders never drooped like Tab's did now, so hopefully Tab was beginning to suspect that nature was getting back at him by tossing a kid into his car door. I mean, you can't lose your car and your job on the same day and not see it as a sign that you've pissed off something.

After Harry hooked the front bumper of Tab's car to his tow cable, he ran around to where the black-knobbed levers were and pulled one of them down. The front end of Tab's car began to rise. I scuttled over and reached underneath the chassis to jerk Gram's cage off the truck's muffler, all a mass of tangled wires now, and totally shed of any signs of cageness. Harry clambered back into his cab, honked, then bulled his way into the traffic. As an independent business operator, Harry could come and go as he pleased.

"Whoa!" Tab suddenly shouted after the tow truck. "Whoa!" one more time, running to his car to grope around the front passenger seat. A moment later he held up a small bundle wrapped in white tissue paper.

In good ol' Tab's case I might have been wrong. The weight of the world could get a little heavier. About one dead canary's worth.

Tab and me left Del to his note-writing and walked the half block to the department store, more or less side by side, all in silence. Despite having to drag the bike all by myself, I couldn't even be bothered hating the guy anymore. When I caught him sneaking a gander at me after I'd stopped to remove my baggie again, I turned the open end to him like I was offering him peanuts.

Tab declined the gesture, muttering, "Fuck me," under his breath.

"Suit yerself," I said, shrugging.

I guess my gesture didn't go totally unappreciated because after three yards and a couple more "fuck me's" Tab tried striking up a regular conversation.

"How long you bin smokin', kid?"

At least he had the decency to call it smoking. I held my cigarette up to a street light, estimated the number of drags I had left, then, returning it to the corner of my mouth, said, "Dunno. Goin' on a while," because that's how Grumps talked to other adults. Goin' on this and nigh on that.

Tab made a noise in his throat, then reached for his back pocket and his can of Copenhagen Wintergreen. He twisted the lid and tilted the can toward me. Inside were the tiniest tea bags you ever seen, filled with smokeless tobacco. I waved away the offer, tapping on my coat pocket. Smokers and chewers—we're two different breeds.

With our courtesies out of the way, and having reached Couch-Newton's in one piece, Tab asked me to give him a minute inside by himself. I was okay with waiting. He could spin events however he liked, as long as it didn't cost me money. I leaned my bike against the wall and perched my ass sidesaddle on the seat. Del, done with his notes, appeared through the cloud of my next-to-last drag and into the light cast by the store.

"You know, I'm almost certain there's a law against that." He pointed a thick finger at the ciggie pinched between my thumb and index finger.

"Prob'ly," I admitted. I took one last hit of my tiny, four-pull butt and dropped the remainder on the sidewalk, also likely against the law, littering or something, and ground it into dust-enough that a gust blew it clean away.

Del poked my bike with his toe. "You okay about getting home? Do you need a lift?"

I hadn't noticed how the front tire resembled a pizza with a slice removed and, rats, I'd even forgotten about the hump back to the farm. Grumps's car was another piece of broken crap at the moment. We were six wheels of crap today.

"Nah, it's cool," I lied. "My grandpa will pick me up."

"You sure?" Del asked. "We can throw your bike in the trunk. Maybe I can explain to him what happened."

"Nah, it's cool," I reminded him. He meant to be nice, but sometimes help is pity in disguise. Which leads to self-pity. I don't have time for that.

"You sure they'll be fine about everything?" he tried again.

"Yep," being pretty close to true enough. "Thanks, though."

A big cop, nobody'd dare smack me in front of Del, but G and G weren't those kinds of—the school calls them "guardians"—people, which was his main concern, I think. He didn't know them well enough, was all. And I did come from Sliver. Del couldn't be sure who had rubbed off on who.

I did regret not letting him help me right then. Sometimes a guy makes a generous offer because there's something in his own life that needs to be balanced again, or set right. Being a cop, Del probably had a few errors in judgment he wished he could take back, and he saw people like me as opportunities to feel a little bit better. But if I'm going to be "opportunity guy," I don't want to get too beholden to any one person and their favours, and have those favours pile up too heavy on one side. Then I start owing—I'd spend the rest of my life trying to get things back to square. I already owed Del from our previous run-ins and didn't want to go deeper into debt.

It was Sliver who introduced me to Del, sort of, after a vet discovered I had a broken wing when I'd just gone there to bring in my dog.

Did I mention I had a dog once? No, probably not yet. Although, if that dog's still alive, it's only thanks to me, even if I got a busted hand because of it. His name used to be Curly.

Sliver's lady-of-the-moment was partly to blame for my hand too, but I can't get too mad at her. She only wanted what everybody in Quinton wanted, the route to a decent home and happy family: a nice kid, a good dog, a decent man. Me and Sliver lived in a wartime house in a neighbourhood of war-time houses. All the houses look the same on the outside. I could understand how a barfly might mistake our house for a peaceful and pleasant place, our house surrounded by ones filled with peaceful, happy people. How could she know the difference from the sidewalk?

She tossed the dog at me one steamy afternoon before plopping herself on a stool beside Sliver's chair. She hadn't been making much headway key-to-the-front-door-wise with him, and so, like they all eventually got around to trying, she tried to go through me. Sometimes, if a lady circled around our house enough times, she might try to get me to call her "mom," thinking this was the secret to Sliver's heart, but all that did was stir up bad memories in him. Those ones didn't last very long at all. Still, the women kept coming over. I can't remember anybody besides barflies liking Sliver, unless you counted Narc Ether. Narc owned the pool hall where Sliver was the runt king of billiards. When Sliv wasn't sucking rye and smoking Exports in the big wing chair at home, or off knacking sick animals their owners didn't have the heart to slaughter themselves, he was shooting pool and collecting trophies. Beside his chair at home, he kept an ashtray that was nearly as tall as I was then, with claw feet, a Roman colosseum pillar for a pedestal, and a brass arch that spanned the wide, deep bowl—in case he wanted to lug it with him to the can. His name, Sliver Pine, was engraved into the side of the bowl, along with the word *Champ*. Narc'd given it to him for being aces. Instead of trophies or ashtrays, I got rabbits and fish tossed at me by barflies, because I was the champ at being Sliver's son.

Any of Sliver's lady friends, if they'd only been circling us for a couple of weeks, considered him charming and me a dear: "Tug on my hose, dear"; "Be a dear and fetch me some Coke for mix." Sliver would eventually get tired of them hanging around, "crowding me," he'd say, and then it was back to just Sliver and me, in a house that I'd always thought had plenty of room for more. Sliver and me were the longest-lasting things in our house. No, scratch that. I was the longest-lasting thing—we were three, two, then one—me.

The dog didn't last a day.

This was my first dog, a pup actually, so it was pretty wild still, like any little thing when they think they're set for life—usually a big mistake. Anyway, the barfly's other gag was to slide a naked toe up against Sliver's foot, make him snarl at the dog more.

"He bites me once and your dog's done," Sliver would warn everybody right before hell broke loose.

She winked at me like this was the greatest game in the world a family could play, but all she accomplished was to get Sliver madder and madder at the puppy—and at me.

This barfly had arms covered in tattoos of hearts and knives and musical notes, no colour left in any of them except black. When Sliver ordered her to fetch him another drink, her tattoos puckered into ink smears as she hoisted herself to her feet.

If she didn't stop teasing Sliver, though, I'd be digging a hole for it soon. I had a spot in the backyard where I buried all the helpless stuff that fell in love with me, when they couldn't stick. When it was over, I assume his gals toddled back to whatever bar Sliver found them in, like how my mom may have toddled off back to where she came from, in which case I don't know why she hadn't ended up at the farm. Not everybody is cut out for the farm life, I guess.

From the kitchen, this current gal hollered, "Where'd you hide the rye?"

"In the freezer."

"Jesus, why?"

"Cuz we're outta ice."

"You're so smart, baby."

"Yeah, I know."

"I love you, Sliver."

"The fuck you will."

I saw that dog's short life flash by in the fraction of a second it took for Sliver's dangling sock thread to catch its eye. I whispered at the dog to stay down, but being very young and stupid, it made a play. I caught him by the tail, but not before his teeth found Sliver's heel. Sure enough, ol' Sliv drove his foot down hard, but that last whisky had him sloppy; he only grazed the puppy's head. Most of his weight landed on my hand, snapping a couple of fingers nearly clean off.

Sliver's lady friend bustled back from the kitchen with a rye in each hand, three fingers deep. She gave one to Sliver and set the other on her stool, then came to where I lay in a ball on the floor. She tried to pry my busted hand off my chest but I had my knees jammed up there tight. "Holy fuck, Sliver. It's pretty bad."

"Ah, he can take it. Right, champ? Champ? You can take it."

Decently, she made a splint out of two pencils and wrapped them and my fingers in a pair of her rank old nylons, although that just about caused me to puke a bucketful. Then she carried me upstairs to my room, which I guess was also decent of her. She didn't know she was already done, even if I knew it.

I'd named the dog Curly because of its hair, and because it deserved to have something on the tombstone I'd have to make it if Plan A didn't work out. Later that afternoon, after Sliver and his gal had passed out, I walked Curly to the animal place, meaning to leave it there for somebody to adopt. Turns out a veterinarian is not at all like the pound, which was a pretty lucky break for Curly and me both, because the vet who worked there said she'd see that Curly got a good home. She even fixed up my hand a little, cutting me free of the hose and rewrapping my fingers in some metal doohickey and a bunch of gauze. Fifteen minutes later she was piling me into a cab and paying the driver to take me home.

Sliver's barfly slapped me something stupid over her missing stockings about five seconds after I walked in. Then Sliver called her off and slugged her good—and, like I already knew, she was done. Del the cop would stop by later that day to have a few words with Sliv. The vet thought she was doing me a huge favour by reporting him. When their convo entered the "kids will be kids" territory, I knew Sliv was off the hook.

Del didn't know me yet, so I don't blame him for not asking harder questions. Maybe that's was why he wanted to give me a lift back to the farm so bad this time around. Maybe he thought if he'd done something other than laugh along with Sliver, he wouldn't have found me living by myself later. I want to tell Del not to worry about it, that things couldn't have worked out better for me. Let him know how me and him are all square. I've had to work on getting people to stick around long enough to see how I'm not as bad as Sliver tried to make me believe.

I wonder too if that's why I'm standing outside Couch-Newton's again, waiting to talk to Mary Lynn and trying to impress her for reasons I'm not really clear on. I guess I'm not much different than any of Sliver's gals: throwing ourselves at someone, anyone, not so much even for love, but just hoping we'll get invited in.

After giving poor old Tab what I felt was a reasonable amount of time to get his affairs in order, I entered Couch-Newton's armed with my own purpose. I ditched the mangled birdcage in a nearby bin. Del'd left me to investigate a broken window a couple of stores down, but told me he'd meet up with me here to make sure Tab and I got sorted out.

As I bulled my way toward the counter through a huddled orange-brown mass of pissed-off customers, I detected a whole mixture of strange yet familiar smells. Some odours were canary-based, and some was the kind of body odour you get from panic and depression, when you've just had the rug pulled out from under you or are about to have one pulled. Some people shouted about store credit, either demanding it be extended or wanting their payments delayed, even when there was no sign of Mary Lynn. Lots of canary corpses littering the floor, though, and a flock of live canaries flitting overhead, heading more or less to the storefront window. Tracing their lines of flight back, I discovered Mary Lynn hunkered down behind the open door of the canary cage, trying to shoo the last canaries from the pen. As a solution to her customer problems go, this wasn't a bad one in an *if you can catch it, it's yours* kind of way.

Like most people found huddled on the edge of someplace troubling and confusing, she looked like she could use a smoke. Still, I wasn't dashing over there with my butt baggie just yet. I'd give her a little more time with the livestock, the kind of company I've always found calming. Instead I circled around to the goldfish tanks, partly because I liked tapping on them, never mind the notice taped to the glass telling me not to. I have stated my opinion about signs in Quinton, and that extends to the ones stuck on goldfish tanks, too. I'll also say how, in every example, the sign is for the benefit of the one who put it there, wanting authority over the whole dominion of birds and fish and little jerks and crazy kids. A sign for the days they're not around to scream at you in person. Even then they don't give you an explanation about what you should watch out for, just shout "Can't you read the sign?" So when I heard Mary Lynn yip "Can't you read, kid? Don't bug the fish," from the canary area, I have to admit I was a little disappointed. I don't think the goldfish gave one stringy crap about me rapping on their glass wall; their expressions never changed. On the other hand, at least she remembered me, and was talking to me about something other than canaries, which I took as a positive sign.

"Howdy," I said, and began a Gene Autry mosey toward the coop.

A dead bird whizzed past my ear, followed by a disappointed snarl. It came from Tab, for missing me with his one shot. The canary bounced off the wall behind Mary Lynn and landed on the floor intact. A couple of the nearby corpses weren't so fresh as Tab's bird. I'll bet their owners dug them out of the garbage pail when they heard they might have been sold a bill of goods.

Now, you ask any farmer about signs and he'll tell you they come in all shapes and sizes, but hardly ever in word form. Quintonians seem to suck at reading signs unless they're written down and posted everywhere. Not a single soul seemed to be able to connect the dots of why these canaries were suddenly keeling over, why all the fish downstream had started floating guts up in the last year, why the towers of logs in the creosote yard were so tall and not going anywhere. Those are signs too, Tab.

I'd very nearly decided to dip into my baggie for the whole cigarette and offer it to Mary Lynn right then, but Del burst through the front door and into the commotion, shouting, "Clam up or I'll arrest the whole lotta ya bums." His arms were stretched high, nearly to the ceiling. One hand waved a nightstick.

"What about our goddamn birds? What about our store credit?" the people bellowed back.

Del boomed over their heads, "What the fuck are you talking about? What are you throwing there?" Some canaries flitted; others cartwheeled, hucked post-mortem.

Actually, I was pretty okay with the whole hucking-canaries business. On a farm there's not much call for the gentle handling of life. "Firm but square," Grumps would say to a chicken. Caught up in the farm spirit now, I hucked a few canaries back in the direction they came from, nailing a bastard customer every time—including Tab. Canaries are so easy to huck they might as well be snowballs, and I've tossed a mountain's worth of those. Winters are boring as hell on a farm.

Between big Del's presence and my killer fastball, we quickly had the united front of canary-and-creosote protesters scrambling for the door. They'd made their point, Del reminded everybody, all the while slapping his nightstick into his palm for the sound effect. I bounded to the back of the store again, to offer the dishevelled but otherwise composed Mary Lynn a hand up. I think she mistook me for one of the mob at first, because she slapped my mitt and stood on her own. Del decently pretended not to notice, herding a few tiny canary corpses into a pile with his boot.

I don't know why I stuck my crooked ol' paw out there for her, except maybe I was flush from the battle and a little crazed with heroism, and wanting her to acknowledge a deed of mine, for once. But no girl in her right mind would want to touch my gnarly hand, the bones running every which way. Sometimes I wished the vet had just cut it off. Then I'd have one of those double-hook thingies, the ones with the wires that run down the sides like the brake cables on your better brands of bikes. It'd have way-cool drawings of peace signs, and the keep on truckin' guy, and the word *love* written in big balloon letters on the wooden stem. I'd even have a couple of Sliver's Royal Reserve rye stickers on there, depending on how far up the amputation was. And nobody'd suspect a thing about what I was missing until the sun hit it and it sparkled.

Mary Lynn did manage a grim "Thanks" when she recognized my offer for what it was, already looking bored with the whole scene of me and canaries. Casually sexy as hell, she tossed her head back to flip her hair out of her eyes. I nearly exploded.

"Hey, that's Veronica Lake!"

From beneath her half-shut eyelids, Mary Lynn's eyes crossed in an effort at pretending she'd never heard of the actress. "Huh?"

So I explained the look: "It's when your hair hangs down from one side of your head and the bangs cover one eye, peekaboo-style, so you flip your head back to get it out of the way. That's Veronica Lake."

I gave my head a flick to demonstrate, even if there's not a lot a brush cut can do to recreate the manoeuvre's sexiness.

"Who, that black-and-white actress? Jesus, kid. How old are you?" The question came with what I felt was a pretty fake laugh. More of a snort really, before sweeping the cascade of blond strands from her eyes, only with her hand this time. Del meanwhile was quietly killing himself in an effort to supress the fact he knew all about Veronica Lake—and sexy hair flips, for that matter. Maybe he was married to a Veronica Lake type. I didn't know if he was married at all, or had a family life he could go home to when he was done bailing me out of jams. I'm not sure what kind of wife Veronica Lake would have made. Grumps told me once she went crazy later in life, and you could sort of see it in her last movie, *Flesh Feast*. Hopefully Del was still single, in that case.

Not that I was totally shocked by Mary Lynn's reaction either. Getting snorted at by women is bound to happen if you've learned your entire repertoire of charming manoeuvres from senior citizens. During our movie nights, after Gram went to bed, Grumps would offer his ideas on why a dame did this or that on the CHEX late show. I think Grumps liked having my company. He had lots of opinions about people's strange behaviour, and part of my job on the farm was to listen, even if somewhere down the road an idea or two of his came back to bite me in the ass. Mary Lynn, being normal, was right to snort. Had she been a kid in my class she wouldn't have left it there, though. She'd have gone into a whole vaudeville routine at my expense, pissing me off beyond repair. Maybe I wanted to hang around Mary Lynn for the fact she knew when enough was enough, when in my space.

"You okay, Mary Lynn?" Del added a wink for me, a heads-up sign that a plan was about to unfold.

"Ya-huh," Mary Lynn purred. She took a quick peek down the front of her blouse, in case, during her dives for cover, buttons had popped open where they shouldn't have.

"That's some arm the Kid has, eh?" He meant my hucking ability and not the gnarl.

"Who? Oh yeah. Yeah, prob'ly."

As good an answer as I could hope for, at that point.

"You want me to call your mom to come and get you?" Jesus, Del knew everybody. He walked toward the counter, where the cash register and the phone sat alongside one of those little bells you had to slap if you wanted service pronto.

"No, sir, it's cool. She's working at the drugstore anyway. I'm to go there after here."

I knew that store. Mostly a hangout for hippies-to-be. I got fries there sometimes, when I came to town with Grumps. He'd also let me stand in front of the magazine rack for a few minutes, which is how come I know anything about girls' developments.

Del shrugged. He reached into a shelf and pulled out a phone book. "Okay, well, I'm gonna try and get the owner down here, find out what's what with these birds. And maybe get you outta here a little early." When a couple more townsfolk showed up with their tiny bundles, Del set down the book and aimed his nightstick at the door, shooing them away. "Okay," he said into the phone at the end of his call and hung up, but immediately brought the receiver to his ear and dialled a second number. He waved me over with the stick. "Last chance for a ride home, kid."

My old bike's last hump into town was done, having carried me to where I wanted to be, in the company of who I wanted to hang around with. I felt a lump in my throat...but it was time for me and Mom's bike to move on, go our separate new ways. I needed time to till the ground here a little. See what I could get to sprout. "Nah, it's cool," I swallowed.

An essayist could keep his personal valuables in essay storage forever; they will run their range of *useful* after one use, however:

I would've felt an awful lot worse had I been riding, say, a peppy three-speed Stingray with a banana seat and ape-hanger handlebars, not this girl's bike. Mostly, I felt bad for Gram. She'd looked so proud the day, six years plus a couple of weeks ago, when she walked the bike out of the shed and parked it against the farmhouse's stone stoop. I'd been scratching circles in the sand at the base of the steps. Maybe I looked bored—or sad. Because I'd only just arrived, Gram couldn't tell the difference yet.

When she tapped the seat, I squinted up at her. Gram spat into a rag and scrubbed the dust from the dull red leather. Then she patted the saddle one more time and beamed. "Here. It's a bicycle," all *ta-da* about the gift, thwacking her rag into the bike like a mechanic to get my attention. But no amount of spit could change the only important fact of life about bikes, so I saved her the trouble of more cleaning.

"It's a *girl's* bike."

She blinked at me like I'd discovered its dirty secret. "How did you know? Did Grumps tell you already?"

"Who?" I shook my head. I was calling them ma'am and sir, to Gram's annoyance. She was big on nicknames for things— baby cows, baby pigs—and would continue the practice until it was time for Grumps to take over an animal's supervision. Some animals didn't come with mothers but from a box or the back of a truck. That's when Gram really shone.

"Your grandfather. You can call him Grumps, if you like. Did he tell you about the bike?"

"No...you tell just by lookin' at 'em." A very old lady by my peanut brain's assessment. I was worried she'd gone simple already.

"Oh." She stared at the bike. "Well, I can't help that." She gave the bike another once-over. "Really?" she asked again, in case I'd just been jerking her chain.

"Yesss, really. Jesus, it ain't because it's got perfume on," I muttered.

"No...no. I know." She sounded doubtful. "And another thing. We don't swear around here, mister."

I sniffed. "Whaddaya mean? That guy swears all the time." I pointed to the house. "*Grumps.*"

"*We* means me and you. We don't swear. That guy, your grandfather...Grumps..." She scowled at where my finger aimed because lunchtime meant the CHEX news noon farm report was pulling a few beauties out of him at the moment. "He's on his own with God."

I snorted something that may have been "bullshit." Then, realizing what I'd done so soon after being told not to, I sighed, hiked my shoulders, and lowered my head. This left my back open, but I'd rather get my back whupped any day than my head.

When several seconds passed without me feeling any punishment, I poked my head out from under my arms. Gram was staring at me like she'd seen a ghost, her hands over her mouth and her eyes wide as the big blue sky over our heads. "Well?" I was getting impatient.

"Jumpin' blue Jesus," she gasped, before tucking her hands into her apron and pulled up a slab beside me. She took a deep breath: "Another thing, mister... Nobody hits anybody around here—ever."

"Whaddabout Grumps?" I had my doubts about him. He had the same wiry build as Sliver.

"No. Nobody. He's just…grumpy. He loves you the same as me. If something's troubling us, we'll tell you." She managed a smile again. "Same goes for you too, mister man. No smacking us if we upset you somehow. Promise?"

Sounded fair. "Promise," I agreed, especially considering we were going to be hanging out more often now. I knew how house rules were necessary, especially in the Quinton pool hall, where they were nailed to the wall, so I was cool with this talk. In fact, I'd already started liking Gram, even before she chose not to slug me.

Gram dabbed an eye with her apron string, then cleared her throat. She rubbed my head, maybe for good luck, before she pointed out another major flaw in the bike. "It's kinda rusty, but your grandfather can touch it up. We got some house paint left."

Great. "Girl's bike," I reminded her, in case she'd forgotten the main sin. Sky blue wouldn't hold second place on the list of everything else wrong with it: having only the one speed, the mostly bald streamers that hung from the handlebars, the fact it was way too big for me. I smoothed the sand between my feet and drew two circles in it, adding a crossbar high between them. "See this? That makes it a boy's bike." I tapped the ground with my stick.

Gram frowned. "Well, that's dumb. Your mom wouldn't have learned how to ride with that thing there. This used to be your mother's bike, when she was about your age."

"I don't have a mom," I had to remind her, a little surprised she hadn't heard yet.

"I know you think that, but you did. She was our daughter. That's what makes you our grandson. At bedtime, when we say we love you, she's one reason why we say that."

My face went hot, nearly to exploding. "How did you know my mom?"

Gram touched my cheek to try and cool it down. "Well... like I said, she was our daughter. She lived here too. We knew her quite a bit. Her bedroom is next to yours."

I knew that room—dark all the time, its door kept closed to trap the sweet-stale smell inside. Their house had tons of rooms that way, growing out of the sides of the main building like warts. Moms and dads and brothers and sisters and friends—these were just dark places, stranger-words I overheard in town sometimes. Sliver hardly ever talked about family unless he was slurring, and those talks weren't very complimentary. And he never said nothing nice about this bike's owner. Had she liked sky blue? As colours went, I decided it would be okay this one time.

"Did she know Sliver?" Being a couple years away from Grumps's animal husbandry lessons, this was the logical, kind of stupid-assed question a young, ignorant kid would ask.

My question sure stumped Gram; she couldn't answer me straight up and pretended to be busy crushing a beetle into the dust with her rubber boot. She crushed the hell out of it too, like it'd done something to really piss her off.

"Can you ride a bike?" she asked finally, like she hadn't heard me at all.

"Course I can," I lied. Until I heard different, lying was on the table among the house rules here.

"I'll leave it to you whether you want her bike," Gram said, then started up the steps. Grumps was howling again. That needed tending. At the door, she caught me edging from the stoop. "Your mom taught herself. She was your age then."

I liked Gram; she wasn't a barfly at all—and she *had* wiped the seat with her spit, which was pretty okay in my book. I'd wait till she went inside before I kicked tires.

At armpit height, the seat was a few years away from my ass. So I straddled the pedals and chugged the bike like a scooter to the end of the driveway. The several times I stumbled I just put my foot down and caught myself, easy as pie, and something kid-mom probably did with this bike too—something neither of us could've done with a boy's bike. Sliver would have hated stuff like that about me, and Mom for that matter, how we'd put our foot down when we had to.

"Okay, pal."

Del decided to leave off pushing me on the hows and whens of my getting home. He'd already experienced some of my shifty cleverness from back in my horse-thief days, and how well I got along by myself for that brief period after Sliver exploded. Besides, I see now, he had a plan hatching for me and stood at Couch-Newton's big glass doors with his hands folded behind his back waiting for that plan to kick into motion, one eye on Main Street's traffic, almost all of it on foot now. Angry, discombobulated feet, stepping in and out of the street lights' circles like starving zombies, shuffling into one another, getting bumped into new directions, crossing the street willy-nilly, little puffs of curse-filled breaths tumbling in the evening's cold. Del could've made a million bucks writing jaywalking tickets. Instead he pressed his head forward to follow a cluster headed up Main, his cap tilting higher and higher on his head, then oops, sliding off. He caught it in his hands, which were still folded behind his back. He was the picture of patience and good planning.

Del seemed to sense that the canaries were the least of everybody's problems now, including Mr. Couch, the guy he was watching for. The canaries' job was over. They'd done what they'd come here to do: warn people the only way they could about how the world was about to change. Del still had to make sure nobody did anything more stupid than bump into each other.

Unlike me and Del, Mary Lynn didn't have time to stand around and wait for the vague death rattles of a bunch of birds to be revealed as something meaningful. All she gathered of their demise was they weren't going to clean up after themselves, and that meant she had a job to do right now. While she sashayed to the supply room, I lingered around the couple of canaries that had returned to their coop. Not a peep out of these ones, of course. Instead, they were locked in a death-row stare at the storefront window, probably not liking what they saw in its reflection. I don't blame them. How does a bird, or anybody really, recover from a scene like Tab and me and the rest volleying their dead mates back and forth? These little guys looked to have a pretty good grip on the fact that life here wasn't the sing-along they'd been making it out to be. And let's not forget poor Bill and Doris and whatsisname. They didn't ask to be dumped at our creaky old farm. Well, two of them. The third had another message, but I wasn't going to under-stand what he was trying to say until too late.

Mary Lynn returned with a broom and a pan, but three sweeps through the feathers and guts and she looked ready to lose her lunch. It's the smell more than the gore that gets non-farmers. I'd already mentioned how I'd gotten used to almost every variety—shit, old grandparent bodies, fresh kills, you name it—advantages Mary Lynn didn't have. Also, with all my smoking, I think my sense of smell might have started to collapse too. I have to give her an A for trying, in that case, and was glad I got to see this side of her in person, diving into manual labour like a farmer. The chowderheads at school would have straddled the broom and zipped away cackling.

Catching her pale reflection in the window, Del asked, "You feeling okay, Mary Lynn?"

Mary Lynn muttered an "uh-huh," but he could tell she was about two seconds away from joining the canaries on the floor. He grabbed the cashier's stool out from behind the counter and set it underneath her.

"Thank you, sir," she said right before dropping onto the seat. This struck me as being exceptionally polite for a teen. As someone only a few days away from being teen-aged myself, I knew I'd have a few hard decisions to make regarding the kind of teen I wanted to be. Until this stretch of getting to know Mary Lynn a bit more today, my teen experiences were limited to Quinton's hippie yokel variety.

Del took the broom from Mary Lynn and passed it to me. "Here, kid. Do her a favour and take over."

Again, not a big deal, especially in the degrading way it might look like to hippies. First of all, Del made sure to sound like this was a request; he already knew about my steely bearing in the face of rotting carcasses, because he'd seen how I was living the day he brought me from Sliver's house to the farm for good. Secondly, Gram handed me manure shovels like she was passing me the peas. I darted around Couch-Newton's battlefield like a fly, and in no time flat had those little peckers and their guts in the dustpan. I grabbed a big pot and lid from the kitchen department and dumped the whole shebang in it, then closed the lid before putting it back on the shelf. Del gave me a kind of sideways smirk, but let it slide. I was right to assume he liked a good joke as much as the next guy.

Unless that next guy happened to be the one who arrived in a '57 Dodge Coronet, yellow, with two-foot tail fins that glowed red when their brakes squealed in front of Couch-Newton's. The car came to rest halfway on the sidewalk. Del went to the door and held it open until Mr. Couch—a short, muskrat-faced man—got out of his car, spit the cigarette dangling from his lips four feet down the sidewalk, and took a sip from a glass wedged between his legs for the drive. Boy, did I sit up straight! Whenever I tried spitting my smokes on purpose they usually stuck to my bottom lip first, before tumbling down the front of my shirt, resulting in a grilling from Gram later over why my shirts had so many burn holes in them. I couldn't tell her they were the result of needing more practice with my butts, so I'd blamed my standing too close to Grumps. (She accepted that answer.) I made a mental note of where Couch's butt landed. Hopefully there'd be something worth keeping when I got outside.

Couch drained the glass right in front of Del and God and everybody, then tossed it into the back seat, clutching his grey houndstooth trench coat tight as he blew past us on his beeline for the checkout counter. After popping open the till to look inside, he fired a cocked eyebrow at Del. Del shook his head. "You weren't robbed."

"Why'd you call me down here then?" Couch slid the drawer shut and took a gander down an aisle. "Who's working? Where's the clerk?" followed quickly by "Where the hell is everybody?" because all the aisles were empty and clean, especially of customers. He'd probably already heard the news about the creosote plant closing. Looking down the aisles was like looking into the future, and he knew it.

"I called you about your canaries. We had a bit of trouble here."

"My canaries? You mean the *birds*? You called me down here because of fucking birds?"

Couch was partly snockered, sounded like to me. I believe Del's phone call had interrupted him on his way to fully snockered.

"Just the dead ones, Mr. Couch." Del retrieved the pot I'd filled with most of those same dead birds and opened the lid.

Couch stared at the contents, which looked like somebody's head had exploded on a pillow. "What the hell is that?" he gagged.

"Canaries, sir. What's left of 'em. Seems you've been selling defective canaries."

Poor old Couch's mouth slung open but he didn't ask anything additional, rightly suspecting that every answer would circle back to canaries anyway. He placed his hand across his forehead, then dragged it down to his chin, pulling with it all the extra skin left over from his flustered expression. When he started fidgeting at the chest area of his coat, slapping one side and then the other, I knew what he was after. Every smoker in the world knew what he wanted.

Del tossed an extra detail or two at him while Couch was fishing through his pockets. "Your customers have been in and out all day with these poor little things. And taking it out on Mary Lynn." He didn't dare crack a smile; the owner's face was at maximum flush already from the booze. Any more and his head would have popped for sure.

"Who?"

"Your cashier."

From the interior pocket of his overcoat, Couch finally removed a silver cigarette case. Fine swirls engraved the surface, and as he held it up to his face to nudge his hair back into place, he remembered who he was and how little he should care.

"Tough hairy nuggets. The birds aren't my problem once they leave the store." Which, you may recall, is exactly what

Mary Lynn told everyone. Couch flicked his wrist; the cigarette case lid flipped open. He removed a cigarette from a row kept tidy under a metal clasp and stuck it in his mouth. For the first time ever I felt shame over my baggie.

"Tough what?" I think Del was running out of patience, finally. "This isn't one or two, pal. You're hanging a lot of people out to dry. I know it's not much, but all things considered..."

"Whoa, whoa." Couch threw his hands up to protest. "It's buyer beware. That's the rule. Maybe all that smoke from the plant got to them, which, in case you haven't heard, that problem has been taken care of. Which also means I'm just as screwed as the customers, all things considered. Who's going to compensate me when people stop coming in?" A flame flickered from his lighter and leaned toward the tip of his dart. His breath being so thick with liquor, he could have exploded that way too. If he owned a canary, it was probably just now falling to the bottom of its cage.

Del placed the pot on the counter. "Be that as it may, you'd better close the store until things simmer down. I've already had one store window broken out there. Just a sec..." The cop signalled me to come over. "Say, kid, this is going to take a while. How would you like to escort Mary Lynn to the drugstore? I need somebody I can trust to see her there safe. Her mom is expecting you."

He might have been thinking about the mob outside when he asked me to be Mary Lynn's escort, but I also believe he meant to give me a boost in the relationship department. I have to admit, I didn't see his plan, amid all the guts and feathers and stuff. Mostly all I saw was how my time with her was about to run out and I'd accomplished dick all.

Couch bent around the large cop's frame and down to the shadowy end of the aisle I'd just finished sweeping.

"Who the hell's that? Did he have something to do with all this?"

"Nope. That's the Kid." Del stated with what could only be interpreted as pride. "He helped me save your store from your customers. And he cleaned up after." Del tapped the pot lid handle as evidence of my handiwork.

"Hmph, a vandal more like," which sounded like an accusation to me and Del both. Del removed the lid and started shaking out the contents. When I passed Mr. Couch on my amble toward the exit, I handed him the broom and said, "That end goes on the floor."

From here to the end I try to get Del's plan out of first gear. Also introduce some union stuff:

Mary Lynn was still inside, gathering her coat and possibly having a word with Del about not needing an escort, so I waited beside Couch's yellow Coronet, using the felt checkerboard elbow of my jacket to buff the tail fin like I owned it. I had one leg crossed in front of the other, and in the corner of my mouth dangled the good-sized remainder of Couch's still-glowing cigarette. I'll bet to anybody walking by I looked like the whole package, anyone with shoulders not so weighed down they couldn't look up. They'd see a cool cat waiting for his tomato. A nice car. A smoke of decent length. Oh baby, they'd think. What we wouldn't give to trade our life for his. Go ahead and try, I'd say. To prove I was serious, I put on a sneer, should anybody raise their head.

When Mary Lynn stepped into the chilly autumn evening, the upper half of her body and most of her face were swaddled in a yellow caftan; if you didn't know it was her, you'd never know it was her. Which might have been the plan. I noticed she wore grey sealskin boots with white fur trim. I knew that style of boot—useless in puddles. Gram told me so one day when I'd stopped at a store window to admire a pair, and had begun dropping subtle hints about how not every piece of footwear in the world was made of black rubber, even if, like my beauties here with their red racing trim, they were waterproof. Oh, my toes got freaking cold in the winter, but at least my socks stayed dry. And not only were they indestructible, but try and lose them— they'd be right there in the mud room the next morning, straight and tall like they had walked in on their own, all ready to take the edge off any shining moment I wanted to stride into. Like after my hotshot-leaning-against-the-car moment, when their signature *wallop–wallop* sounded my hustling to intercept Mary Lynn, who hadn't noticed me by Couch's car. By the way, the rubber is stiff as death, so I could never walk very far without chafing the tops of my toes and my heels. At least I wouldn't be humping alongside Mary Lynn on my mom's bike.

My cigarette's glow, boosted by the dark, was my one attraction that registered positively with her. She pulled the hood of her caftan back from her forehead so her entire face—round, soft, perfect—could sit in its feathery frame.

"You smoke, kid?" she asked.

"Yep."

"Aren't you kinda young?"

I took a long drag, using the time to roll her question around in my brain, beat back the undertone that came with something you weren't sure was an insult or not. Only a grade older than me, the "teen" slapped onto the end of the number to her age instantly made her more world wise, in her fellow teens' eyes at least. "There's no bad age to start," I drawled, finally.

Mary Lynn clicked her tongue at my truth, then turned toward the bridge. I shoved my smoke back into my mouth and shuffled up next to her, my boots *ca-whuffling* softly through my approach, a sound barely noticeable above the clomp of the mob's workboots as they streamed toward the bridge. I had no reason to believe she might make a break for it to be shed of me, but if she did I'll bet the mob's stomping helped change her mind. They had strength in numbers, but no sense of purpose more than getting to the other side of the river. They were a mob, no longer in a union.

Actually, Mary Lynn and me were somewhere in between at the moment. I had a sense of some purpose, just nothing too solid to hang it on; Mary Lynn had a sense of some direction, just one not necessarily her mom's drugstore. We were walking east together, so for the time being that wasn't half-bad.

When Grumps wasn't helping me enjoy the facts of life as presented in *Flesh Feast*, he'd plop me down in front of the tube for a little schooling on broader social issues, as witnessed in the movies *The Grapes of Wrath* and *How Green Was My Valley*. My main takeaway was, as Preacher Gruffydd in that last one said, "With strength goes responsibility, to others and to yourselves." I was never sure what type of strength Grumps thought I had, or why I should be responsible with it. I just knew enough about Grumps and speeches that it probably wasn't superpowers, or even the regular physical kind, which was too bad. I could lift my weight in hay bales already. I'll bet he was thinking about those stupid chickens, how I'd hopefully learned that we shouldn't take advantage of weaklings just because we can. It was Gruffydd's point that always stuck with me best then, because just before reciting it, Grumps would slap me on the knee and go, "Listen up, you." Those also being the only times Grumps would lay an open hand on me.

Mary Lynn and me got about ten feet before she stopped and put her hand on my chest. She could feel my heart pounding pretty good, I'll bet, which was partly for the fact of her hand, but also I had lungs like two peas. We farmers don't run much. "You know, you don't have to walk me to the store. It's not that big a deal out here."

"I know. I'm only doin' it cuz Del asked me to."

"Well, he shouldn't have bothered. How do you know Del?"

"Oh, we go back a ways." I threw my thumb over my shoulder just before wedging my smoke back between my lips to make the heater wink. Mary Lynn couldn't take her eyes off it, so I asked the obvious, because the prettiest girls in Quinton all smoked. "Would you like one?" I squinted, my eyes becoming a little teary from Tillsonburg blowback.

"Sure," she quickly accepted.

I turned my shoulder so she couldn't see me fishing through my jacket pocket. I knew I had a whole cig or two on me. "Here. You like Luckys?"

My hope was she'd just shrug because she'd never heard of them. Otherwise she'd know them as old-man smokes, which would reignite an earlier point she'd raised during the Veronica Lake whoop-dee-do. Tough hairy nuggets for her, in that case, because if I had a whole cigarette in my baggie it was bound to be one of Grumps's Lucky Strikes. As it turned out, she didn't offer an opinion one way or the other, just scooped it up like a chicken on a grub. I passed her Couch's old butt to use as a lighter and got her batted eyelids for thanks. She stared down the length of the Lucky, going cross-eyed with each try at planting the heater against the tip. Her cheeks would fluff in and out whenever she thought she was close, but only when I reached out to steady her hand was she able to get the Lucky lit. The cigarette, minimum a month old, was dry as cornflakes, and by rights should've burst into flames the second she got it going. She kept her throat composed pretty well, all things considered.

"Thanks," she finally managed. "I'm more used to matches or a lighter." The exhausted words billowed around her head.

"Yeah, me too. 'Cept I don't own a lighter and it's kinda windy for matches." I was glad she didn't ask me how mine got lit, because we'd have to go back to the store and ask Couch.

The wind picked up the nearer we got to the river; it flipped the loose corners of her caftan across her face and nearly knocked the Lucky from her mouth. I suggested she tie the hangy bits off somehow or else she'd get a burn hole. She couldn't argue against the wisdom that comes from bad experience, so she looped the ends a couple more times around her neck before making a knot. Nothing fancy, but the effect was she looked like she was wearing a mink stole, the kind an old-time, black-and-white movie starlet would wear. I must've been pondering too hard over what actress she resembled and from what movie, because while I mulled it over, she ducked off the road and started jogging toward the docks.

"Where you going?" I wheeled on my boot heels and bound from the sidewalk after her. "I'm not swimming across."

"What? No, dummy," she hacked back at me. "I've just started my smoke. I don't want to get to the store too soon." What she meant was, the drugstore where her mother worked was just across the bridge, barely ten puffs away at any sort of clip at all.

"Yeah, nobody knows I smoke either," I said, which was only true if Gram and Grumps were as clueless about my habit as I've always hoped they were, and you ignored everybody downtown earlier, or every random day at the canal with the boaters. Despite not having a whole cig of my own to enjoy, I was okay with this detour. She could finish every butt in the bag for as many laps of the town as she liked, if it meant we got to hang out for longer.

A little bit on the local Quinton setting would be useful, and how some people choose to kill time in it:

The Quint River divides the town into two segments: east and west, more or less. And no matter if anybody's travelling north or travelling south across the bridge, from one side to the other, everything is overseen by the bridge's troll. None of the cardinal directions could be said to actually run true; these were the generally accepted directions, as they read on a compass. In fact, the river swerved every which way, the way a river will, along practically every compass point. Some of the creosote flock had churned toward the east side, the same as us. They reminded me of birds pushed out of their nest for the first time, flying around the tree for a revolution or two, listening for a call to come back. Everything I knew about abandoned nests, though, told me there'd be no happy reunion at the plant. The workers were on their own and would have to start from scratch, collecting what little scraps they could of what they'd learned slapping tar onto logs, and locate some vacant branch.

We turned down the pathway leading to the public docks, where pleasure boats parked in season. Tonight only a few aluminum fishing boats were tied there, like dogs waiting for their owners. The little boats putted up and down the river with their jacklights blazing, trying to draw fish closer. Pickerel season was in full swing, but once the river started to freeze there'd be nothing for Quinton's main sports heroes to do until the ice got thick enough to support their fishing shanties, at which time they could start sport drinking all over again. Sliver wasn't a fishing hero, not as far as I knew. I mean, he never got his picture in the paper for being able to hold up a big fish and smile at the same time, because if he did, the picture would have been taped to the hall of fame—that's what he called the fridge door. I wasn't on it. There were tons of pictures of Sliver holding up a pool cue, or him and his various trophies. He was a pool-shooting son of a bitch. Everybody said so. I hadn't gotten into pool by the time Sliver blew up, so the only sport to speak of for me was fishing, self-taught, like my bike riding. That's why you'd never catch me fishing down here below the plant. I practised my sport at the canal, far away from the creosote plant and the cancer fish.

I hung out at the canal quite a bit. When I wasn't in school, or if I was skipping a class or two to blow off steam, that's where I'd be. Sometimes swimming, if the weather was warm, but usually sitting on a bollard and wetting a line for mudcat. Gram cooked my catches with handfuls of the shelled green peas we grew in the garden. She'd cut the fish into tiny morsels, then stew them in cow's cream with the peas and salt and pepper—oh yeah, and onions too. Everything she made I liked fine, except whenever we had onions she'd tell the same goddamn story about the time I pulled all the onions out and then tried to stick them back in, green side down. It didn't matter that I was a shit-faced six-year-old at the time, Gram got a big kick out of the memory, enough that I think she only grows onions now so she can retell the story for the yuks. I guess that's okay. If I can entertain Gram with a cheap onion story, it's sort of like my pay for room and board. No big deal. I'd put up with a lot worse when I lived with Sliver. Gram's soft chuckles are the sound of me getting off easy.

I should mention that I haven't been to the canal since a year ago September. It's not that I got sick of fishing or wouldn't like to go back, but has to do with the bully I might find there.

That last visit, after I'd stuffed my catch into my backpack and fired up my celebration butt, I decided to go for a tromp through the paths around the canal rather than wait at school for my bus, which wouldn't arrive for another hour. I caught shit from my teacher all the time for the fishy smell of my notebooks, but I didn't care. She could suck my potatoes—and saying so is what'd guaranteed me a trip to the principal's office, by which I actually mean the canal, because I'd just kept walking out the door rather than sit there listening to that schlub. The thing is, a guy can't keep his various outrages in check forever. He's got to defend himself once in a while, physically or verbally, or else he'll explode.

Around the canal are about a million paths, every single one with the same general end point at the canal's block walls. The paths' beginnings, on the other hand, could be from anywhere in the world—maybe even Spring Valley, Saskatchewan. Even though at any number of points the paths intersect, there's not so many people out mid-afternoon on a weekday, so the odds of running across another person are kinda long. What I mean is, nobody expects to meet another soul while on a stroll, let alone have them ruin your good time.

So I was a little surprised when I spied a tall, lumpy, sad-faced man walking alongside a little girl, loping along his own path toward the water, his eyes fixed hard on the ground. Anybody here this time of day was either hatching some kind of pervy plan or, like me, had been banished from somewhere else as the result of a criminal act, like my "suck my potatoes" advice. I followed the man and little kid mainly out of curiosity, but also a little bit of concern. I knew they weren't up to anything fun because they didn't have fishing poles.

The little girl would have been practically invisible if she wasn't such a yappy little weed-rustler, her bright red hair going *flip–flip–flip* above the tops of the greenish stalks each time she jumped, about every other step. She was skipping a length of doubled-up grey rope, her helium-voice hollering, "Leg up! Leg down... Leg up! Leg down..." Jesus, little kids can't walk anywhere like normal people; they have to skip and sing and hop. That's because for the first few years, they're pretty oblivious to the dirty tricks of people and nature; they have tiny, oblivious brains that can't reckon with the dangerous world as it roars by and sometimes sucks them in. This kid sang up such a storm that the lump of a man had to shout at one point, "Hush, Donna Mae."

My ears perked right up. My favourite cartoon strip was *Peanuts*, and I'd just handed in a killer theme essay on why Charles M. Schulz decided to ruin it by adding "the little red-haired girl" character, and making Charlie Brown crazy about her. Although he was married to another woman at the time, I proposed Schulz had introduced the girl because "he secretly lusted for an old flame, some red-headed gal named Donna Mae." The new character was "his horn-dog way of weaselling back into her life." My teacher called the essay's subject matter and language inappropriate for Grade 7, even when its thematic thrust went straight to the heart of child abuse. What I mean is, and I'm quoting myself again here: "What gives Schulz the right to torture Charlie Brown, readers like me, and original Donna Mae (probably) by dredging up some old hard-on? Why would he sink a perfectly good comic strip for the chance at a screw?" My main argument was, why drag us readers down with him and his unhappiness? Along that reasoning, I didn't trust this guy with a Donna Mae either.

At the canal's lower end, bulrushes sprouted between the jumble of rock left over from the dredging operation a million years ago. I found Lumpy staring into the water beyond the gaps like he'd dropped his wallet. Donna Mae squeaked up at him: "Whatcha lookin' for, Daddy?"

"Nothing, honey. Go play for a bit."

He might as well have told a kitten to lick cream, because she immediately jumped onto the wet, shimmery stones to rattle those same cattails, squealing, "Meow-ow! Meow-ow!" until her father had had enough and bellowed, "Donna Mae, hush!" He pulled out a jar of apple juice to stick in her yap, which only kept her quiet till a sailboat putted by on a two-point-five horse. Donna Mae squealed, of course, then scrambled to the wall to watch. Her father stayed put, testing the heft to various rocks. Only once did he turn to look at the couple sitting in the back of their boat. When they gave him the "look how insanely well-off we are" salute that people in big boats normally handed out, he didn't gesture back. On the other hand, Donna Mae flapped and hollered like a maniac.

She wasn't alone in seeing them as something special. I'd stare at the passing barges and shitty sailboats too. Sliver said once that he'd married a gal who took off upstream. I don't know if he meant my mom or some other dame, or if the canal was the stream he'd meant. Sliver wasn't much for communicating verbally. Then again, we didn't have a lot in common, so there wasn't much to talk about. I liked to talk, though, so when I was canal-side I'd shout at the boats and the occupants would shout back, *where you going, do you know so-and-so*, the usual chit-chat. Sometimes they'd point upstream, if they heard something different than what I asked.

The boat gargled from view; Donna Mae's dad took one end of the rope and tied it to the prize-winning rock he'd selected, and then looped the middle around his big ol' beer gut. He snared his daughter by her thin waist with the flimsy slipknot at the other end, then scooped her up and walked to the edge of the wall—and didn't stop. A lone waterspout splashed straight up. I poked my head out of where I was hiding in the weeds. I really noticed the quiet when Donna Mae stopped yakking.

No matter if I happen to be showing off a "don't give a fuck" attitude, I'll still stand up to an asshole judgment. Not coincidentally, it was that kind of thinking that brought me to the canal that day, so it also felt like fate. I stumbled down to the wall shrieking, "Goddamn you!" partly at Charles Schulz, but mostly at Donna Mae's dad, because here was another jerk dragging a kid into misery without her permission. I'd developed a real soft spot for red-haired Donna Maes.

Tiny frothy bubbles, not your larger, gulps-of-air variety, crackled where the pair had entered the canal. I jumped in feet-first too. (I can't dive worth shit.) Being a seasoned canal swimmer, however, I *could* touch bottom no problem. Jagged rocks and beer cans were the usual highlights down there, so there wasn't ever much to look at. But now I had to keep my eyes open, no matter the pain. Two hard kicks was all it took to find the wispy strands of orange seaweed hair I wanted, and with one dog-paddle more, I stared into a surprised face. Donna Mae had that semi-delighted look kids get when a new kid wants to join in their game. I mean, that's how crazy kids can be—that one'd float here happy as a piglet in slop, till the air in her lungs gave out, convinced life was great because her jerk dad and her were in the middle of a crazy-assed game together. Speaking of assholes, her dad's had hit the canal floor first, pinned by the stone he'd chosen for this very job. By the time I arrived, he was sitting in a cloud of muddy water, calm as hell, holding on to his daughter by the rope like she was a balloon. Fortunately, he'd made a crappy knot—he hadn't expected company, I'll bet. Plus, I knew knots inside out; we used them all the time on the farm. He did grab for his daughter's leg, at least, when the rope went slack and she floated away. A short game of tug-of-war followed, which must've thrilled her to no end, before he surrendered and sat back down, defeated.

Me and Donna Mae popped to the surface and bobbed around like a couple of muskrats, of which there were already plenty in the canal—brown shifty ones I hated to turn my back on. (They resembled the rats I hunted in Gram's chicken coop, only way larger.) Muskrats were an occasional pain in the ass when I wanted to swim in peace. We got along about the same as me and the rats because I've chucked a ton of stones at both in my life. So, just in case they recognized me and decided on revenge, I grabbed Donna Mae by the back of her soppy green dress and booked it for shore. The muskrats whirled circles beside us until they spotted the calm figure of her dad on the bottom and dove in that direction. I pushed his kid up the rock wall by her butt, and then clambered out and flopped down beside her, just in time to see big bubbles explode through the muskrat rings. With zero oxygen left myself, and a snout full of water, I began hacking a ton. Out of the corner of my eye I caught Donna Mae's beady kid's eyes on me. Every time I coughed, she did the same, except she was just saying the words "cough-cough." Crazy kids and their games.

What priests called "the eternal stillness" arrived, cutting into our little game. Donna Mae hadn't heard about *that* yet and started screaming the alphabet song to the beat of her sneakers' heals bouncing against the stones as she squinted into the canal's shimmery swirls and bubbles. The half-full bottle of juice sat within arm's reach, so I passed it to her; I needed quiet to think. Donna Mae's hands trembled putting the glass to her mouth. Little kids have no heft—they're mostly volume. They feel the cold sooner than most.

"So…your name's Donna Mae?"

"Yep," she said, her eyes fixed on the water.

"Neat. That's a great name."

"Thank you, sir."

Sir. Pretty good manners, this one. I liked her right off and was glad I'd saved her. "Do you know where your home is?"

She gave me a look like I'd just insulted the hell out of her. "Of course I do," she sniffed.

"Kay. Just checkin'. It's just that some kids don't. Come on. I'll take you home."

"Nah, Daddy will." Her bony arm waved to where the two of them had gone in.

"Nope, he's gonna swim home underwater," I said. "We're 'sposed to race him!" I tried to sound excited—practically impossible when you're cold, soaked, and forced to babysit.

Predictably, Donna Mae hopped right up. "Come on," she insisted through chattering teeth. "We can win."

Dead-serious kid's eyes—they'll get you right *here*—so off she skipped for her house. I paused to remove a two-inch butt from my plastic baggy and fire it up. Then I was off behind her.

She headed into a neighbourhood full of identically whitewashed wartime homes. Impressive, I thought, how she picked the right one out straight away. If I'd been pressed to do it, I might have been able to pick out the home me and Sliver used to live in—it was around here somewhere—but I hadn't had any cause to revisit that period in my life yet.

Donna Mae stopped in front of the gravel driveway and looked up and down the maple-lined street, her eyebrows bonking together above her nose. I got that look when I did math, when stuff didn't add up. Hers probably meant the same. Like, how exactly could her father swim home, and where would he pop out of to declare himself the winner. He struck me as the kind of jerk who would make that kind of declaration.

"Looks like *we* won," I gasped, having finally caught up.

Donna Mae crossed her arms and tapped a finger on her chin. "May-beee," she said, stretching the word thin, before making her first hesitant step onto her driveway.

To hurry things along, I clapped my hands and shouted, "Run!" to make her think her dad was hot on her tail. Donna Mae didn't stop till she reached her front door. There she flung her hands into the air and shouted, "Hurray!" Her green dress, nearly black from the wet, stuck to her narrow frame like a cabbage-roll skin. She let out an "eep!" when a mother-type dressed in a nurse's getup reached through the door and yanked her inside. The nurse re-emerged alone a second later and glared the length of her driveway to where I stood, possibly memorizing me for a lineup. In *that* case, there was no point in waiting here, dripping with heroism, for an invitation to come in. I hightailed it, *toot-sweet*. I recognized the look of someone determined not to hear true facts just because they didn't like the look of the messenger: a kid with a butt sticking out of his mouth and stinking like canal water.

All of which was perfectly understandable, so I never held a grudge. I was mostly disappointed I couldn't stay to hear Donna Mae's spin on events—everybody jumping into the canal, me pulling her out, her daddy swimming home. A hoot for sure, but I had to get lost before the cops showed up. Cops lived for events like this—even good cops like Del. Also, my getaway vehicle (the school bus) was likely waiting to drop me into whatever equally impatient world tapped its toes for me at home. I'd have to offer Gram and Grumps a defence of my essay, my follow-up "potato" rebuttal, and possibly explain why my clothes were wet. But I'd keep this latest Donna Mae business to myself. I'd already written one killer Donna Mae–based theme essay on what happens when some jerk comes along to try to ruin it for everybody, and that had gotten me booted from school. A second essay wasn't going to do any good, if everybody'd missed the point of the first one.

Of course, as everybody on board with me now is hopefully realizing, grade A material can't be kept in storage forever. I can even feel Grumps's hand slapping me on the leg, telling me "good job" for figuring out how Preacher Gruffydd's line can apply when the time comes.

Now seems like a good time to bring up the importance of a balanced approach, when building themes or building relationships (rather than diving headfirst into those shaky waters):

The docks in Quinton are nothing fancy, just a series of wooden platforms kept afloat on empty oil drums and tied to a main pier by iron pins, which makes them tippy as hell and therefore a blast to stand on. I hustled past her and ran to the end of one, standing spread-eagled and rocking side to side. (My black rubber boots had excellent grip.) I called to Mary Lynn, hoping she'd join me, but she shook her head violently and took a step further back from an edge she was in no danger of going over. She planted her less grippy sealskin boots on the grass and folded her arms across her chest, only unfolding them once, briefly, to take a drag from the cigarette squeezed between the first two fingers of her right hand. Very Bette Davis, I thought, but I kept quiet about the look this time. Davis was a cool customer too, though, like in *Jezebel*, when she slugged Henry Fonda. I didn't want Mary Lynn slugging me so I didn't ask again. Henry Fonda, as you may already know, was in *My Darling Clementine* too. He was also in *The Grapes of Wrath*. These were not so much coincidences as they were signs, except the point they were trying to make was escaping me at the moment. I had no idea Henry Fonda movies kept popping into my head every nine feet, although I think they probably had more to do with the actresses who played opposite him. Had she come out to the end of the dock with me, I would have asked her what sorts of movies she liked generally, even if I wasn't ready to discover she liked *The Graduate* or *Who's Afraid of Virginia Woolf?* two movies that, even if they ever make it to TV, I would never in a million years be allowed to watch with Grumps.

You don't want to find out too much too soon about the other person in a new relationship. You don't want them backing up the dump truck when you're not sure how much you can stand, everything being pretty flimsy yet. Like, if she had been standing here with me, I wouldn't have brought up movies at all, but instead pointed out all the gas bubbles I'd stirred up, how they looked like glazed-over cow eyeballs. They were filled with swamp gas and often gave off interesting fart smells when they popped. We could have discussed that. Unfortunately, not even farts were going to get discussed because when she finished as much of that crusty cigarette as she could tolerate, she flicked it onto the grass and scrambled up the little sloping shortcut to the bridge, seizing on the opportunity my preoccupation with the dock and its gas bubbles had presented.

After a salvation detour for the remainder of the Lucky, which had two inches and now a little bit of lipstick on it, I broke into a full gallop to try and head her off at the pass, otherwise known as the bridge. She had pretty long legs compared to mine and was very nearly to the platform before I'd finished scaling the slope.

"Don't like water, huh?" I hollered, to signal that I was catching up and would be there soonish.

"No," she snapped. She really stretched her legs now.

"Yeah, not me. I swim here all the time. Well, not here… the canal. The water's cleaner."

"Uh-huh."

"Yep. I'm a good swimmer too. Whaddabout fishing? You like to fish?" I was starting to wheeze, but was so close I didn't want to stop and catch my breath.

"God, no. Look, kid, you don't have to follow me. I'm perfectly capable of walking a few hundred yards by myself."

"I know, 'cept like I said, Del asked, so…*ta-da*." My feet felt like a bloody mess by the time I caught her. I'll bet her feet were perfect. "Those are sealskin, aren't they?"

Something unintentionally accusatory in my tone caused her to slam on the brakes. "What?"

"Your boots…they're sealskin."

"Yeah, so what?"

"So nothin'. I almost got a pair once—they're no good for farm work, though. You don't mind wearin' sealskin?"

"No, why should I?" she huffed, sensing there might be some non-cowhide outrage coming next.

I kept my point rational. "Well, you shouldn't, that's why. Just, some people don't want other people wearin' sealskin. Not me. We kill stuff all the time on the farm. People gotta eat. Cows, pigs, horses—we club them with an axe."

"Eew, you kill horses? That's terrible!"

"What? No! Well, there was that one...but he was real sick. Anyway, it wasn't us that killed him. We hired a knacker."

"A *what*?"

"A knacker. That's what they call the guy who goes farm to farm to kill animals you can't eat because they're sick, so he disposes of them for you."

Mary Lynn gave me a look that could've been ten dressed pounds of horror, so I did what I often find myself doing when I'm in Quinton—explaining things, slowly.

"Jeez, no. I mean, no, we don't eat horses. Nobody does. That horse's name was Ted, and me and him were pals. He just took sick and nobody had the heart to whack him. So my grandpa hired a knacker. The guy caught him right here, clean as a whistle." When I showed her the prime real estate, if my skull had been Ted's, her eyes practically spun in their sockets.

This is what makes being both a witness and a theme writer so hard, those times when what you are witnessing is the shortcomings in people you planned on defending in your essay. It seemed that Mary Lynn, like all the other Quintonians, didn't spare a second thought for farmers and what we did for a living.

"My dad used to be a knacker," I pointed out in an effort to tie a bow around the subject of animal slaughter. It wasn't effective.

"Wow, what a shock. What is he now, an executioner?"

"No, he's dead. That's why I had to move in with Gram and Grumps."

"Oh, sorry." She looked to the eastern shore, where she wanted to be more than anywhere else, clearly. "Mine too."

"Oh yeah? Cancer?" I shouldn't have sounded so excited, but once again, Sliver's death was the only part of our relationship that seemed to pay off and get her talking.

"No!" she snarled. "What makes you think cancer?"

"That's how most people in town die. I took a stab."

Because the creosote plant was on the upstream side of the bridge, most of the cancer patients in town lived downstream. With the plant's closing, maybe upstream and downstream Quintonians could finally share a common fatal infirmity. I've already mentioned suicide as the likely candidate, so I won't suggest it here, like I didn't suggest it to Mary Lynn, which was a bullet I didn't realize at the time I'd dodged. I'll just point out how Quinton's cancer patients were like their canaries, for how nobody read those signs either.

"Nope. He drowned." Mary Lynn's voice had fallen to just above a whisper. "I suppose cancer's how your dad died?"

"Nah."

"Oh, heart attack?"

"Nah."

"Jesus, fine. How then?"

"Axe."

A three count later she sputtered, "Bullshit."

I made a chuckling sound at having been called out correctly. How he died would be hard for anybody to believe. Axe, on the other hand, was equal in its bluntness and precision to an instrument of death. Hardly any follow-up questions came when I told people that, which usually left me free to steer conversations where I wanted, someplace far away from Sliver. Such as now: "Your boots are nice, is all I meant."

She flicked a reflexive look at my black beauties, poking out from under my stylish bell-bottoms, then redrew the caftan around her mouth without a word, compliment or otherwise. Of the three choices she had at her disposal, I guess silence was the best I could hope for. I'd gotten plenty of insults at school, and lots of compliments from Gram— and Grumps in his grumbly sort of way. Silence was a new experience for me. In the middle and non-committal.

The bridge forms the middle hump on Main Street. The swing section's base, what the cars ride on instead of real road, resembles a giant cheese grater; you can see through it to the water below. Mary Lynn stopped at the seam between where the pavement ended and the metal began. She peered through the grate into water the colour of tar.

"Don't be afraid," I offered. "It's solid." I jumped on the platform to prove my point. It didn't budge an inch.

"Yeah, I'm not five, kid." Even so, she flinched every time I landed.

"So what...you never crossed before?"

"Yeah, of course. It's just...I don't know, spookier, at night."

"That's weird. Nah, I'm kidding; it's okay. Hey, did you know this looks just like the killing floor at the slaughter-house? Only they use theirs so blood and crap can pass through to a trough underneath."

"Please shut up," she groaned, then took a deep breath of cold river air before edging her way onto the sidewalk's metal weave. A few zombie slash newly unemployed plant workers passed us as they headed to who knew where on the east side, scowling at the dark outline of the plant and its eternal towers of wood hulking there astride the shore. Mary Lynn kept to the safety barrier while she crept along the sidewalk, actually a narrower grate of the same type as the road, so probably not much better if you had concerns about what was under your feet. Zero surprise to me when, barely halfway across, the bridge's bells start to ring. The zombies knew what was what, and broke into trots that carried them in a timely fashion to the other side. We, on the other hand, were fucked.

"What the hell's happening?" she shrieked when the bridge shuddered.

"Better get yer ass movin' or you're goin' for a ride," I encouraged her. She just gripped the railing with both hands and slammed her eyes shut, resigning herself to wherever the bridge wanted to take her. The red and green navigation lights on the downriver side lit up, and through the bridge's canary cage of guy wires and rebars, backlit by his shack, stood the troll on his catwalk, staring toward the bay, a tiny pin light glowing hot between his lips.

"Let's go," I yelled into her ear, and grabbed her hand.

She wouldn't budge, collapsing into a snug ball, her head buried between her knees. This was a perfectly acceptable defence for a baby chick or a bunny in their natural surroundings, but she was none of those. Easy pickings, in other words. The platform's sprockets and gears ground their teeth and our perch began a slow separation from Main Street, carrying me and Mary Lynn with it.

"Neat, eh?" I whistled.

"Are you nuts?" she cried, mostly into her lap.

"Nah, it's cool. Getting stuck here happens all the time... Well, some. But you usually have to plan for it. This is my second time today." I'd always been of the opinion that the town should charge admission rather than trying to keep people off.

A loud blast from downstream drew my attention to the bay, where one of Northwestern Shipping's barges, loaded with coal, was just now plowing into the light cast across the water from Quinton's east side. Not sure where it was chugging to this late in the season. Maybe Peterborough.

Maybe farther west? Most trips upstream included a stop at the creosote plant to dump a load in the yard. Not tonight. To the disappointment of the handful of locals scooping leftover coal into potato sacks, the barge would steam toward the canal without a thought. Me, I took advantage of Mary Lynn covering her eyes to root through my baggie for something calming. Getting it lit was a challenge here in the crosswind, and cost me nearly a whole book of matches, spark after spark briefly hopeful, then zilch. It took the accumulated heat of about a million match heads to finally do the trick and start my butt. That first puff was pure sulphur, but the next wouldn't be too bad. "Here. Take a drag on this."

Mary Lynn muttered into her pants, "Can't you ever stand still?"

"The bridge is just swinging. It'll be heading back in two shakes."

"Just stay put. You'll tip it... I don't wanna drown!" She looked up at me with teary eyes so big they caught the lights from the troll's nest. Kind of heartbreaking, when I think about it now.

"No, no, no... Jeez, you can't tip the bridge. It can't go up and down this way." I tilted my arms up and down like a teeter-totter while jumping up and down on the lip. The bridge more resembles a flimsy birdcage, even when it's locked into place. If someone is afraid of drowning, though, there's probably not enough common sense in the world to make being suspended over open water feel like a perfectly regular position to be in. And what does anybody know about tipping points unless they've been out on the edge to test one or two?

I'm not suggesting that Mary Lynn doesn't have some mechanical knowledge. Working in a department store, she probably knows a little bit about things like toasters, vacuum cleaners, irons, plumbing supplies, math. Some of those I'm familiar with too, some not so much. And now, after sharing this bridge-riding experience with me, she can add tipping points to her areas of expertise. She can look back on tonight and be grateful, if she ever finds herself in a similar predicament.

When presenting an essay in public, exude confidence in the material. Good posture and an appropriate tone help:

Because I know more about non-department store things than Mary Lynn does, and am no stranger to offering advice in these areas, I've found that a key tool when presenting something people might find strange, or boring, is patience. Most of my theme essays, unless they are personally riling, like my Schulz essay for example, are read out loud using a very calm and soothing tone. My grandparents were the first to demonstrate that method, after I experienced how patient they were with ignorant, fresh-from-Quinton me. Quintonians only know best-before dates. Gram and Grumps managed to pass along all the farmer ropes of how things really got planted, grown, harvested, or slaughtered. Mainly, they taught me that there's no arguing with the weather, dirt, sickness, or death. There's no amount of pleading or negotiating or prayer that'll change a course set by nature, once nature has sunk its teeth into a thing. Bad weather is bad weather. Good is good. Nature doesn't have an opinion about anybody or care what anybody thinks about it; it doesn't give a rat's ass about labels like best-before dates.

It's also important to not sound too self-centred about knowing so much more than the people you're trying to educate. Sometimes my tone might drift a little toward brainiac, not taking into account what my audience knows and doesn't know. It's a result of having so many important things to say, which even I didn't realize I had until I got away from Quinton. I knew hardly anything about Mary Lynn's experiences after Bruce. Those canaries were kind of unusual, but as a topic of conversation with a girl, they may have run their course of usefulness. (Thank God I smoked. Nobody gets sick of that! I held out what I knew we had in common and waved it under her nose. She took the cigarette butt, slipped it between her slightly-less-tense-now lips, wincing "Thanks," after her opening drag.) Not that I haven't been storing what I've been learning about her. Since leaving Couch-Newton's I know, besides how we share an interest in smoking, that we share an interest in dead fathers. And now we've ridden a bridge together, so can add ignoring stupid Keep Off the Bridge signs to the list of shared experiences unrelated to Bruce. These make for fine starting points, or prompts, if like me you think in those terms. As we had about ten minutes to kill on the bridge, I thought I'd try to find us some more common ground, by throwing a little of my historical perspective into the mix. Hopefully she'd have a few thoughts of her own during the question-and-answer period at the end.

"So, you know I live on a farm, right?"

"That's great. Don't care."

"Well, it's true. Not forever, but starting when I was about five or six. I was just a little kid, so pretty stupid about what was going on around me."

"Wow, look at you now."

Her indifference toward we farmers was typical Quinton, a barrier we'd have to face a few times before we could settle into a nice, coupley, routine. I was ready. If Gram and Grumps have taught me anything (besides farm stuff), it's that the people your lessons are meant for can come away wiser and not even realize they've learned anything. "Yep, so one morning, really, really early..."

The tinny rattling Gram made while gathering the morning's pots and pans travelled through the same wrought-iron grate that, in the wintertime, let the heat from the kitchen into my bedroom. I also had the warming benefit of a heavy chicken-feather quilt, a thick grey fuzzy blanket, a comforter, and a thin white sheet that pinned me to the bed Gram had tucked me into, so normally in the morning I'd have a good sweat going from trying to wiggle out. On the sky-blue dresser over by the window sat my next-day clothes, folded. I'd stopped being surprised to find them there after living with Gram and Grumps for about a week. I was more used to having my clothes lay where I'd dropped them the night before, but in this house, somebody had been coming into my room after I'd fallen asleep to pick them up, fold them, then set them on the dresser for me to find. Sometimes the clothes weren't even the ones I'd peeled off, but brand-new ones, or at least cleaner ones. I'd stand in my underwear and bare feet and stare, because even the simplest things, like getting out of bed, had changed and took getting used to.

The five-in-the-morning pots and pans, for example, took some time to figure out, but eventually I got to the point where I could sleep right through Grumps's breakfast, before he went off to do whatever farmers did so early in the goddamn morning. The big mystery on this particular morning was that the noise I heard through the grate wasn't part of the usual kitchen hullabaloo. It sounded like Gram's radio got stuck between two stations and both stations had guys playing saws. Nobody could sleep through a saw duet. I got dressed and headed to my door, stubbing my toe on my piss pot. (We farmers use piss pots after we've gone to bed, so we don't have to hike to the outhouse at night.)

There weren't doorknobs anywhere in our farmhouse—all latches—and in the middle of the night they clack like crazy. It took some mean B-and-E skills to open a door without making it sound like I'd dropped a milk bucket full of bolts. None of which mattered that morning, because Gram and Grumps weren't going to hear me over all the racket. The kitchen was the only room in the house that didn't have an actual door; I slid a finger between the two curtains and peered in. There was Grumps, running his butcher's knife across his whetting stone. That was the sound. He was sitting next to the stove, his chair leaning back against the wall, a half-smile on his face and a cigarette in his mouth. Every so often he'd drag the back of his thumb against the knife, check the knife for curls of fingernail, and begin again. It's a very hypnotic sound. Maybe Grumps liked hearing it as much as having a sharp knife. Sliver played the harmonica; maybe Grumps played the knife and stone. I didn't have a hobby back then, not even smoking, my days already full to spilling with all the exploring around the farm I did whenever I wasn't trailing Gram while she performed her chores. I mean, good luck trying to find time to practise anything. I'd forget the bits I knew and have to start all over. It'd drive me crazy.

But all good things must come to an end, even songs, and Grumps slapped his knee and announced to the world, "Time's a-wastin'," which got him a sharp *shh!* for a reply, Gram's wooden spoon swirling in the direction of the grate between me and them. He made a sort of ducking motion at the memory of me, then pulled himself up out of his chair with a more subdued *whoosh-uff* of effort. Clearly this warm place was going to be better than anywhere he was headed to in the dark of early morning.

He swallowed his teacup's leftovers on the way to the basin, set the cup and saucer beside it, and then carried on toward the mud room, grabbing the axe propped beside the door. Because I couldn't very well follow him through the kitchen, I tiptoed across the living room to a chorus of Gram's pots and dishes clashing in the sink. I stopped at the side window that overlooked the barn and located Grumps inside a circle of lantern light, the axe's head flickering on his shoulder. In a leather pouch on his hip slapped the knife. He paused at the side door to the barn, the one that led to the milking room, to turn down the wick on the lantern, then disappeared inside. With the coast now clear, I snuck out through the company door, what Gram called the one that faces Victoria Road (because nobody ever used it except company), and reached the barn just as Grumps was throwing the breaker arm. Every light bulb in the barn came on. My first concern became that he was going to load the hayloft without me. We'd planned on sending hay bales up the conveyor later today. My job was to ride the bales up. I dragged a bale over beneath the window of the milk room, but found it was empty, so I dragged the block of hay beneath the window that looked across the large main floor. There were the cows, all tucked into their stalls on either side of the aisle, some shuffling, some dozing. It took a second to spot Grumps down at the last stall, the one we used to separate cows about to give birth—or sick ones—from the rest of the herd.

Grumps had the one in there now by the tail, slapping her on the rump to steer her toward the aisle. The old girl's name was Ethel. She began a slow waddle toward the double-wide doors that opened to the corral, which also happened to be where I was standing on my bale. Me and her stared eye to eye for a second. I practically fell off the bale when she mooed at me to open the goddamn doors. Grumps had other ideas, though, yanking her tail and pointing her toward the slaughter room. Grumps once told me he called it the slaughter room because that's where he tore apart all his old, broken machines, and true enough, hanging from the walls and rafters were tire rims, bars, chains, metal discs, long narrow spikes, and just about every kind of whirligig you could imagine. The floor in that room was spotless but for a little bed of straw lying under a chain-and-pulley system strapped to the main roof beam. By the time I'd dragged my bale to its window, Grumps and the cow were standing in the straw, Grumps stroking her wide forehead. He might have been talking to her but his back was to me, so who knows. Gram talked to me when she stroked my forehead, so anything was possible.

Turned out all he was doing was picking a landing spot for his axe, which he drew back barely higher than his shoulders, then swung down square on Ethel's head with the blunt end. She dropped to her front knees while her butt stayed up for a second or two, then it flopped to the floor as well. When her front knees gave out, her giant head smacked against the floor. Quick as lightning Grumps had her hind legs tied to the pulley, and a couple dozen whirls of rattling chain later, Ethel was swinging free and easy above the straw. After he steadied her swing, he removed the knife from his pouch and slid it across the side of her throat. A spout of blood, nearly as wide as the water from our kitchen pump, shot across the room. That's when things got hazy— and then disappeared completely.

I came to inside the slaughter room, propped against Ethel in the straw. Her body was still warm as toast.

"Morning there." Grumps's smile was a thin, tight line and his eyes were sternly fixed to mine, waiting for them to stop bouncing off the sides of my skull. He had blood up to his elbows.

"Sliver? I thought you was dead," I coughed.

"I'm not your dad, son."

Grumps closed his eyes through a long inhale of tobacco. He removed the cig from his mouth, which like I said, he hardly ever does, and pointed the damp end at me. "Here," he said. "Take a little puff. Short and gentle. It'll clear your head."

I did like he told me. My head swam a piece further, partly from the tobacco, partly from the dream, before my focus could settle accounts with the sticky sweet smell to the room.

"Don't say a word to your Gram about this, or she'll see to it I end up like the cow."

I shook my head that I wouldn't. I liked that we were going to be a team in this one thing. I'd never had a partner before.

My grin, when I'd finished sharing my slice of farmer life with Mary Lynn, was about a mile wide and full of hope that she'd see what made me *me*—and what we had to look forward to together, if she picked up on the sly and wise "partner" message buried in my tale's conclusion.

"And?" was how she began her response. Not a question I'd anticipated.

"And what? That's it."

"So you pass out watching cows get their throats slit. Big whoop. Who wouldn't?"

"No, it's about the first time I smoked," I said. "Plus other stuff." I was a little crushed that her only takeaway was how I'd fainted at the sight of blood.

"Hmm, okay," she said, tapping her chin. "Then how did he find you outside if he was inside?"

"Ah, I guess when I fell off the stupid bale I banged my

head pretty loud on the wall. He found me and carried me inside."

"Ha," she sneered, still hung up on the fainting angle obviously. "When was this? Yesterday?"

"No, a long time ago." Fact was, I'd seen a lake full of blood on the farm since that day. Besides, it wasn't the blood that got me woozy, but how Grumps had suddenly turned into Sliver. But of course Mary Lynn had only zeroed in on the part when I was weakest. "And anyway, you're not one to talk. I'll bet you've never seen anything die right in front of you."

In looking back, I think this will do as a good example of me being self-centred.

It's also why most things, not just cigarettes, should have filters on them. Drowned dads, cancer diagnosis, factory closings, canaries... What if all that unpleasantness slipped through charcoal-activated, menthol-flavoured felts of alternative possibilities first—Heaven, or Medicare, or UIC—and came out the other side with hints of hope? I've smoked roll-yer-owns and I've smoked things I'd found between the cracks in sidewalks, and no matter how crusty they'd gotten, even a sidewalk smoke with a filter doesn't come close to the eye-watering experience of a rollie. Thanks to Mary Lynn's filtering effects on my day, I was having a hell of a decent time, despite all my humping back and forth and then breaking my bike by smacking into Tab's car. As for my filtering effect on Mary Lynn, well, that was still a work in progress. A guy can hand out life memories and butts until the cows come home, but sometimes he just has to wait to see what sort of impression they've made.

She hoisted herself to her feet and stared through the grate into the flickering water beneath us. I expected her to bring up her dad as an example from her own life, but she didn't. Instead, she shifted her gaze to the creosote plant, its stacks of telephone poles and railroad ties in shadows, where yesterday they'd been basking in a secure glow.

"They're all out of work," she said.

"Yeah, I guess."

"What are they going to do?"

"Dunno." I shrugged. "Fish?

Mary Lynn slowly adjusted her gaze again, more or less in my direction, but her eyes didn't meet mine, rather settled a little over my head, like she'd just heard the dumbest noise in the world but didn't want to acknowledge the source's existence. Biting her lip she waited for the road to creep into alignment with the bridge. East side Quinton was the busiest it'd been in forever, if you counted all the people standing around doing nothing. I left her to her thoughts about her fellow Quintonians and went to the bridge's edge to enjoy the gut-tickling shudder-and-rumble that came when it aligned with the pavement. The bells clanged "Hooray!" the way bells will, and the lights on the black-and-white wooden arm flashed, letting the whole waiting world know it was going up. Too bad Mary Lynn hadn't joined me.

A bridge in the process of closing is quite the production. It's no wonder I was too distracted and didn't catch the sound of her flying the bridge-coop, the feathery-soft muffle-and-shuffle of sealskin boots rustling being barely a whisper compared to the clatter of the bells and the grinding gears. Looking up I glimpsed her yellow caftan flapping goodbye, and wedged between her fingers *our* cigarette, burning against the night like an engagement ring on fire.

Thankfully, of the zombie mob she was charging into, most had splintered into smaller factions, depending on what east-side distraction tugged hardest at their wish to fill their sudden free time. Some headed for the deli counter at the drugstore. Some slipped into Ether's place to shoot pool. Some walked the extra block to the hotel that featured dancing girls. Technically, I was only under contract with Del to see to it Mary Lynn got to her mom's work in one piece. She was about sixty feet from bringing that contract to a close. Thematically, I still wanted to explore and expand on what I'd started six years ago with her, learn what sort of union would work best for us, since I knew so little about the non-labour varieties. Because there was still plenty of work to do in the various fields of love, I was actually pleased to watch her and her bright yellow caftan light on the side of the road opposite the drugstore, and appear in no hurry to cross the road. Her reasons were probably unrelated to me, but so what? An opening was an opening. After giving my legs a shake to restore body to the corduroy bells around my boots, I bounded after her.

As most of Quinton has discovered today, there are times when even a union is not a picture of stability, and we have to find and celebrate brotherhoods and sisterhoods where we can:

When Grumps wasn't explaining farming and old movies to me, he liked to rail against scabs and union busters. I was never clear about why I should care until this exact moment, when a lanky, pimple-faced greaseball stepped out of a cluster of zombie mobsters and slid across the road. Before I could scream, "Look out!" he was pulling our cigarette from Mary Lynn's mouth and sticking it in his own. Pretty intimate gesture for a scab, I thought, especially considering he'd done nothing to earn the smoke—he'd jumped the line, bold as brass. Worse than anything, though, when he finished his drag he dropped the butt on the ground and twisted it into dust with his running shoe, just as me and my rubbers were stumbling up to the curb, him leaning in like he was about to kiss her on the mouth or something. The loose tobacco got caught up in a cold gust of wind arrived off the river and whirled away. I curled my lip.

"I'm sorry," I'd heard her say, just before she planted a peck on his cheek. "Maybe something better will come along."

Trawl (his name was painted on the side of the lunch pail dangling from one hand, as well as stitched onto his green nylon jacket in white lettering, green and white being the high school's colours, and a year under that which put him beyond an appropriate best-before date for Mary Lynn) passed up the opportunity to kiss her because, I hoped, I was that "something better."

"You didn't tell me you had a little brother." He winked at Mary Lynn. "You know this twerp?" He sneered down at me from at least a foot above, in case I missed the double slam of being both brotherly and a twerp. I was too steamed over the cigarette's loss and what a piss-poor job Mary Lynn had done of protecting our property to return a slam of my own, however.

"Jeezuz, you again." She seemed genuinely surprised to see me parked at her shoulder, like I hadn't been parked at her shoulder off and on for most of the day. "I dunno...*the Kid* or something."

Trawl sniffed. "Hello, *the Kid*. You got a real name?"

I did, but as Mary Lynn would shortly delight in discovering, my first name was pretty susceptible to abuse, so Trawl sure wasn't going to hear it from me.

"You a mute?" He poked my chest.

A normal twerp would have walked away when the finger

landed. I didn't budge. I blame love. Some people run away from that too, skedaddle into the sunset rather than hang around a little longer to see how the world turns with him still in it. I refused to even consider the possibility that the person I wanted already had somebody in her life. I suppose it was pretty stupid of me to think that Mary Lynn had been twiddling her thumbs before I got here. Then again, if I'd known the facts, I might have jumped on that last barge, broken-hearted and steaming west.

I'm not someone given to shouting myself stupid from a rooftop about my feelings. I'm a declarative-in-essay-form sonofabitch instead. Think of me along the not-so-obvious-unless-you'd-seen-the-movies lines of a Clark Gable with Claudette Colbert in *It Happened One Night*, or possibly Margaret Sullivan and James Stewart in *The Shop Around the Corner*. Either of those types might do the job here, because I'm pretty sure I heard a shift in Mary Lynn's tone when Trawl poked me, which, had I not seen those movies, I might have missed completely. She was that subtle about me.

"Leave him alone. He's just walking me to my mom's work." Mary Lynn pushed Trawl's hand from my chest and pointed across the road to the drugstore.

"Ah, me and the kid are cool. Ain't we, kid?"

I swear, if he'd scuffed my head right then, I'd have dropped him. I'd be punching up a weight class, but I'd do it.

Instead I said, "Yep," and took a step back, just in case. A lot of people can't help themselves with brush cuts and I didn't want to plow him in front of Mary Lynn—didn't want to reveal uncontrollable violent tendencies, if I had any. Decently, Trawl stuck out his greasy paw, intending for me to take it, which I very nearly did until something on the wind caused him to jerk away his hand.

"Shit, you smell like a farmer." He made a big production out of sniffing. His obvious point was that Quintonians had a smell and farmers had a smell, and if you were the only farmer in the Quinton crowd, yours was the standout smell.

Ask Gram about Grumps's smell and she'd let out a great whoop: "It's what we live with. It's our air," she'd say. It never occurred to me that the air that caused Grumps's smell might have soaked into me, but because I'd started to like Gram and Grumps a fair bit, things like the air we lived in didn't bother me as much as it should have. To return to my point about gradual shifts into affection and unions, for anybody who hasn't been paying close enough attention: maybe the reason Mary Lynn never mentioned my air was because she was starting to come around to me in a Claudette Colbert slash Margaret Sullivan sort of way. Which was good, because if we were going to be an item, whatever that item turned into, I couldn't have my gal's eyes watering up every time I walked into the room.

I did take Trawl up on his invitation to shake before he changed his mind completely, gripping his hand with all my bale-lifting strength and squeezing like I was still that kid who'd just flown through a car window, lost his bike and his birds, found out his gal had been stepping out with someone else. I'd taken about all the slippery turns I could handle. Not to mention the fact Trawl was a scab who'd just crashed a meeting of the union of smokers.

Trawl's mouth tightened as he tried to jerk himself free— little tugs at first, then more panicked when he realized I had a point to make. When his knees started to wobble the same way cow Ethel's had, Mary Lynn tapped me on the shoulder: "Hey, kid, just let it go. Everybody's having a bad day."

Like I'd said before, mine had actually swung to pretty okay, but telling someone to let it go is not always the good advice people think it is, because the second I did, Trawl threw down his lunch pail and raised both fists. He looked itching to throw one.

Mary Lynn stepped between us: "Jeez, he's just being a punk. Don't take your stuff out on him."

"Yeah, no. I think I want to." He stared at the top of my head, striking a pose that looked copied from every grainy boxing picture in the world.

I pulled my own fists up, but more like Tommy Douglas than Tommy Ryan. According to Grumps, Tommy Douglas was also some sort of boxing champ in Manitoba; he fought out of the One Big Union gym. Mary Lynn slapped at my fists first, which was very distracting.

"Whaddaya think *you're* doin', Kid?"

"I got this," I said.

Trawl snarled, "Great, cuz I'm fixin' on plowin' ya, farm-boy." Pushing forward, he nearly pinned Mary Lynn between me and him.

"Both of you—just grow up." She had that look girls get when a guy is fixing to do something immature, her mouth hanging open and her eyes half-shut, like she was about to yawn.

Trawl saw an opportunity. He shoved her clear and came over the top with a cheap shot to my head. Fortunately, being very skinny, he didn't pack a lot of heft. If he'd been a steer on our farm, we'd have axed him for that lack of vitality alone. (Skinny steers don't fetch their weight in what they eat up to auction time.) That didn't stop him from clasping his hands over his head like some sort of champ, right before screaming, "Jesus!" and pulling his noggin-slugging hand against his chest.

I'd punched enough hay bales under Grumps's eye to know that the best way to dislocate a thumb is to tuck it inside your fist before you swing. It'll pop out right at the big knuckle. Trawl squinted back his tears, his face glowing like a freshly washed beet. None of which is a good look for anybody in front of a girl—or an opponent. At least he found enough of the brains God gave gravel to slump away, muttering that cheesy villain's line about me not seeing the last of him.

For my heroics I got a half-assed cuff across my lunk from Mary Lynn, before she scooped up Trawl's lunch pail and ran it to him. They shared a smooch and a few words, some I think meant to be relayed to me. She lunged those baby blues my way, hooded under severely angled eyebrows, and in three strides was on top of me, her arm reloaded for another cuff. I ducked, telling her, "Easy, toots," like Bogart might've done if his doll, Bacall, had already cuffed him once and meant to do it again. I don't think she was thinking of either Bogart or Bacall when she dropped her arm mid-swing and slid it into her pocket.

"Nah," she said, smirking. "Too much trouble." From her pocket she pulled out a stick of spearmint gum, stripped it, then popped it in her mouth, the whole time staring at my face, like a hundred little light bulbs were going off in her head. Folding the gum with her tongue and shoving it to one side, she only tossed the mildest insult ever at me. "Don't you have any friends?"

Thankfully she didn't stick around for an answer and was standing on the other side of the road before I could spit out a roster of random kids in my class. I shuffled after her but kept the list to myself as I waited in the drugstore's light beside her for the spearmint to take hold of her breath. Between the two of us, the smell of cigarettes was pretty thick.

"You're lucky he didn't kill you, kid." The first wisps of her sweetened breath assaulted my nose.

"That's not luck, sister. I was all over it. How old is he anyway?"

"Old enough."

"Can he drive?"

"Yeah, of course. He has a licence. He has a job... Had."

"Great, so he can drive himself to the unemployment office."

Mary Lynn held her palm up to her mouth and blew. I could have told her her breath was perfect but didn't get the chance. She pushed me to one side with another insult of the mild variety: "In case you haven't heard this yet today, you're kind of a jerk, you know."

I'd come to the conclusion that she wasn't very good at insulting people. Or at least not very good at insulting me, which I blamed on her not knowing me well enough to say anything decent. When she ducked into the drugstore, I was right behind her.

Mary Lynn's mom, in her blue pinstriped Bob's Drugs and Stuff uniform, was on the other side of the door when we walked in. She hadn't witnessed anything of across the road because she gave Mary Lynn a peck on the cheek. She didn't have her daughter's blond hair, at least anymore. It was mostly rust-coloured, with a little grey poking through here and there under her white kerchief. Also, around her eyes were a ton of worry lines Mary Lynn will probably have one day. In fact, there's probably a whole other theme essay in me about patience, tolerance, sympathy, and how much shit you can put up with before it starts to show. I'd call it "An Explosion of Lines" or something equally clever.

Mother and daughter did share eyes to die for, I must admit. People got those eyes when looking at a roadkill cat—*Poor little bastard, never had a chance*—that general theme. For Mary Lynn's mom, the cause of why she looked at me that way was pretty apparent—she'd been talking to Officer Del. Seems I was the topic of his second phone call, so not a hint of surprise on her face to see me trailing her daughter. Skipping the intros, she pointed to an empty booth and commanded, "Park it."

I expected this moment, but didn't see it coming. You couldn't get more official notice that your obligation was over than have it come straight from the top. I couldn't believe how far short of my goal I'd fallen—which I partly blame on never having a clear goal in mind. This brings up an important *Hinterland Who's Who* moment for theme essay writing (cue the flute)—pick your theme ahead of time. Otherwise you'll spend a lot of the early going stumbling around, looking for things to say until you get your footing.

As I stood in the doorway with my thumb up my ass, my delivery duties complete, I probably looked like one of my mudcats after being caught and placed on the ground: opening and shutting my mouth, nothing coming out. Since nobody ever invites the mailman in for a cup of tea, I removed my thumb finally and reached for the door, my half-hatched dreams of Mary Lynn's companionship all but busted like so many teacups on a sticky drugstore floor. With a long hike ahead of me, even with the few shortcuts I knew, I figured I'd be back at the farm in about a month.

I didn't get very far.

"Whoa, mister."

Out of the corner of my eye I recognized the approach of a determined hand, and I dipped my head accordingly. The hand was just there to spin me around and escort me to the booth, however. "You plop yourself down with her."

"Yes, ma'am," I practically cheered.

"Leona," she corrected me, tapping the name tag on her blouse.

She followed me to the booth, her hand on my shoulder the whole way, not realizing how unnecessary that was. She steered me onto the bench opposite Mary Lynn and gave us a briefing. "Now, I got about fifteen till my shift is over, so you guys wait here. We're giving you a lift home when I'm done."

Mary Lynn exploded. "Mom, I got stuff! I made plans!" I'll bet she meant with Trawl—something about a tankful of gas, a mickey of rye, and a cornfield echoed in my head.

"Well, sweetheart, now they're going to include him for a little bit."

"What? Him? Why?"

"Officer McCabe—Del's last name, obviously—asked if we could give him a lift and I said we'd be glad to."

"So we're giving rides to every mutt who follows me home now? Mom, I get one night. That was the deal."

"I know, sweetheart, and I'm sorry, but sometimes things come up." Leona swept her hand over the room, in case Mary Lynn hadn't noticed how just about everybody in the drugstore'd had a thing come up.

For future reference, if a guy ever needed a place to hide in a rainstorm, he could do worse than to park himself under the lower lip Mary Lynn produced. She could pout aces. Pretty nice to look at, if I ignored her "mutt" crack and the lasers she was burning into my forehead.

"Jeeeez." Mary Lynn sagged impressively into the booth's padded bench, crossing her arms over her chest in a leave-me-the-fuck-alone posture.

I shuffled a couple of inches at a time along the bench until perched, barely a cheek and a half's worth of ass, on the edge. It had a covering of gummy red vinyl, the kind that made hilarious fart noises whenever an ass moved a certain way. Grumps and me had entertained ourselves at this very booth in the past.

"So, what about you, handsome? Want something while you wait?" (Leona called me *handsome*!) The joint was nearly full with the town's recently made miserable, every one of them grumbling like a deep, steady drumbeat, so she had to practically shout. Which got me thinking about how her whole day had probably been spent yelling to be heard. On the farm, when we yell to be heard, it's because of all the empty space between us, although lately Grumps has been mumbling a little bit too. I've always been kept pretty busy at the farm, so haven't had a lot of free time to think about the business side of farming, which I'm sure is important too.

"Hey, kid. My mom's talking to you."

"What? Oh, sorry. Yes, ma'am. I mean Leona. Tea, please."

Mary Lynn rolled her eyes. Her mom walked away with a chuckle, stopping at another booth before continuing on to behind the lunch counter, where she began fiddling with knobs and steam and stuff.

Mary Lynn saved her fiercest look of the day for this moment.

"What?" I demanded.

"How old are you? Nobody under fifty drinks tea."

"Whaddaya mean? We drink tea all the time."

"Pffft," Mary Lynn sputtered. "Well, nobody in town."

A little bit of her judgment spit landed on my neatly folded hands. She spent the next minute sending heat beams at it, trying to evaporate it. The bubble didn't shrink, and I wasn't about to wipe the little darling away. The hippies at school talked about swapping spit, and while this wasn't exactly what they meant, I was pretty pleased with the exchange. It got me thinking about a smoke, like the characters in Grumps's *Argosy* magazine stories had when their encounters were over. But there was no cool way around rooting through my butt baggie. The Lucky Mary Lynn'd tossed back at the docks was the only decent-enough sized one left. And wouldn't that've been perfect, her lipstick on the paper like a crime-scene bloodstain.

An ashtray sat against the wall at that end of our booth. It was clean, unfortunately. I slid it to the middle of the table anyway and twirled it around with my finger, the action causing the spit bubble to burst finally, which was the break Mary Lynn had been waiting for. With one push she was at the edge of her bench, then beelining for her mother, to hash out the particulars of her new evening. That gave me the time I needed to dip into my stash for something in the two-inch-or-longer department, since it looked like I'd be sitting by myself for a minute or two. There was a lot of arm-flapping on both sides of their debate, Mary Lynn's mom possibly introducing whatever Del may have told her about me, things I'd have preferred not be revealed without being able to filter them first.

The sulphur cracked when the match head burst and that farty smell (also good for a laugh in the right crowd) filled the booth. The butt, perched at the full extension of my lips to avoid me giving myself a burn, was just long enough that I could guide the flame to it accident-free. Seasoned butt smokers know what I'm talking about. I settled back on the bench to enjoy what tasted like a curb-Players and take in the ambience of the most miserable drugstore diner in history. A minute later, Mary Lynn was carving her own swath through the misery, a glass of Coke in one hand and a cup of tea balanced on a saucer in the other.

"Here," she groused like every surly server in the world as she set my tea in front of me. She pointed at the condiment tray. "The milk's in one of those plastic things there. There's the sugar."

I removed one thing of milk and four things of sugar. "Aren't you going to tell me to have a nice day?"

"Why the hell would I do that?"

If she wasn't sore with her mom, I think she might have laughed, or at least insulted me a little. "It's a joke. You were being my waitress, see? That's what they say." I went ha-ha-ha but it came out wheezy and fake.

"Okay, whatever."

Mary Lynn wasn't much for games with me yet, settling over her Coke to stir the hell out it with a paper straw, sparing an occasional snort for my tea. Frothy brown bubbles exploded around her ice cubes.

I took a long drag on my cigarette, hoping she might recall the good times we'd had as smokers together, about twenty minutes ago. Instead, a flicker of panic crossed her face.

"Don't let my mom catch you. She'll kill us both."

"Nah, people don't care what anybody does. I smoke everywhere and people don't say shit."

Her hair whipped across her eyes, Veronica Lakeish again. "No, you're way wrong as usual. Some people care a lot about other people. They just see to it you don't know about it."

"Like your mom?"

Mary Lynn shook her head. "No, she'd let you know. Also, she used to be a nurse at the hospital before it closed. She's used to commanding people to stay healthy for their own good."

"Yeah, that's not the same. She got paid. Otherwise, if you don't deal with things yourself you might better let the knacker come and haul you away. That's what I think. Unless they're getting paid, people don't do shit."

Mary Lynn's face became one giant knot. I stabbed my cigarette into the ashtray and suggested she relax. "It's just a conversation," I said.

"You mean like your cow-killing conversation?" She nearly smiled, but it died on the branch.

Her point was kind of on the nose, though. Some of my theme essays tend to miss the original mark. That wasn't always my fault. People's takeaways can go only as far as what they know. And like I've said, Quinton has been a very limited town, in my experience.

I took the four things of sugar and opened them at the same time, then began pouring them into my spoon. Ordinarily I take four teaspoons of sugar in my tea. A thing of sugar didn't give me barely one. I made two full teaspoons with the four things and dumped them into my cup, then tore open another two. Mary Lynn watched, quite mesmerized, until whatever I was doing wrong in her eyes pushed her over the edge.

"Jesus, you're supposed to dump the sugar into the cup. You don't need the spoon."

I blinked at the illogic. "And how do I know how much is in a packet unless I fill up the spoon first? I would've been short almost two whole spoons."

"You just know."

"Well, guess what? On the farm, our sugar doesn't come from little packages, so sue me." I took the spoon and stirred the whole muddy mess. I thought I was in the clear once I clinked my spoon on the saucer, but Mary Lynn practically fell out of the booth when, next, I poured a little of the tea into the saucer and raised it to my mouth. As I blew across the surface, I realized I was eye to eye with the next round of scorn. I lowered my tea. "What now?"

"You're drinking it out of the saucer. God, who does that?"

"I dunno. Lots of people."

"Hardly. In fact, nobody, that's who. Is it a farmer thing too? Farmers don't use cups?"

"It cools it down faster. Otherwise I'd have to sit here longer in your stupendous company, waiting for it to cool."

"What's wrong with my company?" Mary Lynn had climbed out of her self-pity long enough to catch the insult.

"Nothing, you're a peach," I said. Same tone; same intent.

Boy, she had me steamed. Or something had me steamed. Maybe it was the tea. I poured what I hadn't drunk from the saucer back into the cup, then put the cup on the saucer. I crumpled the empty paper packets and stuffed them into the little milk container and set it on the saucer, then shoved everything—cup, saucer, garbage—toward the aisle end of the table, so her mom could reach it. I could have lit a butt with my face, it felt so hot, so now I had to worry about bursting into tears or something over how I'd wasted the golden opportunity Del and Leona had presented me with to figure things out with Mary Lynn and not act like a pissy twelve-year-old. I buttoned my red-and-black checkerboard hunter's jacket up to my chin to brace for a long cold walk and swung my legs out from under.

"Lookit, I'm sorry you got stuck with me. I'm sorry I ruined your plans. I didn't ask Del to call your mom. Tell her thanks for the tea and the ride offer, but I'd rather walk." And now my voice was cracking. What a piece of work.

Mary Lynn sucked in air sharply through her teeth, clearly pricked by some terrible thought. She swivelled her head over her shoulder, toward where her mother was washing dishes.

"My mom said she'd drive you. What am I supposed to tell her when you're not here?"

"I don't care. Tell her I drink tea out of a saucer. She'll

probably be thrilled she dodged *that* bullet."

Mary Lynn's forehead wrinkled. "She's gonna be sore, you know."

"Maybe not. She seems nice."

"No, sore at me."

Now, I wasn't a rash-acting fellow in general. I didn't make rude choices all the time, and by that I mean choices that might affect another person in unintended ways. Seeing the consequences to my actions is a kind of gift, like how some people can do math in their head, except instead of being able to say what nineteen times forty-three times three times five hundred and sixty-seven is without the use of an abacus, I see how the choices I make might affect other people before I make them. Which is not to say I wouldn't make them anyway; I'd just be disappointed with myself after.

Okay, so maybe it's not as cool a superpower as the math thing, which I'd kill for, by the way. And sometimes the superpower is to simply *not* to do a thing at all if it means harm—like being the cause of Mary Lynn's mom screaming at her. It's really just the superpower of not being a jerk all the time, and being more considerate generally. And since I've already been accused of being a jerk by Mary Lynn once today, perhaps it was time to try heading back to my main purpose. So yeah, not so much a superpower or a gift, just the experience of being on the other side once or twice. I unbuttoned my jacket and slid my ass back on the bench. I stayed near the outside edge, though. I think my gesture worked, because Mary Lynn said, "Thank you." Then she took our relationship a step toward a direction I wasn't all that fussy about:

"So, what's your name, really? I know it's not *the Kid*."

"Nope. But it's pretty dumb, so I'd rather not say yet."

"Yet? What are you waiting for? The Christmas card?"

"Nah, just not yet."

"It must be pretty bad. Is it Dorcas or something?"

"What? No. It's a real name. That's just a made-up name. Nobody's called dorkus unless you mean it for an insult, like 'Hey, dorkus, what's with the head?' You know, like that."

"Ya-huh. My aunt's called Dorcas. Auntie Dorcas."

"Bull."

"Nope. It's true. It's from somewhere…the Bible or something."

"Well, I wouldn't know about that."

"Where do you go to school?"

"St. Mary's."

"Hey, that's where my aunt teaches. How can you go to St. Mary's and not know about the Bible? It's the law there."

"I manage. Anyway, bull on that too. There ain't no Dorkuses teaching at St. Mary's. No, wait a mo— We have a ton of dorkuses teaching there. Which one is she?"

"She doesn't go by that name now, dummy."

"Wow, what a surprise."

"No, she's a nun. They change their names when they turn nun. She's Sister Mary Madeline. Nuns are all Sister Mary something."

"Holy smokes, no kiddin'? She's my teacher. Oh man, that's great. I can't wait until Monday."

"No, you can't say anything! It's a sin or death or something if their real names get found out."

"Nah, it'd be a sin *not* to blab something that good." I was practically rubbing my hands together.

"Just don't, okay?" Mary Lynn with her doe eyes, she sure knew how to use them.

"Ah, okay. Hey, you're a Mary. Mary Lynn. You plannin' on being a nun with good ol' Auntie Dorkus?"

"No, not ever."

"Ah, too bad. You'd make a great nun, I bet, for how you like to cuff people."

Mary Lynn raised her hand like she meant to slug me to prove me wrong. "You don't know a thing about me."

I told myself she meant to be playful, that she wasn't really going to cuff me, but the second I saw the shadow pass over my head, I pulled my head down. Again.

Mary Lynn gaped. "Jesus, what? Did you think I really wanted to slap you?"

I felt stupid as hell, of course; there's no recovering from ducking from a girl. "Nu-huh."

"Ya-huh, you ducked." A crooked little smile appeared. Not a full-blown gotcha smirk or anything, but more as if she'd caught a taste of something and seemed to enjoy it. Suddenly afraid that she might try to pry deeper in that direction, I pulled out the only distraction play I had: "It's Kaspar."

"What is?"

"My name. It's Kaspar."

"Casper? As in the ghost? Bull."

"No, that's Casper with a *C* and an *er* at the end. Mine has a *K*, with an *ar* at the end. K–a–s–p–a–r."

"Holy cow, that's awful."

"Yeah, I told you. Now you know."

"Jesus. So...when Auntie Dorcas calls your name out, she actually says something like, 'Kaspar, quit being so stupid!'"

"Nah. She goes, 'Kap, quit being stupid.' Most everybody there calls me Kap."

"Cap? Like the little hat? Jesus, this just keeps getting better." Her turn to rub her hands together, I guess.

"No...well, yeah, I guess. 'Cept you'd have to spell it with a *K* to be correct. Otherwise yeah, just like the hat."

"Holy cow."

"Yeah, you said that already."

"Oh, oops. It's just…I never met one before."

"Well, *ta-da*!" I threw out my hands for the umpteenth time today.

"Ha. So who are you named after? You gotta be named after somebody. Got anybody in your family who acts weird?" She raised her eyebrows real high and made a new and prettier smile just before easing up on me. "Nah, I'm teasing. But nobody does that to a kid unless they're paying off a debt or something."

(This was another new step in our relationship, letting me know when she was teasing.)

"I dunno. It's Russian, I think. Maybe back there."

"A commie, eh? Are you an immigrant or something?"

"No, I don't think so. I mean, I'm not sure when that applies." My class at school did take social studies, but its focus hadn't left Quinton yet.

"If you came from some other country, like maybe you've escaped a war…and ended up here."

"At the drugstore?"

"No, goof. Bigger here. In Canada."

"Oh…" I scrubbed my chin, trying to figure out what she was implying. I wondered if there were different types of immigrants, local ones as well as the flown-in-from-far-away variety. Because I thought I qualified, if you could immigrate to a farm from Quinton. Telling her some long, boring story about that part of my life might come off like self-pity. She wouldn't find that very attractive. "Then no, I'm not that."

"Well, why Kap and not Kas? Even Kap doesn't make sense. I think Kas makes more sense, don't you? Even for the shorthand. Why jump to the P when the S is sitting right there? It's not even logical."

"About as logical as Kaspar, I guess."

"Yeah, that's the truth. I think you could be called Kass. Like Mama Cass, only with a K."

"Who's that? Your grandmother?"

"Jesus, listen to music at all?"

"Nope. Do you think it's better than Kaspar?"

"No, probably not. But not as bad as Kap." She winced. "I can call you Kass from now on, if you want."

"Fine with me," I said, especially since it came with that hint of a future together.

The whole name thing had been beating me down for years, much of it coming from school. I think Mary Lynn picked up on that now, because she left off teasing me just as suddenly as she had started. I went back to worrying about what her mom might've told her about me, the unfiltered facts. Gram went quiet like that around me sometimes.

"Okay, Kass it is," she said at last, sliding my tea back in front of me. "You'd better drink more of this. Mom will be disappointed when she comes back and all you've had is half a saucer." Her laugh this time had a considerate ring to it, which lasted about two seconds, a world record for us.

The tea was ice-cold but I held the saucer to my mouth and blew anyway, mostly out of habit. I'd also caught out of the corner of my eye, and below my saucer, a yellow knitted toque rising like a fluffy sun from the edge of our table. A pair of green, crystal-sharp eyes appeared next, and once the chin was high enough to rest on the table, those eyes latched onto me and wouldn't let go. I lowered the saucer slowly, so as to not spook the little stray.

"Hiya," I said, keeping my surprise to a minimum. As an uninvited guest in Donna Mae's latest game, I decided to play it cool until I knew what her rules were.

"Hello, sir," she answered without batting an eye.

Mary Lynn flicked a casual eyebrow our way, then went back to her Coke. "Hey, shortstop. Is Mom ready yet?"

"Shortly, young lady," Donna Mae declared, obviously mimicking what her mom must have told her moments before she spun off in search of us. But here now, and satisfied that we were who she wanted, she went back to staring at me. Seemed she'd leave it to me to break the ice any way I chose.

"I like your sweatshirt," I said, pointing to its dancing-bird picture.

"It's the bird from Charlie Brown," she stated matter-of-factly.

"I know. He's my favourite."

Donna Mae tugged down on the bottom of her shirt to give me a second longer to enjoy it.

"Are you here to take our order?" I asked, fake seriously.

"No, sir. I don't work here. My mom does, though."

Mary Lynn interrupted with the fill-in information that Donna Mae hung out here sometimes, on non-school, no-babysitter days.

"In that case, would you like to sit with us?" I started to shove down, but the words barely left my mouth before Donna Mae sunk out of sight and then popped up from under the table on my other side, turning so her knee was against my leg, her hands folded on her lap and her gaze comfortably locked on my profile.

Mary Lynn choked on her drink. "You have a pal... Donna Mae, take off your hat. You're making me sweat just looking at you." I figured this was her way to make the intros.

"Kay."

"Donna Mae is a great name," I said.

"I know."

A magnificent explosion of wavy red hair flew up with the static when Donna Mae yanked off her knitted toque. It drifted weightless as an auburn halo before settling over her face and shoulders. Mary Lynn, having anticipating the effect, already had her palm licked, and reached across the table to brush away hair so she could at least see. "Dim, you'll embarrass Kass, staring like that." (Dim was for D.M., I figured out.)

Donna Mae threw out her chin and said, "No I won't," before she tapped her chin with her thinking finger. "Wait a tick. Kass?" She probably had an imaginary name made up for me, something gallant to fill in the fourth chair at her pretend tea parties, so really any other name was going to be a disappointment.

Before I could defend myself by blaming Mary Lynn, Mary Lynn chimed in with an explanation. "It's short for Kaspar."

Her sister exploded so hard that she nearly landed in my lap. "That's not right! You gotta call yourself Kap for short! Kap is the nickname for Kaspar. Not Kass." Donna Mae's pointing finger settled directly under my chin, its demand that I explain myself.

I tried pleading ignorance. "Really?" I said. "That's good to know." I looked at Mary Lynn, who shrugged. "She's your friend."

A solemn Donna Mae bobbed her head. "Yes, it is. Do you know where it comes from?"

As this was the still-fresh ground I'd tilled with her big sister and my ignorance was all warmed up, I told her, "Don't have a clue."

"It's from one of the three wise men's names—Gaspar. Can you name them all, cuz I can. There's Gaspar, Balthazar, and the other guy. We learned about them cuz they're going to be in our Christmas play. Not the real ones...just us. Can you come? What do you want for Christmas? I wanna bike."

Shit, I'd forgotten all about my bike. "Yeah, a bike'd be great," I agreed. "I guess I'd want a bike...and a birdcage, since you're asking."

Donna Mae puckered her face, clearly disappointed with my second choice. "Nah, a birdcage is no good. If I got a bird, I'd just let her go anyway. Why don't you wanna bird?"

"I don't?"

"Nope. You said you wanted a birdcage. You didn't say nothin' about a bird. That's dumb. Do you already have a bird or somethin'?"

Mary Lynn slapped the table, a little touchy about birds yet. "Donna Mae!"

"Nah, she's right," I said, coming to Donna Mae's defence. "It's dumb to want just a cage."

Donna Mae jabbed her tongue at her sister.

"I guess I meant a birdcage first, so if I decide I want a bird, I'm ready, set, go. I mean, you gotta have someplace safe for it to live first, right? Who gets a bird and doesn't have someplace safe to put it?"

Donna Mae rubbed the dimple on her chin again. "Well, okay. You can't hold a bird in your hand forever... It'll die. Anyway, I wouldn't have a bird if I was you. We had one once and it died."

The superquick glimpse Mary Lynn and I exchanged was spectacular, one of those unspoken moments like Gram and Grumps shared between them by the ton since I arrived. I don't remember Sliver ever having an unspoken moment with anybody, so by that measuring stick alone this was going great! Mary Lynn ended it by correcting Donna Mae.

"No, Sly died a long time ago."

This was a logistical error Donna Mae couldn't let slide. "Nu-huh, Mil. Not a long time ago. Cuz that's the same day..."

"Hush up, Dim!" Mary Lynn slapped the table so hard, this time my cup and saucer both jumped, sharp enough that it pierced the usually unpoppable Donna Mae bubble. She shrank into her seat, grabbed her toque, and wedged it over her head down to over her nose, creating a tutu of red hair around its brim. She sucked her lips inside her mouth, a useful trick, to keep from spilling things everybody at our table might regret.

"It's okay," I said, and actually put my hand on Mary Lynn's in case she meant to reload. I only left it there for a second, but if I'm not mistaken this was our first skin-to-skin, non-smoke-or-smack-related touch. To be safe, I pulled my hand away before she keeled over from affection, or in case I spilled something I might regret, like present my theory before it was ready in essay form on why I believed hers and Donna Mae's canary died.

Into the quiet created after Donna Mae sunk below her toque rushed the voices of those creosote-plant workers who had been biding their own newly canary-free time here, who couldn't bear the thought of going home to break bad news, and needed a community of similarly damaged folks to build their confidence up. Smoke and bullshit piled over the heads of the men in the booth behind Mary Lynn. The big guy with his back to hers was the loudest; everybody else had to wait until he stuck a smoke in his mouth to get their two cents in. I expected her to lean forward to get away from the syrupy sweet odour their clothes gave off, but she wasn't put out at all. If anything she appeared to be taking deeper breaths. Personally, I found the odour pretty annoying, but speaking from personal experience I'll never be surprised by what people can get used to. Like, if I'd brought up Trawl's smell back when he brought up mine, I'm sure he'd have no idea what I was talking about.

The workers' conversation moved on, topics about debts, how to pay them, and what sorts of skills a guy could carry from a creosote plant to another job. Because she was closer to the men than me, she shook her head when overhearing the answer to that last one, and when I asked her what useful things they'd thought they'd learned, she told me, "Nothing at all."

"What was that? What'd they say now?" The corner of her mouth had gone up. I hated being on the outside of a joke.

"Somebody said they should've seen it coming, how the one thing that won't last when you make things that last forever will be your job."

"They mean the preservative."

"You think, Einstein?"

I nearly made a witty comeback, but she was looking at her mother now, standing between two stacks of dishes. When Mary Lynn swung back over her Coke, she took one more deep breath, then exhaled slowly, her mouth hovering over the straw. She didn't take a sip, so I kept quiet. If Sliver was here, he'd tell her to suck it up. Then he'd probably slug her. A better habit, especially for a theme essay writer, is to always take plenty of time to think about what you want to say. You'd never hear me say "suck it up" to anybody, even on the spur of a moment when I've just been insulted.

Yeah, I was a little pissed off at the creosote men for ruining our good time, but they weren't totally to blame. Some of it was Mary Lynn's fault. Certain people, depending on their background, will think they don't deserve to feel upbeat, and the second they feel that way, will beat themselves up about it. I used to be that way, for my Sliver experiences. But I got over it. Or people lifted me over it. Donna Mae didn't seem to need anybody to lift her, but she was still just a crazy kid. Who knew what they thought? I wondered who Mary Lynn had who could lift her. Her mom was busy all the time. Her dad was obviously out of the picture. That left scrawny Trawl, and from what I'd seen, he couldn't lift shit.

The booth behind Mary Lynn had worked itself into enough of a froth that Leona had to come over and smack her receipt book in her hand a few times. She pointed to our booth and told them to keep the cursing down. They'd said nothing me and Grumps would consider offensive, but I appreciated the gesture on Donna Mae's behalf. The way Leona wielded her receipt book reminded me of Del with his nightstick, one part threat and one part good humour. Gram said you can tell a lot about a person by how well they hang on to their sense of humour when things turn squirrelly. Now I've seen Del in action with his canary squirrels, and Leona with her unemployed squirrels. They were like two peas.

My old pal Tab's name was the first thing to come up after Leona left and the men had recovered. Turns out he was the shop steward. Tab the stewie. Tab the shop stupid. Those guys had tons of nicknames, not many of them complimentary. The men were wondering where he'd gotten to, why he wasn't around to answer a few questions. I was dying to tell them that if he was on his way, it was going to be on foot, but I kept my yap shut. Somebody brought up the commie next (that's the man above the stewie in the way of union rankings, according to Grumps), and the table went quiet instantly again, even without Leona's receipt-book intervention. One or two men blessed themselves and peeked over their shoulders at our booth, which I didn't understand at all until the big guy looked around to make sure their waitress was out of earshot. Then he angled his body over their table. "It'd be better for Tab if he sunk himself in the canal too."

When Leona strode by right then, everybody's clams slammed shut and their eyes flicked every which way, but she was only here to count heads at our booth, sparing an extralong look at the toque-shrouded puffball beside me.

"Are you in there?" she asked, flustered and red-cheeked but together enough to joke with her youngest daughter.

"Yep," Donna Mae's little voice peeped from under her toque, having no doubt at all that the question was meant for her.

"Are we ready yet?" Mary Lynn huffed, gathering her caftan over her shoulders and shuffling off the bench. "Because I got plans."

"No, so change those plans, Mil. I can't leave yet. I'll let you and your friend go ahead, though. We'll catch up."

"What? To that farm? No way."

"No way-ay-ay," the hooded Donna Mae echoed absently, banging out a rhythm against the bench with her boots. Not sealskin like Mary Lynn's, but yellow rubber with a white fur trim. Every little kid in the world wore boots like that.

Her mom blinked. "No, not his farm. God, grab a brain."

"Grab a bray-ay-ain."

"Hush, Donna Mae. And quit that." (Her mom meant the kicking.) "You two,"—she pointed at me and Mary Lynn—"can go to *our house* and hang out. I've got to stay for an extra half-shift. Donna Mae and I will be along shortly..."

"Shortly, young lady!"

"Hush. I've already cleared it with Kap's...grandmother, is it?" She had to pause because she'd just run into the high brick wall where my archives were stored.

"I live with my grandparents, ma'am...Leona." I'd never been the subject of so many phone conversations outside of school before, so this was quite the honour.

"Ah." Her head tilted back, away from my wall once more.

I bet when she was younger, Leona looked like Donna Reed. She kinda looked that way now, just a little more haggard, like how Mary Hatch looked haggard when she became Mary Bailey, when her husband, George, slipped that sprocket and she realized what sort of kook she might be married to. Mary Lynn's mom had the later Mary Bailey look. Mary Lynn and I slid out from our booth, and because she needed to debate with Leona a little more, once again I was leaving a store alone.

A discussion about loss and longing and betrayal should prove useful here:

For the second time in a matter of hours, Mary Lynn stepped out of a store and into the night looking none too pleased with who she found waiting for her on the sidewalk. I couldn't blame her. She had her own social schedule and would resent anybody who got in its way. Technically I'd been given a schedule too—a couple, in fact—that just happened to conflict with hers. First Del scheduled me to see Mary Lynn to the drugstore, and now Leona slotted me in for a walk with her daughter to their house. Normally I don't have a social schedule. Living on a farm so far from town, what I have resembles my school bus route—last stop, me. My familiarity with what other kids' did on their days off came from what I picked up in scraps of conversations at school. So I knew that some of my fellow Grade 8 clowns were going to the same field party Mary Lynn'd planned on attending with Trawl. It'd be easy-peasy for me to go too, since the field was in my neighbourhood.

To avoid an explanation of how I already knew where she lived, I let Mary Lynn take the lead on this part of our journey. It was tough keeping quiet about the route she chose, though, because she wasn't going close to the right direction. I used casual small talk to get a handle on her plans for us. "So, you live this way, eh?"

"Yep," she said, short and sweet. The way a lie should be told.

"Is it very far?"

"Yep, so if you'd rather be someplace else..."

"Well, now that you mention it, I do have to make a pit stop."

All I meant was that my tea had worked its way through my system, and if we were going on a mystery tour I'd better deal with the call here, where facilities were nearby. On the farm I'd have just whipped it out where I stood. In Quinton, that's a crime of some sort, though. But more important than a whiz, I'd also planned on picking up a few supplies, and by supplies I mean something more inviting than the stubs in my baggie.

"You should have thought of that before we left," she scolded, before adding a "Whatever."

I should have been suspicious. Instead I toodle-oo'd, "I'll be right back," confident she'd stop thinking about me as an inconvenience when I returned with two packs of smokes, one for her and one for me. I ducked into the five-pin bowling alley and hit the can. Next, I went up to the counter where they rented shoes and sold cigarettes, and purchased two packs of Export "A"s, the kings. I'd never had five bucks to spend on anything before today, let alone two packs of Export "A" kings. I'd never even bought anyone a gift before, at least not with my own money, or without being nudged in a certain direction from Gram or Grumps, depending on the occasion. Tonight I finally knew somebody well enough to get her what she'd really like. Plus, after taxes, along with the packs of daisy-fresh nails, I had nearly three bucks in change, which I could use for other treats as needed. Gum, for example. All thanks to Bill and the gang, who were sort of becoming like ancestors to me, for how they kept factoring into my major milestones.

Waving the Exports over my head, I burst out of the bowling alley, proud as punch for my good deed. The gesture was to go unappreciated.

"Shit."

Main Street was the clearest it'd been all evening, if you didn't count the steam rising out of the sewer grates. I walked to the curb and looked up and down both directions. Mary Lynn and her long legs were long gone, a predicament that called for the kind of clear-headed rethink only a brand-new, full-length smoke could provide. I pulled back the flap that sealed in freshness on my pack and caught my first whiff of Tillsonburg the way it was meant to smell. I removed a king-size tube of that farm country's fine product and fired it up. Like I thought it would, my head cleared immediately, and options galore poured in. If I eliminated Mary Lynn's less likely avenues of escape, like toward the hotel (with its drunks), that only left a couple of dozen points on the compass. I inhaled Export-deep a second time and eliminated the bridge as a direction. Going back to the drugstore was also a long shot. At least, I hoped she hadn't gone that way, because Leona'd be pissed, especially if she saw the reason we'd become separated dangling from my mouth. The narrow laneway right here, between the bowling alley and the pool hall, seemed like a possibility, if someone wanted to get shed of me in a hurry. I jogged to the lot at the other end of the alley, then stopped to catch my breath, unbuttoning my deer-hunter jacket to let some cold air in. A cloud of steam poured out of me.

If you needed someplace to bury a body, this would be it. Or if you needed rink scrapings from the arena to put in a road cocktail, or were looking for the road leading to the water filtration plant that sucked up Quintonian shit, purified it, and dumped it into the river, they were here too. Oh, and my school was up the hill a little piece. Nothing out of the ordinary for the ass-end of town, in other words. Unfortunately, that meant no yellow caftans and sealskin boots and beautiful mysteries. At least, not that caught my eye from ground level. The field here had a mixed bag of trees—cedars, willows, Manitoba maples—glorified weeds really, and certainly nothing that could hold me to a point high enough for a good view. Too bad. I'm one hell of a tree climber, a skill I'd learned at Sliver's house but perfected on the farm.

On the farm we have real maples, giant ones with nice, thick branches perfect for climbing. I'll bet Mary Lynn never had the chance to climb a real tree in her life, or to know what jumping in the leaves felt like before you torched them, or cared what a pile of burning leaves smelled like. I'd have loved to show her stuff like that—what made me tick. The row of maples along mine and Gram and Grumps' driveway aren't all the same height, but close enough to be within a few years of each other. At the very end of the row, closest to the house, there's one little tree not much bigger than what I found back here. I helped Gram plant it after their dog Laddie died. "You can't climb the Laddie tree for a while," she'd said. Gram was a piece of work. She even named her trees. Some kind of German shepherd and sheepdog mix, their dog accidentally fell asleep against one of our hay wagon's wheels, and when Grumps pulled away on the tractor—*ker-pop*!

"Who are those other trees?" I had to ask, since she brought it up. "Do they have names too?"

"Oh my," she sighed, seemingly unprepared for what she'd just stepped in, conversation-wise, maybe reminding herself that she'd have to be more careful with what got said in my presence. "Well, okay," she decided, and took my hand. "I'll make the introductions." We walked down the driveway, to the tree closest to the road. "This is your uncle Alexandru's tree. People called him Alex for short."

"Where's Uncle Alex?"

"He died."

"How did he die?"

"He fell out of the hayloft and hit his head."

Then we turned and walked toward the house, stopping at the next tree. "This is your uncle Ionut's tree. People called him John."

"What happened to him?"

"He got measles—a lot of people died of that back then, but nobody does anymore so don't worry your little head." She mentioned that last bit when she realized she'd stepped in something else. At the third tree, the smallest of the climbing trees, and for that reason the one that had my swing tied to it, Gram patted it and said, "This one is your uncle Mihai."

"Is he dead too?"

"He died very, very young. Right after he was born."

"A baby?"

"Yes, a baby."

"What did people call him?"

"Just Mihai."

There were no other trees. Maybe Gram got sick of planting them, or only planted one when she absolutely knew the whole story, like it wasn't enough for someone to just disappear. That's no kind of ending. You only got a tree only when you were definitely done. Grumps pitched a lesson on this to me when he sat me down for a little speechifying over Laddie's accident. "The Occupational Hazard of Being a Farm Dog," he could have called that speech. The dog never got called by name throughout his lecture, Grumps being a vague and big-picture speaker. Sometimes this dies, sometimes that dies. Very general, a broader topic than why one dumb dog was never coming back. He never talked about the trees at all, but when he finished he slipped me a puff on his cigarette, which had kind of become our thing by then. I'll bet dollars to doughnuts nobody ever sat Mary Lynn down for a rationalizing butt after her dad drowned himself. I think it would be useful if everybody carried a butt baggie on them. Not to smoke yourself, but to have at the ready in case you run across somebody about to slip into melancholy. You could hold out your baggie, let them select something sizeable enough to snap them out of their one- or two-inch funk, then off you go, on your merry separate ways again.

I also want to be careful here, don't want to turn this into a mom-hunt just because of a few trees, because then I'm writing a memoir otherwise. But it's hard not to bring her up to support a point or two. The fact is, I've thought about my mother more today than every other time put together, and maybe Mary Lynn is partly to blame, with her coming, going, running away, leaving me all alone in Quinton, just like Mom. And now I got a knot in my belly, which is not how I'd normally put it, but because whenever Gram lost one of her baby animals a knot was what she called the feeling that came to the pit of her stomach. Sometimes animals got out because I forgot to close a gate, and I felt bad when the dumb animal got a switch to the backside because of my mistake. So in a way, their getting walloped was my punishment too, whether or not Grumps intended it to be seen that way. Sometimes I think he did. His lessons came roundabout more than telling me anything directly, keeping his fingers crossed that I wasn't a complete stump when it came to picking up life lessons on the difference between life and death and running away. Grumps didn't have to worry. I was the king of life and death. And anyway, cows and sows have pretty thick skin.

I shouted Mary Lynn's name, not totally discouraged when she didn't come snuffling up to me right away. Lots of times Gram's lost animals didn't come the first time she called. I did draw a couple drunks out of the alley, though, who hooted, "She's not here!" before they staggered into the pool hall through the back door.

An important note on why a pool hall is not the same as a union hall:

Sliver's people hung out at Ether's Billiards Lounge. I guess that made them my people too, and the damp cloud of smoke twenty cartons thick that poured out when I stuck my head indoors, chased by a bellow I hadn't heard in years: "Close the goddamn door!" That'd be Narc Ether. I remembered enough about him to do what I was told.

The pool hall was exactly how I remembered, so not much to look at in any interesting way, except now I noticed how the setup here resembled our cow barn, only instead of stalls Ether had pool tables, two rows of four green-felt tables with a single centre aisle. On the two short walls hung pool-cue racks and chalkboards instead of pitchforks and twine. A waist-high wooden drinks rail ran along the two long walls, and at the corner opposite where I was standing sat the canteen. People paid for tables, bought smokes and beers, and sometimes sat and waited for their time out to end if they'd made the mistake of setting a bottle down anywhere but on the rail provided. Back when I dined here regularly, the canteen also sold bags of plain potato chips, and there was a Dutch oven that held hot dogs afloat in grey water. Sliver would perch me on a high chair and push it against the counter. This wasn't the kind of regular high chair a little kid might sit in at suppertime but a bar stool with extrahigh legs, intended so a guy could watch the action at the tables without having to stand. It made for a long drop to the ground. Sliver always bought me one of those hot dogs and a Coke in a paper cup.

Narc's face was much rounder and fatter than the last time I'd seen it. He still sat in his little corner opposite the canteen, his eyes squeezed shut against his cigar's smokestack. He liked that corner because his house rules were nailed right over his head for everybody to read. He'd point straight up whenever he caught sight of an infraction, and shout, "You're done." The main rules were: A cigarette had to be in an ashtray when taking a shot. No trick shots allowed where the cue tip comes in contact with the felt. Nothing but elbows on the table. Even so, all of Narc's tables bore long scars and brown stains, and polka-dot holes from cigarette burns. Balls mumbled and rumbled when they rolled over the lumpy felt.

I shuffled against the wall to keep clear of any cues in backswing mode. I'd grab a dog and do a lap of the lounge on the zero chance that Mary Lynn had ducked in here. I think a small part of me was only using her as an excuse for one more stroll down Primrose Lane. ("Primrose Lane" was the theme song to the one TV show I had to watch with Gram that wasn't a soap opera, about some sap-happy family who acted all pleased with each other all the time. The song wasn't bad, and because I knew all the words they'd pop into my head at the worst times, like in a pool hall.

Even though I'd kept it to a hum, I still felt Ether's stare. When his muskrat teeth were done gnawing at his memory, he hollered, "You there. Kid."

Everybody else in the joint looked about a hundred years old, so I pretty confidently answered, "What?"

"Come here." He stabbed his crooked finger toward me, then curled it back and forth. "I know you, don't I?"

"Doubt-er."

"Don't shit me, kid. I've seen you before. You're Sliver Pine's son, ain't you?"

What a day. Twice now somebody'd remembered Sliver Pine just because of me. "Yeah, I guess. So what?" Poor old Sliver was probably spinning in his grave over what his legacy turned out to be. I suppose it won't be long before I'm spinning too, every time I get lumped together with Sliver. I kinda hope this essay will keep my revolutions to a minimum.

"Been a long time. You've grown."

"Some, I guess." And a second later, "Thanks."

"Sorry about your old man. If you don't mind me askin', how'd he die?"

"Nah, I don't mind. Axe," I said, because it usually raised a laugh, given what Sliver did for a living.

"Bullshit." His rumbling chuckle, once he realized I was playing him, was like a gravel truck on a dirt road, if the truck's engine erupted into a violent coughing fit at the end. Guys who coughed like Narc usually had cancer, especially when they spent the majority of their time downstream of the creosote plant, like everybody in this pool hall.

Maybe I should have told people Sliver fell out of a tree. Sliver didn't leave me much else to hold on to, memory-wise, besides a middling joke about a knacker with his axe. That's not much of a foundation to build on.

"Jesus," Ether suddenly yelped out of the gravelly blue, like the house rules board had broken from its nail and landed on his head. "Wait here. No, follow me."

He slid down from his perch and waddled toward the canteen, disappearing into the shelves beneath the counter, then bobbed to the surface holding a cardboard box. He pulled out one trophy after another, examining each one before lining it up on the counter beside the last. Some trophies had a man perched on a pedestal with a cue stick in his hand. Some had the man bent over, as though lining up an invisible shot. Some had two people, one standing, the other bent over. "Aha," he cried at last. "Here, kid. Take this. I guess it belongs to you now."

"What is it?" That is to say, I knew what a trophy was. I guess what I really meant was, "What's it for?"

I thought I knew all the awards Sliver'd won, because I'd melted them all down myself in our backyard for the gold I'd need to fund my escape. Turned out trophy gold wasn't real gold. My six-year-old brain's plan was to take the money from the melted gold and skip town. Sliver was as disappointed as I was to see the smouldering blob in the backyard, he being the other sight I'd hoped to avoid by being long gone before he got home. I had to stand there and watch as he stomped on the flaming pile of past glories and screamed, "Oh my fucking God! What did you do?" as the last little figurine sank out of sight. The other thing about trophy gold is how, when it's hot and melted, it sticks to everything and still keeps burning. Naturally, the flaming goo stuck to the bottom of Sliver's boot, and then his axe when he used that to try and beat out the fire before it spread to our shed. Sliver used the shed as a smokehouse for jerky, which he made from leftover animal hunks he brought home after knackering them. When the flames crept up the axe handle and singed his hands, he was forced to drop it in the goo and all that remained of my escape plans.

For a knacker an axe is like a best friend, so I guess Sliver had a right to be heartbrokenly pissed off to watch his burn. On the other hand, somewhere out in the country the poor old horse who was supposed to feel its sharp edge the next morning got an unexpected extra few hours of life. Me? I got a few hours of being dog-chained to the tree out back. Sliver'd deal with me later, he said, and went inside to fix himself a rye and ice.

Ether passed me the one and only reminder of what a star Sliver was. "It's for mixed billiards," he read, dragging his thumb through the dust on the engraved plaque glued to its base to remind himself, although the babe on top was a good clue. "He said he wanted nothing to do with it. I kept it in case his teammate ever claimed it. Forgot all about it until now. Congratulations," he said, and, after he passed it to me, shook my hand.

I'd never seen a pool trophy where one of the figurines wore a skirt. That's quite a hoot to think about even now, because no lady in her right mind wears a skirt while shooting pool. I rubbed my thumb against her boob bumps to remove the smudges. I'll bet guys entered the mixed tournaments just for the chance to win a trophy with one of these pin-up babes on it. The bumps also reminded me of why I was in the pool hall in the first place. Mary Lynn could be miles away by now. I had to skedaddle.

"If you wanna stick around, I'll give you the next table. I'll bet you have a little Pine in you." He meant pool-playing Pine. I tucked the trophy in my pants pocket and said, "Nah, I gotta run." I meant it too, and not just to chase Mary Lynn. Who needed to find out he had a little more Pine in him? That's why they called him Sliver, for fuck's sake. I'd nearly made it to the door before Narc was coughing at me again. "I liked yer old man. He was a good player."

A shrug was all I had to say to that parting shot. If your only basis for deciding if someone's a good person is their pool-playing skills, then maybe you should leave the pool hall once in a while.

A blast of semi-fresh air smacked me in the face. I readjusted Sliver's trophy so it was between my belt and my pants and closed the hall door behind me before Narc yelled again. The scene on Main Street was the same as when I left it— cold, poorly lit, and Mary Lynn–free. A light fog was rolling in, though, which I took as a cue to fire up another thinking butt and assess where I stood now, in relation to where Mary Lynn might be standing. My position was easy—I was in the exact same spot. On the other hand, she could be halfway to Peterborough by now. But thanks to my head-clearing Export, I realized that wasn't likely, not with a field party to attend. I was further able to deduce that she'd have to go home to change out of her Couch-Newton's duds because, knowing fields like I do, you want to dress for the location, not the occasion. If she was at her house now, great. We could pick up where we left off, which was waiting for Leona to take me home, so I could show everybody where I lived, introduce my people to their people. And if not, then hopefully I'd at least get there ahead of her mom and Donna Mae. I wasn't looking forward to that meeting if Mary Lynn wasn't home yet. Donna Mae's disappointment at walking in and seeing me without her sister would be tough to take. Her heroes were in short supply. I didn't want to turn into someone else she couldn't trust to walk a girl home.

By my third thoughtful drag, I was detecting a flavour that didn't belong in any cigarette fresh out of the pack. My first worry was that my baggie had somehow leached creosote into my Exports, as that behaviour was a common side effect of production at the plant: creosote leached into the water table and into the river, smoke leached across the sky. And speaking of the sky, Quinton's had developed a definite haze, even in the dark, and particularly over the plant. A man jogging past just then, with a folding lawn chair tucked under his arm, informed me that the creosote plant was on fire again.

Around Quinton, any news containing the words *plant* and *fire* in the same sentence wasn't to be taken literally. It was like how you'd say "the sun's setting" or "the moon's rising." There's some truth to all three, in as much as a sun and a moon and a creosote plant have done certain things enough times that "rising" and "setting" and "on fire" aren't actually true but just ingrained into the Quintonian way of speaking. To be one hundred percent accurate, he'd have told me the towers of creosote-soaked telephone poles and railroad ties stacked in the yard next to the plant were on fire. Which they were about ten times a year.

Mary Lynn's neighbourhood (and mine and Sliver's old one, for that matter) is just past the plant, her house two streets in. I wasn't technically taking a detour therefore when I joined a few clods of grey ash and some chair-toting locals to track the reds and yellows dancing on the parking lot across the road. The Quinton River had already turned a brighter shade of orange in the fire's glow, and when I entered Murphy Street I noticed some fishermen had anchored next to the plant, to fish in the warmth and bright light of a roaring fire. They'd stay for as long as they could tolerate the stink, or until they caught their limit of oil-soaked pickerel.

"Creosote stink," the ingrained, airborne Quinton landmark, is something I haven't talked much about yet, outside of the humans it infected. How some towns have plaques to indicate the birthplace of poet laureates or founding fathers, or to mark where something of historical significance had occurred, the sort of stuff proudly included in Chamber of Commerce pamphlets. Quinton has its stink. The best the poor sap occupying the tourist booth could hope for was that the towers of logs were actually on fire when tourists stopped by—or a fire was so nearly due, he could suggest they stick around for a day or two, the event being a little like Old Faithful. By the time I got to the fence that outlined the storage yard, lawn chairs were already parked in the best spots, although the audience was more subdued than what was normal for these occasions, probably a little distracted, possibly a little torn over which side they should root for once the fire department arrived. Butt baggies would have helped this crowd come to terms with their dilemmas.

Haystack-sized clouds of black ash poured from the tops of the towers and sailed across the moon and fat fists of creosote-filled sparks churned, launching themselves up with the ash. These oil-reinforced flame balls orbited the yard a few times before sailing away to die in the river, unless the wind was coming from the river—like tonight— in which case they scattered to the surrounding neighbourhoods, where they touched down on lawns and rooftops. The neighbourhood homeowners who had moseyed to the fence made predictions about the paths the sparks took.

"Looks like that one's headin' to your house, Jim."

"What? You think?"

"As long as the wind doesn't shift"—he made a whoosh-ing sound tinged with bad intent out of his mouth—"then yeah, maybe. Oh, wait...never mind."

Sometimes, following a particularly loud crack, there'd be suggestions as to the kind of animal a flurry of sparks looked like and where it might land if it didn't burn itself out before it got there.

"That one looks like a cat, headed to Al's house."

"Yeah, I see it."

"Should somebody tell him?"

"Hey, Al!"

"Yeah?"

"Ah, forget it."

As the fire grew, so did the size of animal it spat out—dog, cow, stampede of horses—and the distance they could travel. A few homeowners, the closest ones, gathered up their chairs and Thermoses of coffee and left the warmth of the fire to go check to see if their garden hoses needed thawing.

The swing bridge started clanging its bell. First we all looked up toward the canal, and seeing nothing glide out of the stone chute and into the river, we waited on the bridge to open and reveal what hid in the darkness on the other side. I caught whispers of hopeful conversations, never mind all the termination notices stuffed in their pockets, that maybe it was a barge full of coal and maybe it would stop at the plant.

The bridge swung away from Main Street. A man seated with his family asked everybody within earshot if anyone had thought to call the fire department yet, as this was around the time in the show when the fire truck arrived and the men in costumes performed a slapstick routine of running fat hoses everywhere, slipping in the oil-slick yard, then spraying silvery arches of water into the logs.

"The fire hall's right there," somebody pointed out, meaning that the building was directly across the river. "They've got eyes." The next question, we all realized, became more specific to the current predicament—how would the trucks cross the river with the bridge fully open?

A bony Claude Rains lookalike (Rains before *The Invisible Man* but after *Casablanca*) emerged from the haze to settle in beside me. A motorist was yelling, "Somebody go tell that guy he's gotta close the bridge." Rains shook his head. His clothes were soaking wet; he looked like he'd just climbed out of the river. His eyes drifted down to the pack of smokes poking out of my pocket. He trembled like a leaf, so when I took out a smoke for myself, I turned the pack to him. Then I offered him a light, but he shook me off, instead stabbing a passing spark with the unlit end of the smoke, huffing for all he was worth until it lit, pinching his eyes hard. Tobacco mixed with creosote is a pretty wild taste explosion, unless you were the troll whose body had already been making accommodations on creosote's behalf.

We stood side by side, enjoying our smokes in silence, until he raised a bony finger toward the retreating fishermen, muttering something about how the fish'd been soaking in poison every day of their fish lives.

"You don't have to tell me," I said. "That's why I stick to mudcat."

When a fishing boat passed under the place where a road should be, somebody shouted at its operator to climb up to the effing troll's hut and ask him if he'sdnoticed that the plant was on fire. Claude Rains leaned into me: "What do you wanna bet he knows that already and doesn't give a fuck?" He was in a bit brighter mood, even if his voice kept its rattle. I recognized that rattle, but I couldn't quite place it.

Betrayal can do that to you. Eat you from the inside out. You can live and work in a place—a house or a town or a farm or a province—your whole life, think you have each other's back. Then one day you discover how that's not the case. For how many people worked at the plant, and for however long, Quintonians pleaded a lot of ignorance. If a few schmucks a month dropped dead, oh well. I guess the troll felt the betrayal more than most, breathing the plant's exhaust all day and night, drinking water pumped straight from the river. I'll bet he hatched his plan to move up in Quinton's pecking order a long time ago and was just waiting for the inevitable tower fire to ignite. Maybe he was bitter about having absorbed all of creosote's killer aspects but none of its preservative benefits.

A fresh explosion of sparks snaked over our heads, and one giant beast somebody named Clusterfuck howled east. The tower it sprang from, the one built out of telephone poles, shuddered. I've seen enough poorly stacked hay bales in my time to know what was coming next, so I backed away before the pole tower collapsed and the resulting heat blast struck. As the logs cartwheeled toward the plant, I was on my way.

A brief anecdote demonstrating why the theme essay format is superior to others:

It occurs to me that a standalone theme essay on Quinton's betrayal of the troll is just the sort of topic Sister Dorkus would disapprove of. She sensed a prejudice in me against the town and she was determined to break it, like prejudice was a breakable bad habit. I blame her upbringing. She probably believes there isn't a habit she can't break—like swearing and smoking, two other parts of my nature she'd like me to deny. She thought anything was possible if I only worked a little harder, buckled down a little more, laid off the mudcat, concentrated. The problem with dorkus-thinking is how it lumps smoking and swearing in with getting angry at ignorant Quintonians, when they're not the same. I just see Quinton for what it is—a breeding ground for subjects of kick-ass theme essays.

And since we're on the subject of who to blame for what, it was Sister Mary Dorkus, likely feeling guilty for all the essay topics she'd denied me, who chose my bench-clearing speech for the Royal Canadian Legion Public Speaking Contest over all the stupid-hippie entries about peace, love, and Bobby Sherman. The speech, a lot of it dictated by Grumps, is the main reason I'm even slightly conversant about Saskatchewan, unions, universal health care, and, yes, betrayal.

My original speech, the one Dorkus and my class heard, was a glowing three-minute-or-less summary of farm memories. At the legion, unfortunately for the legionnaires, my new and improved speech, boosted by Grumps's further recollections, included tearing new assholes for a number of people, including Lester B. Pearson and the Queen, whose giant mugs scowled down at me from the legion hall walls, like the wedding photographs of a married couple who had no intention of living together.

Grumps was an old union man, sort of, except for him being born at the hospital in the big city of Moose Jaw, then raised by the Saskatchewan Farmers Union, although he'd say he was less a union "man" than a union "son of the soil." So when school speech season arrived, he suggested my speech should be generally farm-related, and I should use it like a springboard to hurry my farming education along. I guess he thought I didn't demonstrate much interest in farming, outside of the basics of dirt and seeds, and suddenly here was an opportunity for me to research farming history and the honest-to-God people behind it. Grumps even gave my speech a title, "Stand Your Ground" (which was so clever Gram said he likely copied it from somewhere). He didn't care about the five-buck prize money if I won at the legion, but he sure seemed excited about the prospect of me reading my speech there.

Everybody in class said my speech was stupid. They were in the union of hippie wannabes therefore knew shit-all about farming, those jerks with their American or British flag T-shirts. I was the only jerk whose T-shirt had the provincial flag of Saskatchewan on it; it's not hard to guess where I ranked. It wasn't even the cool kind of full-flag T-shirt, just a cheap Couch-Newton's department store brand tee, where the tiny clumps of wheat sat in a corner near my armpit. And, since I was two years away from growing into it, the flag usually ended up somewhere in my pit, which meant my shirt mostly looked like a plain white one. Sad to say, Gram was thrilled to pieces with her purchase, having ordered it special because the department store didn't carry apparel from her favourite province, if that shocker can be believed. I gave her my pleased smile, even though it didn't fit. People shouldn't go around breaking other people's hearts just to make a personal point about what kind of uniform is acceptable, especially when you're not really sure yourself.

The legion version of my speech started out pretty calm and on script, with a little pile of manure about how cat's ass Saskatchewan is for being the birthplace of free doctors for everybody. I had the whole blue-blazered crowd bobbing their wrinkled heads, probably because they were so close to strokes and heart attacks and such. The other difference between my school version and its legion divergence was nobody in the school audience had a cigarette dangling out of their mouth. At the legion, distracted by the ashtrays brimming with beautiful, glowing butts, I'd gotten my speech tangled up with one of Grumps's monthly harangues about the plight of farmers in Ontario. His screeds leached into mine, over what a raw deal farmers were getting generally when compared to the rest of the population, with special attention paid to the latest straw breaking Grumps's camel's back, the Ontario Milk Marketing Board. From there I kind of lost my farm footing and branched out into expounding on why Quinton didn't have a hospital, why we only had a swing bridge, why I had to go to the canal to fish, why should anyone give a rat's ass about the Queen, and, well, that's when the judges began tapping on their wrists to indicate that my allotted three minutes was well past up. Some went into coughing conniptions, others stood with arms akimbo—my speech vexed the room that much. The final freak-out arrived when I leaned down and plucked a butt out of some guy's ashtray and started sucking on it—I knew that only tobacco's sedating powers, as practised by Grumps and me on the farm, could bring this explosion to a close.

The drive home from the legion was super quiet until Gram cleared her throat, finally, to observe that the apple didn't fall far from the tree. I expect she had more words with Grumps later, along the lines of how do you suppose a kid could inhale that much smoke and not cough his lungs all over the legion floor, and Grumps would know enough to stay quiet until she was done. Hiding with me in the barn after, he slapped me on the back and told me, "Good job."

I didn't get a slap on the back from Auntie Dorkus the day after my speech, that's for sure. She pulled me aside and finger-waggle-reminded me that she was the one who'd promoted me to the legion and that I had not only embarrassed the school, but her too. When I hit her with my "suck my potatoes" comment for my Charles Schulz theme essay a few days later, and she kicked me out of class, that was her way of telling me my leash was only so long. I wonder, if she reads this, whether she'll realize that had I not written my Schulz essay in a way that offended her, her niece wouldn't be alive. Life is funny like that. You may never know how one thing can be tied to another, for bad and for good.

Now I'll explain why everybody needs a union hall to call their own:

As the last constellations either burned out while whirling around in the sky or snuffed themselves in the river, and the townsfolk had begun trickling away like so many streams of rendered oil, I started my trek northwest again, to eventually hook up with the same street I'd raced with Donna Mae back when. In this part of town every street—and every house—looks the same as its neighbour. Every street has wooden telephone poles spaced fifty feet apart, with thick black, droopy wires joining one pole to the next, and skinny black, droopy wires running to every house. Every house has a narrow one-car driveway on the same side of the yard and the outside of every house wears the same identical white siding. A large single-pane picture window lets you look clean into the living room from the sidewalk if you want. Every roof is steep, every shingle black. And when I lived in this neighbourhood, and took secret looks from the sidewalk into the living rooms of other houses, I believed that, if I ever got invited inside one of those others, I'd find myself among a perfect family, small and complete, the exact opposite of what I had.

I wasn't thinking about being invited in when I arrived at Mary Lynn's house (which technically I already was, by Leona). What had my immediate attention was the thin stream of smoke coiling over the roof ridge. It appeared to be coming from the back, so I ran to the rear yard. The little flames on the roof barely qualified as a fire at all—just a patch of shingles burning for the time being—but things would get a whole lot worse if I didn't pull my socks up.

Her family didn't have a shed, but they did have a tree with some kind of structure in it, nothing fancy, but better than anything I could have built. Maybe their hose was hooked up to a tap, maybe curled around some bush. Nope. Not even a bush. I pounded on the back door's window; a wisp of smoke leaked out from the eave above me. That wasn't a good sign. I pounded harder and the window broke. Rather than get pissed off, I yelled, "Mary Lynn!" through the hole, before drawing my trophy from my belt and busting the glass the rest of the way, reaching through to unlatch the deadbolt. On the threshold I yelled again, "Anybody home?" even though the house was dark. I ran past a sink filled with dishes into the living room, where I nearly knocked over an ironing board. The iron fell, landing in a laundry basket overflowing with clothes, so no harm, no foul. I yelped, "Mary Lynn," at the stairs a couple times, and one "I'm here!" for the thrill, then went into the basement to look for a hose.

I found it balled up beside the washing machine. After screwing the hose into the laundry tub tap, I tossed the main ball through the basement window, then jogged up the stairs two at a time before turning around and going back down because I'd forgotten to turn the tap on. After one quick stop at the fridge to borrow a can of Orange Crush, I was soon standing in the puddle that had formed around the hose—it was the one and only time today my rubber boots actually came in handy.

All these wartime houses are storey-and-a-half jobs, so the eaves aren't too high up. I found a wooden stepladder propped in their garden, except they'd decided it made a better set of shelves for flowerpots than something you could climb. I shook off the pots and placed the ladder under the eave, then tugged the hose behind me as I climbed to the top step. By pressing my thumb against the hose's open end, I could spray the whole one side of the roof. Fortunately, the flames had taken their sweet time gnawing on the shingles, which were pretty badly curled anyway and probably needed replacing. In other words, the fire wasn't going to be a terrible inconvenience as long as Leona was in the right frame of mind when she and Donna Mae came home, which is being not easily bummed by small stuff. As you're learning, that's a good frame of mind to be in most of the time, as there's enough big stuff out there to be bummed about.

The top step of their ladder slash flowerpot shelving unit was rickety as hell. I didn't want to spend all day up there. I was already doing a lot of tap-dancing just from whipping the hose back and forth, and thanks to the curled shingles some water wasn't even going where I aimed, redirecting instead toward a hole in the roof the flames had made, over a bedroom if my recollections of my old house were correct.

Water bubbled over the eaves and dribbled down the ladder steps. By the time I got the fire out, I thought I might lose my control thumb to frostbite, and I actually managed to get down two rungs before my feet slipped and I fell, cracking a shin against the second-from-the-bottom one, tearing my pant leg enough that it lost all its bellness. Lucky for me, I had that big puddle at the bottom to break the rest of my fall. The ground got peppered with some first-class blasphemes, I'm not embarrassed to say.

I wiped myself off as best I could, removed my muddy boots and set them beside the door among the broken glass, then flipped the kitchen light on. The coast was clear of any smoke, so I pulled out a chair at the table, planning to have a butt and wait for Mary Lynn to arrive.

Since my can of Orange Crush was floating in the puddle outside, I went to the fridge for a fresh can. This time, I noticed the door was smothered with all kinds of crap: report cards, banana stickers, crayon drawings signed by the artist DM. She was lucky. I never got to have my art hung on a fridge door, partly because I'm more of a theme writer than a finger painter, and also because Gram's fridge isn't really a fridge as much as a layer of condensation over several blocks of ice. Nothing noteworthy about me would stick to that. For anything of me to stick, people would have to know how to read.

I borrowed a tea saucer from the sink since there weren't any ashtrays about, not a mind-blower given what Mary Lynn had told me about her mom's impression of smokers. I also turned on the water to let the dishes soak. Ms. Leona wasn't going to be too thrilled to find a sink full of crusty plates. Any money the dishes were Mary Lynn's chore, so if nobody showed up by the time I finished my smoke, I'd do them for her. I mean, never mind she was going to be so in love with me for saving her house, clean dishes would be the cherry on top, whenever we got around to listing all the Kass Pine cherries I had to offer.

I pushed down on the Orange Crush's button tab using my frost-bitten thumb, then took a swig from the can, chasing it with a lung-coating drag of my butt. The sigh I made was the king of sighs, I'll bet. It was the kind of sigh that signals the last job well-done in a series of jobs well-done was done. In other words, I was in total waiting mode—for Mary Lynn, Donna Mae, Leona—the nearly whole, nearly perfect family.

I enjoyed my next drag when I took it, just not as much as the first one. Thoughts unrelated to future plans together were creeping in. Where did Mary Lynn get to? What did she find so objectionable about me that she had to ditch me all the time? Maybe I was worrying for nothing. Maybe I was just tired of going everywhere on foot. I let my head drift down until my chin was parked on my chest. If I dared close my eyes I'd have been snoring in two seconds. That wouldn't look good to anybody strolling in, so I focused on the shiny red puddle on the floor between my socks. As an expert in blood puddles, I realized pretty quickly that it had to be mine. I pulled up the pant leg and poked around. When my brain finished exploding, an actual eyeballing of the area told me my leg was torn pretty good.

As any smart, paying-attention person will have already concluded (I'm still miles away from my main conclusion, so please just sit here beside me as quiet as you can), it's possible for someone to chug along merry as shit and not even realize they're wounded. That realization is saved for the moment you get to feeling really comfortable and be-lieving all the shit is done. That's how some wounds work, especially the sneaky occupational-hazard ones. I never felt sorry for myself whenever I discovered I'd been wound-ed—physically or otherwise—because really, if my own body doesn't feel sorry enough to tell me I've been walk-ing around maimed, why would the rest of the world give a rat's ass? Mary Lynn seemed pretty good at keeping her wounds to herself. Maybe that's why she preferred walking away instead of hanging out with me, and doing something we'd both—me mainly—regret.

Fortunately for me and this leg wound, Grumps had cut himself enough times that I'd picked up a few first-aid basics. I got a rag from the sink, soaked it in dish soap and water, then scrubbed the blood from around the darkest part of my shin. I didn't touch the cut, which would've been crazy painful. I just cleared enough to see what I was dealing with, depth-wise. Whenever Grumps had a deep cut, he yelled to Gram to fetch him a clean cloth bandage. She knew what he meant and kept a whole stockpile on hand. After I'd dabbed the cut with the water, I went for the one stockpile here I knew was clean: the hamper in the living room. Rooting around, I pulled out the longest, stretchiest item I could find and limped to the couch to bind my wound. The couch, I quickly determined, was supercomfortable, but I'd left everything I needed in the kitchen. I limped back to the kitchen, grabbed my smokes and my pop, and a second later was nearly swallowed whole by cushions. A little light spilled from the kitchen, bright enough that I could get a feel for what a regular family in one of these houses liked for decor, not so bright that I didn't dare close my eyes for a second.

The living rooms in these houses are much smaller than what we have at the farm, and this one in particular was extra-cluttered with toys and clothes. Photographs sat on the TV and a few more were tucked on a bookshelf. Pretty typical for any family, I'd imagine. The photos all looked posed, and their dad was absent from every one. Don't know what was up with that, unless Donna Mae spilled the beans about our canal deal. Maybe they went looking and found him holding on to his rock and his rope and wearing his dopey expression. That sort of behaviour would cost anybody a place in a family gallery.

Why it's important to preserve the minutes to your meetings:

Moments of comfort on the farm last about fifteen minutes. That's about how long it takes me to remember what chores I'd forgotten to do. I lasted about that long here before my thoughts drifted back to that stupid hamper with all its stupid, wrinkled clothes, and the only thing I could think of from that point on was *they ain't gonna iron themselves*. The need to be doing things is partly why so many farmers smoke, because our hands want something to hold on to—a smoke, an axe, a chicken, manure—something. As farm chores go, though, ironing isn't high on my list, although I have pitched in on occasion. Gram does it in the kitchen, on top of a sheet on the table. No fancy ironing board for us. If I want to eat dinner sooner rather than later, I have to help.

The first trick is to lick your fingertip, then tap the plate to test the heat. If the plate makes a *hiss* sound, the iron's ready. Pants are a breeze, T-shirts too. And since I'd never scorched a pair of Grumps's coveralls, it seemed logical that my techniques would apply to whatever this hamper had: hold down, press hard, count to ten, shift and repeat. These clothes were less hefty than what our basket held, however, and a couple things in the hamper, like the underwear, didn't take well to being held under an iron for the standard amount of time. But once I got into a rhythm, I had a pretty sizable stack of wrinkle-free clothes on the couch.

I'd moved off the delicates to wrestle with a skirt when I heard a faint cry—a tiny, terrified "eep" to start, then a full-throated shout, "What the hell?"

I was pleased to recognize Mary Lynn's voice without having to turn around. Before I could mention how relieved I was to see her too, she was on to her next big concern. "Who are you? What the fuck are you doing?"

So many questions. I peeled the skirt from the iron and tossed it into the hamper, and gave Mary Lynn a minute to calm down.

"Who do ya think it is?" I asked from the darker half of the house.

"Who are you? Who are you?" She kept repeating herself. At least she'd crept further into the half-lit living room, possibly to let her eyes adjust to the sight of someone else doing her chores.

"It's me, Kap...I mean Kass. Jesus, relax. I'm doing your ironing. I thought you'd appreciate it. Oh, I saved your house too, by the way. And tore my good pants while doing it. So, you're welcome."

My eyes were already adjusted to the dark, so I noticed right away that she was standing in muddy socks, her pants below the knees also wet, like she'd just finished a "Singing in the Rain" dance routine. Or perhaps, like me, she'd been putting out a house fire somewhere because the fire department's truck hadn't crossed the river yet. That seemed more likely than the first, although neither would explain why she smelled like diesel and dead fish. I didn't get a chance to ask about that either because she'd rewound herself.

"Jesus, who? Kass? You? Are you stupid, kid? What are you doing here?"

I know I can be forgettable but I didn't think we'd been apart *that* long. I left off ironing and went to the coffee table to have a drag on my smoke. I spoke slowly through the exhale. "Your mom said to bring you home, but you took off. So I came here to wait. Did you hear what I said about your house? I put out your house."

"No! No! You don't walk into somebody's house," she sputtered. "Kap? How did you get here?"

"Oh, um...Leo—I mean your mom—gave me the address in case you tried to pull something slippery." Pure quality manure I was shovelling there.

"What? When?"

"Yeah, at the drugstore, your mom, in case we got separated. Relax."

As a rule, though, excited people really take offence to being told to relax. A lot of times the suggestion only leads to further unrelaxed behaviour. I don't think the fact that it rhymes with "axe" is a coincidence either. Try telling a headless chicken to relax.

While Mary Lynn was busy turning purple, I returned to the ironing board with another article of clothing. That cleared her head.

"Stop that. Stop that. What the hell? What do you mean, you put out the house?"

One more trip to the coffee table for a drag, only this time I flicked my cigarette into the saucer to gather my thoughts before breaking down what had taken place since my arrival. It was like reading the minutes of a previous meeting. Tedious, but necessary:

I told her how I went looking for her because it was my duty. I listed all the places I'd gone looking, like the pool hall and the creosote fire. I told her about all the flying sparks and how some were heading this way, so I came here straight away, rather than keep looking. I also mentioned, purely out of spite, that her mom had slipped me the address because she suspected Mary Lynn might pull something, which, I noted, she did. Then I went into details about the fire and the garden hose and how come their window got smashed. I added that I was good for the damages so she shouldn't worry.

"I put out your roof by the way, but I think there's some

damage upstairs too, so you should look into that sometime. Oh yeah, and I took a couple pops outta your fridge... I'm good for those also. Then I decided to do some chores around the house—you weren't here to do them—while waiting for you. That's when you walked in and started screaming. And *ta-da*! Here we are, all caught up. Oh yeah, and I tore my nice pants."

She managed to come around enough to dip her eyes occasionally and unclench her fists. That's because I used the voice Gram used when talking to a panicky baby animal, kinda singsong. A singsong voice is the best one to use when trying to calm someone. They will either like what you're singing and settle down, or worry you're more nuts than they are and relax out of concern they might rile you up more. Either way, my song worked like a charm. "Lookit, just sit down on the couch for a tick and catch your breath. I'm sorry I scared you, but like I explained, it couldn't be helped."

"That's your explanation? Jesus, kid. Rather than sit on the step and wait, you decided to break in." Mary Lynn was nearly back to normal. Damp and stinky, but normal.

"I broke in because I needed a hose to put out the fire on your roof. Pay attention."

"The house looks just fine. Except for the goddamn back door."

"Okay, don't believe me. Just don't throw a fit when you have to go to bed in a puddle of ashes."

She turned and looked toward the stairs, hesitating momentarily just in case I'd been jerking her then concluded what would be the harm in investigating, even if she couldn't admit it.

"I have to go change," she said, and stomped up the stairs.

I took a seat on the couch to wait for the show to start.

The second round of shrieking filtered into the living room almost immediately, so I removed another smoke from my pack and set it in the saucer with mine. By the sound of things, she'd need one. I pressed the little button under the lampshade near my head, giving the living room a soft, romantic glow. I kept my fingers crossed.

When the stairs creaked I looked through the railing balusters, where freshly socked feet eased their way onto each step below like they couldn't trust what was underneath them. Grumps walked downstairs the same way, but he was in his eighties or thereabouts. When she reached the last step, I saw that her cheeks were soot-smudged, with long streaks under each eye. She went directly to the hamper and began tossing clothes willy-nilly.

"Can I help?" I offered.

"My room is destroyed."

"Oh. Sorry. Would you like me to find you something?"

"Oh Jesus, shut up."

"Kay, it's just that I already ironed some of what was in the basket, so if you want ironed stuff it's not there; it's here on the couch." I tapped the ironing beside me and tried not to look come hithery.

"Oh God, what'd you do that for?" she groaned.

"Um, I think I covered the 'why' already."

Refusing the labours I'd offered, Mary Lynn rooted even deeper into the hamper, garment after garment sailing across the room. "Shit," she said. And a second later, "Shit."

I cleared my throat and tried one more time. "What you want might be here." (Tap-tap.)

Mary Lynn whirled and stomped to the couch, snatching the entire pile off the cushion and darted back upstairs. I'd have said something complimentary about how nice she smelled, but not everybody thinks of the canal the way I do.

Girls are funny like that, I mean about their perfumes and their clothes, what surrounds them, and all the whys to how to you should behave when in their vicinity. It has to do with being invited in, only in no way do I mean invited in like how Sliver's gals wanted me to invite them in. From experience I know the girls at school hated it whenever I snapped a bra strap, or made witty comments about their underwear waistbands, or guessed the perfume they're wearing was called Eau d'Toad. You can't stroll into someone's space and tug on something personal just because one of you thinks it'd be funny as hell. Like saying "relax," this is the kind of behaviour that can push the other person off their personal deep end. If I had the time I'd do another theme essay that's just a list. Most people would find that useful.

A whole new series of unfiltered cussing roared down the stairs. I think she found the underwear I'd singed.

I slid my saucer-ashtray to the edge of the coffee table so it would be nearer her side of the couch, putting Mary Lynn's cig in easy reach when she took the empty cushion beside. I settled back once more and took a drag on mine, one wary eye still on the stairs. My heart pounded like crazy. A guy on his prom date probably felt like this while waiting on his tomato to come down the stairs in her floor-length whatever. This would be good practice, I told myself. My grade-school prom night wasn't too far off, that half-assed deal our school put on for every stump who managed to graduate into Grade 9.

The meaning of a uniform, for a union whose sole purpose for getting together is smoking:

In fact, Gram had already started sewing the little number I was to wear to the big event. I saw the picture on the cover of the pattern's package—a not-half-bad set of duds, I must say. The pants were nice and wide at the bottom, and there was a matching five-button vest complete with belt loops meant for a belt, preferably one with a gold buckle, like the picture showed. And while I know Gram meant well when she offered me one of Grumps's bolo ties for around my neck, I nearly gagged right in front of her. That shit might fly in Saskatchewan, but nobody in Ontario wears bolo ties. Style-wise, she might as well give me one of his shoelaces. She promised to make me a scarf from the leftover liner material instead, plain brown, so it'd match the pants and vest, both of which had a jazzy, green-brown checkerboard pattern. It was an ensemble nice enough to be buried in.

My prom-date illusion ended the second Mary Lynn clomped down the stairs under a big head of steam, having replaced her wet pants with dry ones, and her Couch-Newton's blouse for a high school sweatshirt, one I specifically remembered ironing—nice thick cloth, very cooperative. She looked great in it, by the way. Only the sweatshirt wasn't what had pissed her off, but the thing she was waving like a highway warning flag. Some kind of shirt, looked like.

"Look at this thing! Did you do this?"

"Hey, careful," I protested. "You'll wrinkle it again." I didn't see the need for her tone either.

"No, you jerk. This!" She took the garment by its shoulders and showed me the back, which had a snazzy triangle design on it.

"Yeah, so?"

"This! That!" Her finger stabbed the offensive decoration.

Not getting where she meant to go with the demonstration, I shrugged. "Beggars can't be choosers." That was another one of Grumps's prime life lesson takeaways.

"B–Beg...what? You burned it, you jerk! It's ruined!"

"Well, if it's burned, how do you know the house didn't do it?"

"The house? Jesus, Sherlock. Look at the mark. It's the shape of the goddamn iron."

I studied the shadowy pattern. "Hmm. Yeah, so maybe it came that way."

"Really? That's what you think? That I don't know what my own goddamn clothes look like?"

Yeah, she'd got me there, though I gave my defence a good run. "Nah, I guess not. Well...sorry. If I did it, I didn't mean to. But don't worry—I'm good for it."

"So you keep saying. I'm starting a list. At the rate you're going, you're gonna owe us the farm in ten minutes. So far it's the window, the stepladder, two pops, one shirt..."

"I got my egg money income. I'll be good." Every morning before school I collected a couple dozen new eggs and when I got home, I washed them, packed them in cartons, and then stood at the side of the road to sell them. As long as the hens kept laying, I'd have me and this household back to square...eventually.

"You sell eggs?" The blue of her eyes rolled into her head for the hundredth time today.

"Yeah, what's the big deal?" I sensed she thought my egg-selling was another nugget to add to her collection of my flaws.

"Oh, nothing. It's *cute*, you selling eggs."

Tone-wise she meant lemonade-stand cute, not industrious-farmer cute. Time to get defensive again. "Yeah, well, at least I'm not selling sick birds to dumb-assed kids so I can break their hearts an hour later. Whaddabout that, eh? Whaddabout all those little kids who thought they had a pet for life? Poor little bastards, bawling their eyes out."

"Well, I'm sorry if you were at home on the farm bawling your eyes out, but that had nothing to do with me and you know it. It's the manager's fault, if anybody's besides the birds."

Oops. "As if I bawled my eyes out," I sputtered. She was pretty quick with the jam; I had to watch my step. "Heartbreaker," I added somewhat weakly, because I actually meant it the way most people would mean it, which had nothing to do with little kids and canaries. Seemed like a good time to slip a compliment into the old convo without too much backlash for its intention.

Mary Lynn smirked. Girls keep one ear on for compliments, even ones that come disguised as the exact opposite. At least it got her calmed down enough to stop calling me a jerk and to instead ask whose cigarette that was in the saucer.

"Yours, if you want it."

Mary Lynn took the cigarette, but instead of sitting beside me, as was the plan, she went to the window, I guess to check the street. I couldn't tell whether she was happy or sad when she saw it still empty. She popped the smoke into her mouth, then immediately removed it. "It's not lit."

"Nope."

"Would you mind?"

I held up my matches and, to indicate that she'd have to come and get them, I put my feet on the coffee table and leaned as far back against the couch as I could. Mary Lynn grumbled over the inconvenience but finally surrendered and pulled up a cushion beside me.

She was a light little thing for being taller than me and hardly made the cushion sink at all. I struck a match and she steadied my hand against her cigarette. Then we both leaned back and inhaled at the same time. I closed my eyes after targeting my smoke stream toward the stippled white ceiling. "Phew. Long day," I sighed, even if it sounded like something a farmer would say after flopping down at the kitchen table to pour himself a saucer of tea.

"Yep," Mary Lynn agreed, and made a little noise like a puff of wind herself, a signal to everybody that all our past minutes were behind us, and we were free to proceed with future business.

A discussion of that future-union business:

"So, about those eggs. How many eggs does a farm boy have to sell before he can afford a new blouse?"

"Dunno. A couple dozen, I'd guess."

"You make a dollar an egg?"

"What? Jeez, no. Maybe a dollar a duz. A stinkin' *blouse* costs that much?"

"Well, they don't cost two bucks. Shop much?"

"Nope. Not at all. Gram does, mostly. Hey, what if I pay you in eggs. You guys like eggs, right?"

"Not *that* much."

"Well, what if I gave you one of her shirts? I mean, some of them aren't bad...I guess."

"Yeah, thanks, but I'm not big on gingham."

"On *what*?"

"Gingham. It's a kind of cloth. Your grandma probably has a closetful."

"Whatever you say. I don't know what all she's got... You like plaid?"

"About as much as gingham."

"Your loss... Lookit, I'm sorry about your shirt. I just thought I was doing you a favour, is all. I didn't want you guys coming home to more work than I thought you could handle. I'll figure out your shirt."

"Don't worry about it." She shrugged, taking a very sultry drag on her cig. As she bent to tap the ash into the ashtray, she paused. "That's one of our good china saucers, you know."

I looked at the saucer, then blinked at her. "How the hell should I know that? It's not like I went huntin' for the best-looking saucer in the cupboard to stab my butts in."

"Nah, I guess," she admitted. "Relax, it's not important. We used to have ashtrays."

"What happened to 'em?"

"Mom chucked them all out, after..." She never finished the sentence.

I'd have chucked them out for memorial reasons too. I'm not sure what my memorial will look like. Hard to say if the thing you think is important about you is the same as what other people think is important about you. Not all memorials are good, in that case. I wouldn't mind an ashtray memorial. Sliver had one the size of a fire hydrant. Maybe somebody here could re-engrave it?

I closed my eyes for just a second when I felt Mary Lynn rustling beside me. I opened one eye and watched her lean forward to tap her cig over the saucer once more. On her way back she gave my leg a backhand, not hard, but still, it was my bad leg.

"My dad used to sit like that," she said to the ceiling after settling back against the couch. "It drove Mom nuts."

"Do you want me to take them off?"

"Nah, it's okay. I don't care. I just remembered now, is all."

"Yeah, I'll bet everybody's dad sits like this. My grandpa sits like this if Gram isn't in the room."

"Whaddabout your dad?" she asked.

"I'm not sure exactly. I don't really remember a lot." I rubbed my eyes because of the smoke between us. "I'll bet he did, though. I don't remember what we had for furniture. I mean, what if we didn't have a coffee table? Where would he put his feet?"

"You don't need a coffee table. He could've put his feet anywhere. Furniture's not really the reason for remembering somebody, you know. It's just a starting point."

Her voice was weary, like she had little strength to spare for me left, especially if I was going to keep reminding her of her past. I didn't like that I did. It was the essayist in me. I sucked on my smoke and blew another stream at the ceiling. The ash at the end of my cigarette had grown to an inch, which I only noticed when Mary Lynn brought the saucer up so I could give it a flick.

"Thanks." My voice sounded a little shaky.

"I don't want you burning the rest of the house down," she said, half smiling.

I don't get too emotional over small courtesies. On the other hand, if I had died right then, Mary Lynn would've been sitting beside the happiest corpse in the world—a corpse who could spew smoke rings like a sonofabitch. I exhale like a pro. Poor ol' Mary Lynn was back to struggling with hers again, despite the freshness being inhaled. I figured her for more seasoning than that. Too stressed to appreciate what she had around her, maybe.

"Sorry," she choked after her latest hack, tapping me on the knee this time. It must have been a harsh one.

"Ah, that's okay. I cough sometimes. You get used to them the more you smoke."

"No, not that, dummy. I mean about calling you a jerk." She took another drag to prove that she could handle an Export "A" just fine, and then exhaled in the sexiest way imaginable. I'm assuming everybody knows how sexily Veronica Lake could exhale, but in case not, it's pretty sexy.

"You probably hear that a lot."

"Not as much as you seem to think. Lately, I mean."

She wrapped her lips around the filter and her half-assed apology. We each had a smile on our puss, in fact, which was cool. I didn't want to be the only one in our smoker's union looking dope-happy over an insult disguised as an apology.

For meetings to run smoothly, it's helpful if everybody shares the same sense of humour. It just won't work otherwise—it's the slapstick comedians versus the brainiacs chuckling to themselves over the latest Duncan Macpherson cartoon. Maybe that was part of the deal with Grumps's stupid chickens too. Most of them acted slapstick, but you could tell the top ones were Macpherson-reading types. Whether Mary Lynn meant to call me a jerk didn't matter to me at all, because she managed to twist it into a little joke, with nice delivery and timing. We were two comedy pros, shovelling witty shit at each other.

Just to be sure, I asked her if she knew who Duncan Macpherson was.

"*Toronto Star*?" she hazarded her guess.

Atta girl.

Some outstanding matters will need to get tidied up before the end. Don't spend a lot of time on them, if you can help it:

"What's that in your pants?" she asked.

"Huh?"

"Under your belt. What's that?" Mary Lynn reached down and tugged on my trophy.

"Oh yeah. Nothin', I guess."

"What do you mean, nothing? You have a goddamn trophy hanging off your belt. That's not nothing."

"Ya-huh."

"Nuh-uh. Like, for example, how did it get there? Pretty sure it wasn't there earlier today."

"Mighta been."

"Nope, you don't miss a thing like that hanging from a guy's pants."

Here in town that might be true, but not on a farm. On the farm, Grumps and me were always hanging things from our pants: axes, hammers, whirligigs. And Gram too—big spoons, butcher's knives, thingamabobs.

"Fine. I got it after you scrammed. And thanks a lot, by the way."

"Sucker. There's a prize for that now?" she laughed.

"Should be, but nah. It belonged to my dad. I got it when I was looking for you in the pool hall."

"Really? Thanks a lot. Why would I be in the freaking pool hall?"

"Well, I don't know. Anyway, I went in and you weren't there, so relax."

"And?"

"Oh yeah. The guy—the owner—he gave it to me. Dad never picked it up."

"Holy cow. And the guy remembered you?"

"Yep."

She raised a single eyebrow at me, some kind of leftover judgment for being famous in a pool hall probably. With her hair as blond as it was, her eyebrows were a little hard to follow. Fortunately, I didn't mind concentrating on her face. I'd noticed how her expressions could bounce between mild curiosity and serious concern on a dime. Her next one was somewhere in between.

"Pool's dumb. I mean, as a sport it's kinda dumb."

"No, it takes skills. Sliv...Dad...had crazy pool skills."

"That's how he got this trophy?"

"Yeah, he won it. He didn't steal it."

"I never thought he stole it." She followed with a backhand to my thigh. Being my wounded leg, I sucked air through my clenched teeth again, this being her third slap on that leg. She couldn't ignore the weakness anymore.

"Ha! Called it. Crybaby."

"For what?"

"You make a face every time I touch you."

"You smacked me."

"What, that? That was nothing. Hardly a love tap."

I should've left it at that. *Love tap*! "Nuh-uh. I can feel a welt. And besides, you smacked me on my wounded leg."

"Wounded? You're not wounded. Wounded how?"

"Don't worry about it—I'll live."

"Exactly. I'm calling bull unless you show me where, crybaby."

Mary Lynn pivoted on her cushion until her nose was barely our two cigarettes away from mine. When she exhaled her smoke this time, it landed in my face, right where she was aiming, and it was just as sexy as I knew it'd be. No wonder some guys think they're gonna get lucky after a cig. Not me, though. My mind was blank. I blurted, "Did I ever tell you about the time me and Grumps hooked the cows up with a bull?"

"Nope. Show me your wound, baby."

"Fine, brace yourself," I warned. I tugged on my pant leg, my shin throbbing like a motherfucker. The dried blood had glued my cut to the cloth; it felt like I was peeling away skin.

Mary Lynn bent toward the bandage. Whatever pity and regret she may have first felt for having doubted my wound disappeared the second she recognized what was covering it. "What the fuck?" she gagged.

"What? Bad?"

"Is that my bra?"

"What?"

"That's my bra!"

"Is it?" I didn't have to act surprised. I really had no idea what I'd grabbed from the hamper.

"What's the matter with you? Why would you do that?" She looked fixing to rip it from my leg in one tug so I shifted my leg out of harm's way. I think she would have yanked if her bra wasn't so obviously beyond salvaging for anything other than how I was using it.

"How the hell was I supposed to know it was yours?"

"So you admit you felt around for one."

"What? Fuck no. I wasn't feeling around for anything. I just grabbed the first thing useful for wrapping. I was bleeding to death." Also the truth, but try and convince Mary Lynn about that at this moment, I could forget it.

The sound she made as she began peeling the bra from my shin was like what an alley cat makes when it comes across another, weaker alley cat. Even so, she used an incredible amount of care, all things considered.

"Ouch," I said, possibly more than once.

"Cram it," she said. I'll bet Leona would have been more sympathetic.

Anyway, after uncoiling her bra from my shin, Mary Lynn carried the bandage at arm's length into the kitchen, returning with a white dishcloth that she then tore into strips. She rewrapped my leg with the strips, taping the ends together with the roll of Scotch tape she'd also brought with her.

"That'll have to do for now."

"Appreciate it," I said sincerely. "You know your stuff."

"Shut up. You've got to do something more about that cut than what I did."

"Why? It looks great." As artwork went, this was about the

best thing anybody'd ever given me. I couldn't see myself taking it off.

"You'll have to take it off, or it'll become infected. Or don't and die. I don't care." Even I didn't believe that last one. However, I was pretty amazed how she knew what I was thinking. "It's bleeding pretty good," she continued. "You'll probably need stitches."

"Stitches? Cool."

"Now you sound like Donna Mae. I have to fix her up too, when mom is at work. Only she doesn't whine as much as you do. Now, lemme see the trophy."

"I didn't whine," I protested, but was happy to tug the trophy out from between my belt and my pants, for a much-needed distraction. "Here. It's just a regular pool trophy, except for the chick beside the guy. Usually it's just a guy standing there alone, holding a cue."

"That's *hilarious*." She didn't laugh when she said it, so hilarious was probably not the word she meant.

"What is?"

"That there'd even be a regular pool trophy. Who cares that much about pool that they'd want to play for a trophy?"

"Lots of guys. It's very popular."

"And so, because it's so damn popular with guys, they figure girls will be equally fascinated and want to play for a trophy, to boot? That's what's hilarious."

"I'm serious. People actually like playing against each other. How else would you know how lousy you are at a thing unless somebody kicks your ass at it?"

"I think competitions are stupid." She gave her hair a flip. "Trophies for everything, just so you can put somebody down by waving one of these in their face." She waved the trophy at me, like I'd won it or something. "Like you. I'll bet you have a roomful of these things."

"Really? Why?" My voice soared a little too much into the upper range, because outside of the occasional feat of strength or my hucking abilities, nothing about me would make anybody think, "I'll bet that kid has a roomful of trophies."

She tapped her chin as she contemplated my reaction. "I dunno, you probably don't. I guess because you said your dad had a bunch of these. I figured you'd want to be like him."

Of the two of us, I didn't think it'd be possible for Mary Lynn to sound more offended at the notion of me wanting to be like Sliver. Since she didn't know Sliver from Adam, she was probably just offended by the general idea of traits being passed down. I didn't say anything yet; this was more theme essay material anyway, on how she was right to be worried about what her old man might have passed on to her. Or taken from her.

Mary Lynn stuck her smoke in her mouth to create the pause inside which I was to show my agreement with her thoughts on heredity. She had a perfect mouth, no matter what came out of it sometimes. It nearly killed me, having to disagree with it so much.

"No, we're pretty different. Pool was his thing."

"So, what about you? What's your thing?"

"Ah, I don't have a thing they'd give trophies for. Nothing on my own, anyway."

"What does that mean?"

"Well, I've got a couple of things, just not trophies. I've got ribbons."

"Ha, you mean blue ribbons, don't you?" she whooped, which wasn't all that attractive, given my latest confession.

My plan was to, in one way or another, love Mary Lynn to pieces, but sometimes, when I picked up one of those pieces and examined it more closely, I saw things that might not work very well in a solid boyfriend-girlfriend relationship, not even a brother-sister or a friend one. Nothing I'd consider a deal-breaker yet, mind you.

"Yeah, as a matter of fact. Me and Grumps, I mean my grandfather, won it for our cow."

Mary Lynn sniffed triumphantly. "Don't you mean the cow won it? You're taking credit for the cow's work. That's all blue ribbons mean, you know. That's why they're just lousy ribbons and not real trophies. The whole thing's a scam."

"Nuh-uh."

"Ya-huh. It's the same for growing the biggest pumpkin or whatever that thing is they take a picture of and stick in the newspaper every fall. Some wrinkled old fart in a straw hat stands beside the blob that ate New York, looking as proud as if he built it with his own two hands. Big whoop-dee-do. He stuck a seed in the ground. Same for your cow. It's...it's... chicanery."

"What?" I'd never heard that word before. Never mind how much I loved being lectured to by a Quintonian about farm-related business, it was nice to learn something new. Talking to Mary Lynn was a little like talking to her aunt, the dorkus, I decided.

"Chicanery. You know, fake business."

"No way. I mean, yeah, we don't build the cows..."

"Exactly."

"But we raise them."

"As I said—whoop-dee-do—like they wouldn't do that on their own." She raised her nose to the ceiling like a queen whose lungs were full of smoke. Whoosh, she went.

"We don't compete using a full-grown cow we plucked straight outta the barn. We could, I guess, but if we want a ribbon then the cow's gotta start as a calf, be cared for properly, given the right feed, groomed, shit like that. Otherwise, you'll end up with a regular cow like every other cow."

"So you mistreat all the other calves."

"What?"

"You just admitted it. You don't care for the other babies properly, don't give them the best food. Only the chosen one, the possible prizewinner."

Hmm. Mary Lynn kind of had a point, I guess, about rearing and/or raising, if she means what makes one calf more deserving of special treatment than another. But if I'm treating that calf more special, it's only so when I grow up and become a farmer, I'll know how to treat all the calves in the best way possible, to make everybody a prizewinner. For Mary Lynn I summarized: "Not necessarily. These are like practice calves. What's to say they aren't getting worse treatment than the regular calves?"

"Big whoop either way, because you're either playing favourites or torturing it. Neither one is right."

God almighty, she sure hated to lose an argument. "Yeah, well, if I gave you a calf for a competition you'd probably just put lipstick on it and paint its hooves, because that's all you know about things."

My charge staggered her, at least to the point she took her cigarette and stamped it half a dozen times into the saucer. "No. I wouldn't."

"Probably would. Because that's all you town girls know about things—makeup and bras and that. There's more to the world than Quinton, you know. There's more than even Ontario."

"Yeah, yeah. You're a jerk. And I'm not apologizing this time," she said. "Calves should be left to their mothers."

Mary Lynn didn't know a thing about what it took to raise a calf. She didn't know a thing about what Grumps and I did to make sure she got perfect milk. I would have made a speech about that next, but she'd gone back to studying the trophy, her way of saying that she'd lost interest in farming. She scratched the little plaque on the base with a painted pink fingernail.

"Aha!" she squealed, jamming the trophy under my nose again. "Did you know they lost? Maybe that's why he didn't want it."

I pushed the trophy away from my face. She'd nearly knocked the smoke from my mouth. "If he lost, then yep. He wouldn't want it. What makes you think he lost?"

"Because I can read. It says right here: runner-up. That means they lost, your dad and somebody named Liz."

"Who?"

"Liz. That's the other name on the trophy, besides Doug Pine. Doug is your dad's name?"

"Can you shut up for two seconds?" I rubbed at my head-scruff to think. "Yeah, Doug. Everybody just calls him Sliver, though...or used to. Lemme see."

She handed me the trophy and tapped on the brass plate with her finger. "See? Right here. Liz Pine. Is that your mom?"

I shook my head. "Nah, I think my mom's name was Beth."

"It's the same name, dummy. E-Liz-a-Beth."

I never saw Sliver's name side by side with anybody's before. The couple on top of the trophy were Doug and Liz Pine. It said so on the plaque. Arm in arm like a normal mom and dad. I could see my reflection on their shiny, plastic gold faces.

"Doug Pine and Liz Pine—Mixed Runners-up—Snooker." Mary Lynn was reading from the trophy. "I thought you said it was for pool. What's snooker?"

"It's a kind of pool game."

"You mean there's different kinds of pool? Well, that's rich. They should just call it pool and get it over with. Who's gonna care what branch it is?"

"Chrissakes, if you're playing in the goddamn tournament, you're gonna care what the branch is. Jesus."

"Okay, relax. Where is she, your mom?"

"Dead, I told you." I hated repeating old news, or even incomplete news. Like I said, I didn't know for sure where she was. Sometimes I said "dead" for the impact, when impact was called for.

"Shoot, I'm sorry. So you're an orphan?"

"No, I'm not." I tucked the trophy under my arm in case it had more information that Mary Lynn could use against me.

"Yeah, I think so, Kass. When you don't have any parents, you're an orphan."

"No, I live with Gram and... With my grandparents. Orphans don't have anybody."

"Yeah, but technically you are. Amazing."

"Fuck off."

"What did you say?" She put her hand to her mouth, like she'd never been told that in her life. But rather than wait for her to turn that hand against me, I leapt up from the couch and went to the window. I almost crossed my fingers hoping that Mary Lynn's mom and Donna Mae would be swinging into the driveway.

"If I don't want to be called an orphan, then you can't call me one. Because you know what? I don't feel like one. In fact, I feel less like one now than when I wasn't one."

What I meant to say to her was this: there are orphans by loss, and there are orphans by lack. I was being raised by two people who seemed to like me a lot, which is the important thing for any kid. And the people I had now were

182

doing a pretty good job, if I do say so. They'd kept me from exploding, at least to this point—though now I was about to explode at any second. I could feel my heart slam against my chest. I told myself to not turn around, afraid I'd shout something more awful than "fuck off" at Mary Lynn, who had the decency to keep quiet for a minute. Stuff I'd really regret too, like what I knew about her dad. So I pressed my forehead against the glass of the picture window to cool it down. The shaky old street lights flickered, or possibly the smoke from the creosote fire had made its way here and was playing tricks. Had it burned itself out yet? Or had the fire trucks finally made it across the river? Had everybody gotten bored and gone home to what was left of their per- manently preserved lives?

I tapped my head against the glass again and again, and tried to not think about anything, which was very tough to do when I've been wading up to my armpits in the best and worst Quinton had to offer. Maybe *tap* is the wrong word. Mary Lynn thought so because all of a sudden here she was beside me, slipping her hand between me and the window.

"Stop it, Kass. I'm sorry."

"Stop what?"

"Hitting your head." She touched my forehead then showed me the red stain. "I'm done cleaning up your blood." She passed me the sock she'd brought with her. "Here. Make yourself useful."

As I wiped down the glass and my forehead, Mary Lynn went back to the couch. She flipped her hair out of her eyes and asked me why don't I sit down and shut up. "You talk way too much."

"I wasn't talking at all."

"Yeah, you were mumbling again. You mumble a lot. Like, non-stop."

She crossed her legs sexily, her hands on her knees trilling her fingers like she didn't have all day for me to get to the point of whatever it was she'd half-heard.

"I was looking at your little tree in the front yard. We had one in our backyard when I lived in town. I was aces at climbing it too."

"That a fact? We've got one in our backyard. It's got a tree fort and everything. If you like, you can go play in it now. It's Donna Mae's but she won't mind. She took a shine to you."

It occurred to me she wasn't really inviting me, just being witty, having put my ability at swinging from branch to branch on the same level of impressiveness as my ironing skills. Good one, in that case. Still, I'd have killed for a tree fort. All I got was a lousy swing. Gram had a deathly fear about people falling out of things.

"Did your dad build it for her?"

"Nope."

"Your mom?"

"Nope."

"For chrissakes, who then?"

"Are you freaking serious? Who's left to choose from?"

"Well, I didn't know. How is anybody supposed to guess you built it?"

Maybe some liberated hippie might have gotten around to her eventually, and I wished like hell I was one for the time it'd take me to think that Mary Lynn might know carpentry, among all the other skills she'd been taking her sweet time revealing. Otherwise, everything I remembered about the workings of Quinton women was what Sliver left me. A guy can't be the sharpest tool in the shed if the only shed he knows is full of jerky.

"You'll really have to grow up some if you want to make it in high school." Her eyes were half-shut, like this was tedious stuff she was passing on. "Four H, or whatever you call it, that isn't gonna cut it there. They have different priorities." She wasn't mad exactly. Worn down possibly, from having to set me straight every time I started leaning Sliver's way. I'll bet she set Donna Mae straight when Donna Mae did something crazy. Keeping her sister out of trouble until their mother came home, and then Mary Lynn could be Mary Lynn for a couple of hours, after the clothes were ironed and the dishes were done. I wonder if it's possible for her to hate her dad and miss her dad at the same time. For me that's no contest. I'm always doing chores I wouldn't normally be doing.

"What sorts of priorities? Quinton priorities?"

"Well, for starters, nobody's going to give a fuck about cows or eggs or whatever you think is so fascinating that you keep going on about it. I mean, Jesus, develop an interest in something that isn't covered in manure."

"I have interests. Lots."

"Yeah, I know. Canaries and tree climbing. Lookit. I don't want to be mean; I'm just trying to give you some advice for what's ahead. It's a whole other world than where you come from."

"You don't know a thing about where I come from!"

"I've heard enough."

Well, I didn't like what I was hearing, that's for sure. Sliver would have slugged her good, if he was standing here. I needed to go for a walk. On the farm I could go for a walk whenever Sliver rose up and forced himself on my behaviour, made me hate the people nearest to me. I found that leaving was the best way to lose him again and quiet my head. Long walks with my head down: that's how I became such a terrific butt collector. The canal wasn't too far away from here. Maybe a barge was passing upstream, and I could hop aboard, and then Mary Lynn wouldn't have to worry about the hazard I might become. Hers and Donna Mae's dad, he was a hazard she couldn't run from. Sliver was still sort of mine. I'd save Mary Lynn at least, if I left her alone and went somewhere peaceful to explode.

I didn't even say goodbye. I ran out the door and jogged down the street as fast as my boots and lungs would allow (so not as far or as fast as I'd've liked). Funny how I could never seem to leave this neighbourhood under my own steam. But I got far enough this time to end up all alone with the dark and cold. Those are the last two things both of our dads would have known too. At least I could smoke. I clomped from a jog to a shuffle, and started slapping myself stupid, harder and harder, like that might make my packs of smokes suddenly reappear. All I had on me still was my baggie. "Shit."

A more seasoned smoker would have tucked at least one of his new packs on his person, not tossed them willy-nilly on every table in a house that wasn't his. I needed two or three drags before I had my throat up to speed with the old routine.

Where I should probably discuss what happens when you lead everybody in the right direction, even if by accident:

So, I was right about never being able to leave this neigh-bourhood. I'm counting the canal as part of the neighbour-hood too, since one of the paths that leads to the water begins at that dead end known as British Chemical Road. That's where Mary Lynn and I met Larry the photographer and Bruce the horse model six years ago, in fact. I wound my way around the crumbled concrete pillars of Quinton's last great employer before creosote arrived, chose one of the hundred channels carved into the waist-high weeds, and soon I was standing on a ledge overlooking the near pitch-black, perfectly calm water. It was a reminder of how I was right to fish here all those times.

I pulled up a bollard and took out my baggie, counted the butts, and realized I might have to ration what was left, if my theories on butts as indicators of economic woes and melancholy are accurate (which they are). On my next-to-last match strike, I caught a glimpse of something yellow bundled on the bank next to the old boat ramp. My last match went to the end of my smoke, before I retrieved Mary Lynn's caftan, folded neatly on a stone. After making sure I was alone, I pressed the caftan against my face and inhaled. It had everything cool about us still trapped inside—cigarettes, Couch-Newton's, the drugstore, Leona, Donna Mae, her house before the fire, hints of Del, a whiff of canary—all tied inside the thousands of knots that went into making it. I bet if I untied those knots, the yarn could stretch from here to the farm and back.

After Mary Lynn and me parted ways the last time I tried running away from this neighbourhood, I'd hoped it was for good. I didn't think anybody could catch a cowboy on a horse. Del had other ideas. When me and Bruce the pony reached the first access road from the canal, there he was, with Larry, standing outside his cop car. The outline of Mary Lynn's head was recognizable in the back seat. Seems her mom had turned us in, after going to the dead end where the photographer had first set up his tripod. The little suckers who'd gone looking for a ride or a picture told her about catching the dust of Bruce, Mary Lynn, and the kid cowboy bolting across the field.

"Howdy," the cop said with a passable drawl as he relieved me of the reins. "You must be *the Kid*."

"Howdy," I replied.

"Doin' a little hoss wrastlin', I see."

"Yessir, I guess. You gonna arrest me, sir?" The notion didn't scare me in the least. I liked the thought of me as a hoss wrestler.

"Nah, no hoosegow for you today, son. I'm only here to take you home." He lifted me off Bruce and waved at Bruce's owner to take the reins. Then he walked me to the car and opened the back door. I slid in beside Mary Lynn, who looked to have just wrapped up a round of blubbering. The car's whole inside smelled like Bruce.

"It's okay about the smell," I told her, just in case that's why she was blubbering.

"What are you talking about?" she huffed, then shuffled down the seat until she was jammed against the far door.

Larry stared at everybody from a little distance away, like he expected the cop to load Bruce in the trunk or something. When Del started the engine, we heard Larry yell, "What about me and Bruce?" so Del stuck his head out the window and told him he'd meet him back at his truck.

A lady was waiting at the truck when we pulled up, her forehead pressed against the driver-side window, her curlers pushed high on her head.

"Hey, is that your mom?" I asked, impressed. She was exactly how I imagined mothers would look, as if suddenly called away to something when they weren't prepared.

Mary Lynn muttered, "Shit," under her breath.

"What? You're lucky," I said, not thinking there could be any debate.

"Yeah, I'm dead, thanks to you," she sputtered just before her waterworks started back up.

Her mother had been killing time between while Del was fetching us by weeding through all the usual crap perverts collected on the seats and the floor of their trucks: nudie books, sandwich crusts, Instant pictures nobody else would ever look at. The second she spotted us, she didn't run over like you might expect and wail on Mary Lynn. Nope, she started yelling at the cop, waving him over, even though he hadn't stopped the car yet. "You gotta look at this, Del! Quick!" She had that red spot on her forehead people got from pressing their foreheads too hard against glass (with which I am now very familiar). He hopped out of the car and jogged over.

By the time Mary Lynn and me had wiggled out of the back seat, Del was knee-deep in pervert crap, scribbling notes, collecting evidence, shaking his head. He was so focused on the truck, in fact, he missed seeing poor Mary Lynn get cuffed across the noggin by her mom, even if, as cuffs go, it was pretty pathetic. I don't know why Mary Lynn cried about it. But the second she could composed herself enough, she spilled her guts to her mom, stabbing her finger at me every third word, it felt like. When Del walked over, that gave her the opportunity to start blubbering all over again, along the same "It's all his fault, ya know!" theme, spouting how I paid for the pictures, where Larry took us for more pictures, how it was my decision to steal Bruce, how she had no choice because the horse was so big and so fast and I was doing all the driving. Del and her mom just stood there with their mouths open. Every so often I'd mutter an "uh-huh" to let them know that everything she said was true, even the part about Bruce being so big and fast, which I thought Bruce would appreciate.

Having finished with turning me in, Mary Lynn fell quiet now except for her sniffles. She did manage to get her mom looking plenty cross, enough that when Leona started walking toward me, I took a half step back toward Del's car before remembering who I was, Gene Autry, and I should stick around for the conclusion of the episode. I closed my eyes and bowed my head in anticipation of getting slugged, but all she did was put her hands on my shoulders as she dropped to her knees. She took my chin in her hand and raised my head. Her watery eyes sparkled in a dark but calm canal kind of way, and she pulled my face right up to hers and planted a kiss on my cheek. I could feel her warm breath and smell her perfume, which was very light and sweet, like roses, and I'm almost certain she left a lipstick smooch on there, if my cartoons were accurate about such things. The last thing she did was whisper in my ear words I'd feel funny repeating, so I won't. I'll just say that after I slid my face out from between her sticky palms I slung my hat low over my eyes and touched a finger to the brim. In my best drawl I told her, "My pleasure, ma'am," then drew my whistle up its braided string until it was snug against my double chin.

Del escorted me to his car and let me sit up front with him. Everything was about to change for me, admittedly for the better, but at the time I couldn't help but think about how if I'd had a faster horse, or even a real horse, I might be at least halfway to Spring Valley by now.

When we pulled up to mine and Sliver's house, Del asked if it was the place.

I stared at the bright red front door, half-expecting it to fly open and Sliver to coming screaming toward us with his broom handle, even though I knew that was impossible.

"It's okay," Del said. "You did a good thing. I'll come with you and explain what happened."

I wasn't listening. I was looking at the maple trees on the other side of the street. The kids who had been climbing them were now perched on the branches like giant birds, everyone glaring at me, like I was the reason they couldn't get their pictures taken on a pony anymore. The tree in my backyard rattled its brown leaves when it saw me and Del climbing out of his car.

Del wouldn't stop ringing the goddamn doorbell. "Do you know if anybody's home?" He leaned across the railing to look through our fishbowl window into the living room.

I almost made up some bullshit about Sliver being out for a while—like at a pool tourney or gone for a walk with the missus. Instead I shrugged and sat on the step with my back to Del. I picked up a piece of broken broom handle and clacked it on the concrete. Part of me wanted Del to leave, but I also wouldn't have minded if he poked around a little bit. I was pretty lonely.

Del quit the doorbell and rapped on the wood, his wide, thick knuckles going *thud–thud–thud*. Not like some skinny guy's knuckles with their *thap–thap–thap*. If I kicked the door with my boot, I might make the sound Del's knuckles made.

"Do you have a key?" he asked, resigning himself to the fact the house might be empty.

I tugged on my whistle. "Don't need one."

Del frowned, then turned the knob. He offered a courtesy "Helloooo" into the crack, pulling his head back when the smell inside hit him. If I hadn't gotten used to the stink, I might have warned him about what was behind the door, which was specifically old meat, dried blood, rotten cabbage, and possibly me, because I hadn't had a bath in a while. In the least enthusiastic voice ever, he said, "Maybe we should step inside and take a look around."

Slipping my whistle from my chin to slide my hat off my head, I led the way, stepping around Del to push the door open.

"Jesus," he gasped. "Who died?"

Not that he thought somebody really had. He just meant it like he'd caught wind of a million farts. When a few dozen flies sailed out of the kitchen and toward the freedom of the front door, Del's demeanour became slightly more professional.

"What's that way?" He pointed toward the doorway that stood between him and a million more the flies.

"Kitchen."

Del stopped under the arch between the two rooms, I think to take a deep breath, letting out a little "whoop" when I toddled around him and headed for the fridge. I was dying of thirst. Maybe Del was too.

From the bowels of the fridge I called out the good news. "There's a beer in here."

"Not right now, son," he exhaled. "But thanks."

"Water?" I brought out the tumblerful I'd been saving for when I got home. It was ice-cold.

"Help yourself."

A big slab of something green and brown sat in the sink, beef maybe. Or pork. Whatever it was it was ground zero for the smell, the flies, and the maggots. Del held his hand over his nose as he studied the sink's contents. A week or so earlier, I'd pulled a reddish slab out of the freezer and plunked it in there to thaw. Pretty useless as food for the first day, I only managed to fry a handful of scrapings. For the next few days after that, though, I lived pretty high off the hog, if that's what it was, slicing big hunks with Sliver's hunting knife, then cooking the meat black. After a while the meat in the sink turned kind of brown and got a taste to it, then kind of green, which was when I stopped eating it. Then the flies moved in and it was their turn. I had to finally eat the cabbage I found rolling around in the back of the fridge, except for breakfast when I had cereal. The milk turned solid around the same time the meat turned green, so I'd been eating the cereal dry.

"Nobody's been eating this thing, have they?" He meant the meat. And me.

"Yeah," I told him. "But not for a while."

The cop angled his head back and forth like a dog who'd just caught wind of a curious scent. "What is it?" he asked at last, stumped.

I told him the same, beef or pork, but added that it could be horse, which, given recent events with Bruce, I felt bad admitting was a possibility. "Sliver's a knacker," I pointed out in my defence. "Mostly he kills horses, more than cows or pigs."

"Gotcha. Who's Sliver?"

"My dad."

"Oh, that's right! Your dad's name is um...Doug. Doug Pine."

"Yes, sir. You met us once already."

"Yes, I remember now. How's your fingers?"

I held out the result of the vet's handiwork. He *tch'd* a little at the sight, otherwise kept it together. "So your dad's a knacker, eh?" (I said, "I guess," unclear of the protocol when someone was only recently disappeared, like how long does a person have to be referred to by his occupation, or his position in, say, a family.) "What's a knacker again?"

So I explained the ins and outs of the profession and why it was logical for the thing in the sink to have been in our freezer, how sometimes Sliver helped himself to a hunk of something before he took the carcass to the glue factory or wherever. Del was an attentive listener. I could tell by the way his eyebrows popped every second word or so. He especially enjoyed my explanation of where the best places to apply a bullet or an axe were. In case you didn't know it, those places aren't the same.

"Sounds like great work," he enthused.

"Yep. We had buffalo once. A whole leg."

"Nice."

"Yep. Want me to show you where he cuts things up?"

That got Del's professional attention again. Or maybe he was just glad to get away from the sink.

I took him by the hand and led him into the backyard. Sliver had a table there, with saws and knives scattered on top. The ground around the table had a stain the same kind of colour as the meat in the sink, only the green was from grass. The flies were different ones, though probably they were all related. Sliver's axe wasn't on the table, though; it was under the tree, right where I remembered it landing.

"See? He puts the meat here."

"Yep, it's a good set-up alright." He swept the dead leaves from the tabletop and checked out the knives, looking down their lengths the way men do.

"He hasn't used the table in a while, has he."

"Nah," I said. "Not for a while."

"How long, would you say?"

Not being one for counting days, I only shrugged. "Work's been slow. Sliver says the world is getting soft. Sliver says if people want a goddamn pet, they should get a dog. I only had a dog once."

Del smiled along with me as he looked around the backyard, maybe even for Curly, settling upon the chain looped around the climbing tree. The other end was snagged in a branch about halfway up.

"Where is he?"

"Sliver or the dog?"

"Let's start with the dog."

My guess is Del was remembering the mystery meat in the sink and wanted to eliminate Curly as a suspect. He didn't wait for my answer, though, and was pressing his fingers into one of the many sneaker prints sunk into the mud of the path worn around the base. He stared at the branches for a second or two, spotting the chunk of chain without its collar, then got back to his feet and brushed the dried dirt and leaves from the knees of his dark blue pants. "I'll bet you can climb that tree."

"Yessir. All the time."

"Pretty high?"

"Almost to the top," I told him.

"How's the view?"

"I dunno. Pretty good."

I only been all the way the once, and the one time I did reach there, my view was of the top of Sliver's head, just before I threw the axe at it. Then I saw the ball lightning explode, and when I opened my eyes Sliver was gone and I was on the ground all by myself. That's not the view Del meant, so I didn't bring it up. Del gave the chain a tug, which caused it to rattle to the ground like an angry snake. He scratched at the end where the collar used to be. Gnarled and blue, the metal looked like somebody had burned it with a blowtorch.

"Any idea how that happened?" he asked. He showed me the burnt end of the chain, waiting for my thoughts.

I stated the obvious. "Lightning."

"Well, that's a good answer. Lightning wouldn't have occurred to me."

I wasn't surprised. Back then, the thought that nature might step up to lend me a hand would never have occurred to me either. Now, of course, I see it all the time. Del went to where the axe lay in the dried mud and pulled it out, examining the metal head, which, like the chain, was scorched to blue. The handle was blackened and split down the middle.

"Ouch," he said as he wiped the soot from his hands. "How'd you suppose that happened? Same lightning bolt?"

"It was a lightning ball," I corrected him.

Del wrinkled his face. (I've since learned not a lot of people believe ball lightning is a real thing. What do they know?) But he'd already steered his attention to the shed. The door only locked from the inside, so he had no trouble breaking in. "Hello?" he called, just for a joke because the shed wasn't very big at all. I smiled.

He found the usual shed and smokehouse crap: a rake, a shovel, plus the chains and pulleys knackers needed to bleed or drag a heavy dead animal, a few strips of rock-hard jerky draped over a length of twine. My sleeping bag was in there too, for when Sliver had his women sleep over. I'd latch the door with a block of wood on those occasions, to keep me safe at night. Otherwise I'd never get a wink. It'd been my regular bedroom ever since that hunk of meat turned. You try sleeping in a house full of dead animal stink and flies buzzing around your head. Can't be done. My sleeping bag was unrolled; the picture on it was Snoopy sleeping on the roof of his doghouse. Next to that was a big stack of underwear and socks. If I'd figured out how to move the TV in there, life would have been the sweetest ever.

"You like camping, I see." I don't think Del got to play detective a lot. He was firing a lot of these half-answered questions at me.

"Never been," I admitted, suddenly embarrassed for being in my cowboy getup, cowboys being famous campers under the stars, after all. There wasn't a star in sight inside the shed.

"Would your dad mind if I took his axe?" he asked. "I promise to bring it right back."

"Nah, he won't mind now."

I liked Del. He didn't lean over when he talked to you. He stood straight and tall, like me and him were two regular guys yakking it up. Sliver's women slumped over when they had something to say to me, like they were doing me this big favour by jamming their round grey faces right in front of mine. I scuffled after Del because he was off again, heading for the back door "for another little look around inside." His hand was hovering over the doorknob when a thought grabbed him. "Why won't he mind?"

Del was pretty sharp, but I wasn't worried. In fact, I kind of wanted a second opinion on my situation. "I don't think he's comin' back, is why."

To his credit, Del didn't ask me right away why I'd think that. He'd met Sliver; he knew my luck with parents. The professional in Del knew he needed a foundation of actual facts first. Otherwise he'd just get another earful about ball lightning. Del removed his cap and swiped his forehead with a white handkerchief, then swirled his whole face with it. "What say we go back inside?" he suggested.

Del held out his hand, so I took it. He let me lead the way back through the kitchen, with one stop at the sink so he could put the meat in the freezer. "We'll throw it in the garbage later," he told me. I escorted him into the living room.

Even for a beat cop, I don't think Del knew a lot about death. As the son of a knacker, on the other hand, I saw death all the time, all the surprised looks from animals too dumb to realize they were sick or old or had outlived their usefulness. When I eventually slid into farm life full-time—which would be about two hours after me and Del walked out Sliver's front door for the last time—I'll bet I was the most well-informed guy Gram and Grumps ever met, at least death-wise.

Half-eaten hunks of cabbage sat on a plate on the coffee table, and beside the plate were a couple strips of jerky. I offered Del one of the strips. He took it and said he'd have it later, stuffing it in his pocket. He looked at the walls and the shelves for pictures that might tell him something. We did have a desk in the living room, and that drew his interest, so while he rifled through it I spun the TV to face the couch.

I waited through a Wheaties commercial. They were making a big deal out of some string bean named Billy Mills. They should have spent the air time warning kids about how lousy Wheaties tasted without milk. (Apparently Billy Mills was some sort of runner—not a sprinter, the more boring, long-distance kind. Superskinny like Sliver, but not a smoker, I imagine.)

Del took a handful of papers over to Sliver's wing chair and sat down, accidently kicking over a bottle of booze hiding next to the ashtray stand. A half-drunk tumbler of rye teetered on the arm of the chair; Del was more careful with that. Out of the corner of my eye I caught him holding it up to the light.

"It's Sliver's." A fact I thought worth mentioning.

Del chuckled through his nose. "Kinda figured. But thanks for clearing that up. He didn't finish it."

"Nope."

"Do you think he meant to?"

"I reckon."

Sliver never left a drink undrunk. Then again, his plan wasn't to chase after me up a tree either. He probably thought I'd be where he left me, so his drink would be waiting for him when he got back. But I was working on my tree fort, because I hated sharing the shed with Sliver's smokehouse. The TV went out when the storm got close, and because he no longer had that to distract him, he remembered that I was still outside. I got as far as telling Del this last bit, then had to hush him twice because my story had come on. Del waited politely silent until the next commercial.

The show was, coincidently, *The Secret Storm*. One of Sliver's women had been in love with Peter Ames, the lead actor, so I watched with her and got hooked. This was its first year in colour, so that was pretty mesmerizing too.

"That chain outside is yours, not your dog's, I guess."

"Yessir. I don't have a dog anymore, remember?"

"Right, Curly. I remember. Why were you tied to the tree?"

"Sliver doesn't like me running away; he says if I'm going to act like a dog then he's gonna treat me like a dog. He says he's tired of hauling my ass home all the time."

Del removed his handkerchief again and dragged it across his face. "So sometime after he went outside he disappeared?"

"Yep. He got mad because I was up the tree. And I had his axe."

"Why were you up the tree?"

"Trying to build a fort. That's why I had his axe."

"Sure, for the wood."

"Yep, and to be a hammer, cuz it has that flat side."

Fortunately the next thing on TV was a public service announcement for Brylcreem, so I could answer Del's question about why Sliver followed me up the tree right away.

"I saw he was mad again, and he was already mad at me once that day. So I climbed higher, where he couldn't go. He climbed to about the bottom of my feet and started tugging on the chain, but the strap broke and got tangled up with him. So he got madder. Plus he saw I had his axe and yelled at me to give it to him. So I threw it at him—and he sort of caught it over his head and that's when the ball lightning came rolling down the tree and everything disappeared. Then I woke up on the ground. I was deaf for a while too."

I showed him underneath my shirt where all the scratches were.

"Jesus, did you get those from falling?"

"I guess. Some of 'em."

"Do you think maybe your dad fell too?"

"Nope, cuz he wasn't under the tree when I woke up. Just me and the axe. I ain't seen him since."

Quinton a small town, if a storm passed over it, everybody remembered, so Del could recall the nearly two weeks since the last big one without being told, which was lucky for him because my story was back on the TV. Instead of keeping quiet this time, though, I started filling in *The Secret Storm* blanks for Del, which were plenty, this being his first episode and all. Who's that guy? What's wrong with that guy? Who's she related to again? are examples of annoying questions you don't want to keep answering for a full hour.

It's hard to fill in the important details to a story that's been running for a long time, because everything is connected in some way, all the way back to the beginning. There's hardly ever one character there for the hell of it this week and gone by next week's show. Pretty much everybody has an important purpose in *The Secret Storm*. If someone important simply disappeared, then everything would stop making sense. When the show ended, Del turned off the TV and asked me to gather up some clothes and stick them in a bag; he was going to take me for something to eat, he said. I reminded him that my underwear was in the shed, so he said he'd get them because he had a little more looking to do back there. When I came downstairs with my bag, Del was outside, over by the fence where the tall weeds grew. I think it used to be a garden, but me and Sliver never planted anything in it unless you want to count the animals his ladies gave me. I started walking toward him, but he raised his voice at me for the first and only time, shouting that I was to stay put. Not because he was mad, I don't think. Scared, it sounded like. He took a moment to poke his big black boot at something in the weeds, took the cloth from his coat, and covered his nose and mouth; he looked about ready to puke for real this time. When he realized I was standing not far behind him, he ran to me before I could get it into my head to go see what the big stink was. Squeezing my hand in his, he nearly dragged me out of the backyard and to his car.

"You all packed?" he asked finally, his voice kind of shaky and his face a little paler than before. He tried a smile when he saw my grocery bag for a suitcase, putting the clothes he took from the shed into it. In his hand was a piece of paper, and once we were in the car he read me a name and asked if I'd ever heard of it.

My eyes popped at the sound, a ghost's name.

"You know them?" Del repeated the names slowly, the pronouncing giving him trouble. Because it ended with a "ski" I could bob my head yes, no matter how much he mangled it.

"I think they belong to my mom."

"Okay, pard. Let's get out of here."

It'd been a long day for Del. He looked worn to the bone, which was how Sliver looked all the time, and also he described the animals he was about to knack. I'd put Del through his paces for sure, so who could blame him for having to catch his breath before we got underway? He let his hand rest on top of my head for what felt like a minute, double-checking the piece of paper in his other hand, until finally we backed down the driveway. I stared at the front door and crossed my fingers that he hadn't locked it. If somebody had a change of heart and decided to come back, I didn't want them to find the door locked.

Sliver's house is located a piece down British Chemical Road. I hadn't noticed the place when I walked past it a little while ago. The yard and driveway were all weeds, and the telephone line to the street had been cut, so I guess nothing connected my eye to the house the first time. Besides, my eyes were pretty cloudy after running from Mary Lynn's house, and I had enough on my mind connecting me to Sliver. I didn't have to go looking for it. But after my visit to the canal, plus a sedating butt, I'd cooled enough that I could deliver Mary Lynn's caftan to her and not do something Sliver-stupid, behaviour-wise. Because a caftan was a scaled-down version of my earlier delivery attempt to their house, maybe I'd actually be successful this time.

The front window had a big sheet of plywood across it, so I couldn't peek inside. Not that I would, except to check if our furniture was still in there. People tend to forget about the furniture when they're running away. I never thought it was such a bad little house. It wasn't bad at all, really, now that the worst of the inside had been exterminated. The outside work wouldn't be much chore, maybe a day for a two-person crew. A lot of the chores on the farm were two-person jobs. Even when I did something by myself— scraping out the chicken coop, for example—I was never far from somebody if I needed help. The only times I felt alone was in bed. Once in a while I got a sense that I didn't always sleep alone. Not every night, and more as if somebody had crawled in next to me while I slept. When I woke up in the morning, it was back to just me so I'd think these were dreams—an arm around me, a mouth breathing against the top of my head…then Bill would start singing and muddy the whole memory.

"This one's not for sale anymore, in case you were thinking of buying it."

Sealskin boots are annoyingly quiet. Mary Lynn had joined me in my circle of street light undetected. She was bundled in several layers of sweaters, the outermost one with a jazzy iron pattern on the back.

"Nah, not enough eggs for that," I admitted. "Oops. Sorry."

Mary Lynn looked at her boots now. "Nah. I am. I get cranky sometimes. I guess I was taking my bad day out on you." Then she delivered a light punch to my shoulder. "Even if you were the cause."

I sniffed my little laugh, then nodded toward the house. "Was it for sale?" I asked.

"Yeah, I think. It'd been boarded up for a while. Mom says the town used to own it because of taxes. Then some lady came along and bought it for a song."

I sucked on the last of my tiny smoke while considering how somebody else was about to take a shot at making something out of my old house. "Maybe she'll turn it into a clubhouse."

"A clubhouse? Why would anybody do that?"

"Lots of reasons. My grandparents go to the farmers' union lodge for bridge night." Actually, I thought cards was just an excuse for them and their escapees from Saskatchewan to get together once a month, exchange cabbage roll recipes, and bitch about the weather, but I left off that part of my reasoning because of how I'd already referred to farmers in the first part. I couldn't keep proving her point. "It'd be a place where people who got along could hang out, shoot the breeze."

"Maybe. Or maybe she's normal," Mary Lynn giggled.

"Yeah, maybe. Hey, how'd you know I was here?"

"I didn't—not until I got to the street and saw you fling-ing matches. You looked like you were trying to set the house on fire."

"It was windy. I couldn't get my smoke lit." I held out the caftan. "Here, I think this is yours."

"Oh," she said, quickly tucking it under her arm. "Thanks."

"Yeah, no prob. You're lucky it didn't blow into the canal."

"I guess. It's old."

"Lucky it's bright yellow too, or I'd never have seen it folded there."

Mary Lynn sighed, suspecting I might be leading some-where. "I just wanted to see if I could stop being afraid. You know, after what happened tonight on the bridge. I didn't mean anything else, if that's what you were thinking."

"No, I know. I don't mean half the stuff people think I mean." I took a deep breath and held it for a few seconds. Then I took a leap of my own: "I'm not like him, you know."

"Who?"

"My dad. I'm not like him either."

"It's okay if you're not. Anyway, I didn't mean anything by it."

"Yeah, but in case you thought maybe. You know, because of the trophy…and shit."

"Nope. Wouldn't even know him except from you bring-ing him up. We don't have much call for knackers around our house."

She let me stand there for another minute of what passed for peace and quiet around me, which was about all she could take of me possibly mumbling stuff. Maybe I don't think and talk the way most people should, by which I mean quietly, to myself. Maybe I'm one of those guys who talks his thoughts out loud, right before getting everything down on paper.

Mary Lynn took my hand and steered me back toward her house. "Let's go. I've got a life too, you know."

I didn't argue, and she didn't hold my gnarled mitt but for a moment. I let it slip free the second she tugged, didn't squeeze or anything. When her house came into view, so did the memory of our last few words there and the realization that she might not be too excited about having me hanging around her for too much longer, let alone her remaining high school years. I decided to offer her a glimmer of hope.

"Look on the bright side. I'm missing so many sacramental badges, your aunt won't want to graduate me anyway."

"She wouldn't care about that."

"I don't know. I don't think she likes me."

"Well, yeah, that I can believe, but she wouldn't care about the sacraments as much as what kind of kid you were. And your marks, I guess. You think they'll hold you back because you don't have all your badges? Which aren't badges, by the way, dummy. It's not like freaking Boy Scouts. Jesus, are you sure you go to St. Mary's?"

"No, I know they're not." I shrugged. "I also told her to suck my potatoes. That might be a last straw."

"You told her to suck your potatoes? Jesus, I'm surprised you're still alive. But you are, so I think you're in the clear."

Back inside, we will settle into our places on the couch and our final roles:

"Can I have another smoke?"

"Oh yeah, they're right there." I scooped the pack from the coffee table and passed her one from the new segment. Mary Lynn licked, then parted, her lips before sliding the filter between them.

"Light, please."

"Yep." I pulled out my matchbook and struck one. Mary Lynn sucked and sucked until the butt was glowing on its own. She sighed and sunk her head back against the couch, exhaling achingly slow.

When she began tapping her chin this time, I was already braced for anything she might have to say, for better or worse. "I guess what I really meant from before was, I think you worry too much about what people think and so don't give them enough time to think anything but what you're telling them. Do you know what I mean?"

"Yes?"

"I mean, let people catch their breath around you."

"Don't I?" I squinted, trying to follow the thread she unspooled.

"Not in the right way, I don't think. I don't know. I suppose all I mean is, just worry about you and people won't bother you."

"Yeah, that's not a problem when you're an orphan. I'm all I have, remember."

"That's not what I meant. Also, it's cool, in a weird way. I never met an orphan before. And it explains so much." Then came the soft titter a town girl would make if she'd thought of something witty to say—and then said it. Girls in Grade 9 can get away with insults like that, partly because they look more mature, so we tend to give their brains more credit than they deserve. From what I'd been hearing, Grade 9 boys are treated like boogers, so we have to either establish a reputation as something more than a booger, or else endure a ton of slags until we can fight back. I wasn't too worried about going into Grade 9 if slags and fights were all I had to worry about. I knew how to recognize real abuse from just pissing around, and I knew how to kick the snot out of people, especially if Trawl was the best they had.

"Just clam up—the best you can—and you'll do fine. Besides, I'll be there. If you get in trouble, which I don't doubt, you can tell them I'm your big sister. I'll say we adopted you."

I wasn't heartbroken by her interpretation, at least not in the way a guy should be when he discovers that he's related to the girl he's been pursuing for his whole life. Mary Lynn had just admitted that we could exist at the same time, in the same space. What's wrong with that? So, not heartbroken at all. Humbled, maybe. Even a theme essay expert has to admit defeat occasionally, or at least realize it when he learns he never had as much control over his theme as he thought he did.

Mary Lynn pulled up her sleeve and looked at a watch concealed there. "Shit," she said, and leaping to her feet, she disappeared up the stairs. A long minute later she was trotting down with some kind of canvas bag in her hand, a peace sign stitched onto the flap.

"What's with the suitcase?"

"It's a backpack."

"Whatever. Are you going somewhere?"

She ignored my question and went to the clothes hamper, separating what she wanted from the rest and jamming them into the backpack without even folding them.

"Got plans for the weekend?"

"Oh, don't worry your big ol' fuzzy head about my plans." She brushed at my fuzz and went back to the couch for her smoke.

"It's just, your mom's on her way, you know."

"I know. Do you think I could bum a couple of these for the road?"

"Smokes? Yeah, I got you a whole pack. They're in the kitchen."

"No shit?" She looked about to jump out of her socks. Sounded like she'd never owned her own pack before either.

"So, what road?" Though I knew already. It would be one of the dirt ones by the farm.

"Found 'em. Thanks!" She walked into the living room waving the smokes in the air, went to a cupboard at the base of the bookshelves, and pulled out a bottle of Royal Reserve and carried it back to the kitchen. There was a sound of running water and the fridge door opening and slamming shut.

"Did you drink my mix?"

"Your what?"

"Did you drink my mix? I had two cans of Crush in here for tonight. They're both gone."

"Oh yeah. I guess I did."

"Ah, shit. What am I supposed to use now?"

"I guess that depends on what you needed them for."

"I told you—mix. For the rye."

"Orange Crush? Jesus, drink much?" As a teetotaller I didn't touch the stuff, but I knew enough from watching Sliver and his women work their way through a bottle or two that the range of mix for rye ran in this order of preference: plain ice cubes, then water, then ginger ale, then Coke. That's all.

"Ah, what do you know about anything?" she growled, back from the kitchen in more of a huff this time. The Royal Reserve was somehow back at its original level, though slightly paler. She returned it to the cupboard.

I held out a dollar from my change. "Sorry about the drinks. Here's a buck." She could buy twice as many pops if she wanted. Mary Lynn stared at the bill dangling there, hopefully a little guilty for snapping at me. Her mood felt brighter.

"I don't want to take all your egg money."

"It's okay. And technically this is canary money."

"I guess we can stop on the way. Thanks."

"On the way? To the farm?" I knew who that "we" didn't include, but a fella could hope.

"Good one. No, I got plans, I said already. Who knows, though, the party might even be in one of your fields. It's that way somewhere. I'm not driving."

"Terrific. What am I supposed to tell your mom? She thinks I walked you home."

"Tell her mission accomplished."

"But you won't be here."

"So tell her I beat you up before I went out."

I sidled over to stand between her and the front door. But she came up fast and rubbed my head—for old time's sake and the distraction—and slipped past me. Like I said, people can't resist rubbing my head, especially a week after a haircut, when it looks most like an orange tennis ball. I've never gone without a brush cut, even as far back as I can remember, at least as far back as my cowboy photograph, which Gram likes to wave under my nose whenever she feels obliged to convince me I used to be a cute kid. Like the onion story, it makes her laugh, so I hang on to the photo, and the haircut, for that reason too. Seriously, if they've only been keeping me around this long for the yuks, I'm okay with it. As for cute, I suppose that's true too. Just not the way an actually cute kid gets judged as cute, posed on a pony all bug-eyed and pale-shiny for the camera like a plop of fresh cream. Back then, I was worn-to-the-bone cute. I'm a little less so now.

I lit a smoke and waved it under her nose. "Whaddaya say. One for the road, toots?"

"Sure, why not," she said, except her arms and coat were so bound up with the straps from the backpack that she looked like a T. Rex. I stuck the cigarette between her lips, which she'd parted for me. Man oh man.

I followed her outside. She walked to the curb and looked up and down the street—first in the glowing downtown direction and then in the direction of the canal. Maybe I should've said something about me and Donna Mae. It might have given me a little more value in her eyes, bought time with all the hugs, until her mom got home. But that's not how real heroes behave, and anyway headlights appeared on that very road. Mary Lynn waved the car in for a landing.

"My ride's here," she said.

"I see."

"Thanks for saving the house and junk."

"Yeah, no prob."

"Are you gonna wait here for mom?"

"Yeah, I probably should. I'll need a lift outta here."

"Are you gonna tell?"

"I...I don't know. Nah, I'm okay with you beating me up."

"Well no, just tell her you did your job. Period."

Story of my life.

The car's tires scraped against the curb before grinding to a stop. Trawl leaned on the horn for about five seconds; his teeth shone in the dark above the steering wheel.

"Tell the whole world, why don't you," Mary Lynn grumbled, which naturally forced him to lean on the horn even longer. Jerk.

Mary Lynn struggled with her backpack again, so I went over to help. Trawl's eyes narrowed when he recognized me.

The driver's-side door popped open and he ran around to grab Mary Lynn's pack from my hands.

"Get your grubby little farm hands off my stuff," he growled. "Sorry I'm late, babe. The bridge is out. I had to take the highway." (He meant the 401, which everybody used to bypass Quinton at 120 miles an hour, unless they absolutely had no choice but to come here.) I could smell the booze on him.

He was wearing a suede coat now, with long suede fringes across the chest and along the bottom seam. His blue jeans had the widest bells I'd ever laid eyes on. The belt was looped around his pants but also about halfway down the crack of his ass, which was a style that had made its way here from Winnipeg. Very hippie.

"I said, get yer…"

"Yeah, yeah, yeah. Yer stuff."

Mary Lynn found herself wiggled between me and Trawl once more. She pushed him this time, which he wasn't expecting. Not very hard, but enough that his heel caught the curb. Down he went, arms flailing every which way. Hilarious stuff. Naturally I snorted loud enough for him to hear.

"Christ, are you fucking stupid?" Trawl hollered.

Mary Lynn glared. I knew from experience she resented being spoken to in such a manner. If she'd had her hammer with her, I'll bet she would've used his head for a nail.

"Don't ever talk to me like that," Mary Lynn seethed, and picked up her backpack.

Trawl scrambled to his feet and opened the passenger door, pretty obviously meaning to slam it shut once she was inside. "Let's go," he commanded.

I saw her shoulders dip a little. I knew the look, recognized it from forever ago, so before she could get to the door I booted it shut. "Maybe she doesn't wanna."

"Maybe you should fuck off. Get in the car, Mary Lynn."

"Do you really wanna go with this asshole?" I asked, because who was I to tell her what to do.

Trawl glowered. "Kid, you're this close to losing your teeth."

"You wanna shake on it?"

Boy, did that piss him off. He came at me with his one good fist up. Remembering how my trophy might do as a hammer in a pinch, I pulled it out of my belt and shook it at him, marble bottom up.

"Calm down," I told him. "Or I'll plant this."

Mary Lynn screamed at both of us to stop it, so when I lowered my trophy, Trawl lowered his mitt and turned his anger on her, pissed that she hadn't yet done what she was told.

"Jump in, I said."

Mary Lynn opened the creaky old door and slid into the passenger seat. Her hair, being clouded by the mist on the outside of the window, seemed to float mid-air, just like Donna Mae's had in the canal, which broke my heart into a million pieces again. I waited until Trawl was nicely seated behind the wheel before me and my trophy went for a stroll around the perimeter of his car, smashing both his headlights and both his tail lights along the way. With my final and most emphatic whack, however, the little figurines broke off in my hand, the heftiest part of the trophy landing on the road in one long, solid piece, leaving Mom and Dad as the only piece still in my hand. Rather than chuck them, I stuck the happy runner-up couple in my pocket for the keepsake-hell of it.

Trawl came screaming out of the car and skidded on the broken headlight glass, nearly falling flat again.

"Are you fucking stupid?" he cried. (I'd lost count of how

many times I'd been asked that question by Sliver over the years, so the insult had zero sting.)

Something I should have anticipated but didn't was him flicking his cigarette in my eye, pretty expertly I might add, which leads me to believe that Trawl and the troll might be related somehow. Maybe Trawl was the troll, or son of troll, like how I have a little Sliver in me. (I worried about that all the time, what kind of adult I'd become, if my past might infect my future spinoffs.) Anyway, when a heater explodes in your eye, you feel the sting immediately, so while I was digging the heels of my hands into my socket, Trawl snatched up the main trophy from the ground and smacked me right across the sweet spot of my temple with its hard marble base.

In conclusion, part one:

In every way possible I'm running out of time now, so to bring this to a tidy conclusion the rest will have to come fast. Trawl took off, natch. The sight of blood will do that to a Quinton coward. He went on foot because of all his car's lights being busted. Mary Lynn ran to me and put my head in her lap, using her caftan to try and stop the bleeding, but there was quite a bit and my head was leaking pretty good, even for me. All she accomplished was to ruin that pretty, no longer very yellow, sweater. I was comfortable, though. Best I'd felt since she'd held my hand. Her mom and Donna Mae pulled into the driveway a few seconds later, so her mom took over the nursing duties, which was fine because Mary Lynn had used up all her ideas in the leaking-Kaspar department. Not that her mom could do much more. We were on a sidewalk, for fuck's sake.

In conclusion, the one for good ol' Donna Mae:

You, good ol' Donna Mae, are as carefree as ever. Your bright yellow snowsuit rustles whenever you move. Look at you, yawning. Poor kid, you should've been in bed hours ago. When you take my hand, you tell me how cold and wet it is, and I guess that's enough to spark your chatterbox, because now you blab the whole canal business and the game we played with your dad, a whole run-on sentence of spilled beans because you're so tired. Your mom and Mary Lynn are too stunned to speak at first, so pretty much it's just you yakking like a champ. Seems they've never heard this part of the story, the part that features me. The deal is big enough to Mary Lynn, though, who finally sees that buckaroo she met all those years ago. I like to think that's your point too. How first impressions don't tell the whole story, and how we should hold off making judgments, or forcing ours on others, until we have the entire body of work to hold the impressions up against. That's what I try to tell you now, in case you want to disagree, but I hear everybody else whispering *hush, Kass, hush*. They can't make out my gurgling, not like you. You've been paying attention this whole time, haven't you? You tell me I should take a nap. You don't quite say our little race is over, but I think I know what you mean. I guess I am a little tired. You are an excellent storyteller, by the way, with a nice, matter-of-fact tone to your delivery. You let everybody know how this isn't about anybody being heroic or brave or unusual. When they are gawking, first at me, then at you, and all your mom can get out at the end of your story is "Why didn't you say something?" either at you or me or us both, you shrug on both of our behalves. "What was he supposed to do?" you say.

In conclusion, for us as one big, happy family, finally:

Hey, Del is here! That's nice. It's like a birthday party with everybody who was invited showing up. He arranges the ambulance. He says he'll go get Gram and Grumps and bring them to the hospital. Better make it the morgue, Del. Ha! Nah, I don't gurgle that. I think Mary Lynn's mom and Del make a nice couple. Everybody looks like a whole family, huddled here around me. I'd have killed to be a part of a nice whole family, but for whatever reason, and nobody's fault, I didn't get to have one, until now, I mean. What I have with Gram and Grumps is pretty good, though not the same as what I've been imagining for so long. I hope I've had a little to do with building this one, if it happens. I'm going to say it will.

I realize that even if you are huddled inside a real family, it's possible you still won't belong. Maybe it's impossible for certain people to be happy for very long. Maybe every family has its shitty stuff: somebody who jumps into a canal, or bolts for Spring Valley, Saskatchewan, or takes swings at kids. Maybe there are no perfect, Primrose families, and "a little screwy" is the perfectly normal way of things. Ah, I don't know if I'd want to include that last bit in this theme essay. I'll leave it up to you to decide.

Everybody except Del piles into the ambulance with me: Mary Lynn, her mom, and Donna Mae, pushing the attendant away to the back. Mary Lynn's mom can take pretty serious charge of a situation, even when she smells like coffee and French fries. She screams all kinds of demands at the attendant and he can only tell her to stay calm, to relax, which, as you've learned already, is a huge mistake. Mary Lynn is the one who shouts, "Don't tell us to relax!" She does hate being told that. Donna Mae pipes up with a reminder for me to not forget about her Christmas play, and just for the hell of it begins humming "I Saw Three Ships," the Christmas carol. That gets me thinking about my real mom again. And the canal. I've pretty much decided that she had to escape, headed up the canal, horse or no horse, and that's fine. I want her to be okay, and since this is my essay, that's how she's going to be: the Pine who made it out alive. This way, when she comes back, after she's found safety or whatever she needed in Spring Valley, she and Gram can plant a Kaspar tree. Gram can tell her, "They called him Kass."

Finally, I should add a bit about how I may have been not totally fair to canaries, or at least may have given people the wrong impression about them. Just because they're the world's cheapest pet, that doesn't mean they don't have value. There's a lot to be said for singing for the crazy joy of living and being nothing more than what you are. It's not up to canaries to throw themselves into burning buildings, to let us know that shit's about to come down. Maybe they're just too innocent to survive. Like how Grumps's chickens didn't know more than what chickens were supposed to know, but got stoned for not knowing what I knew. So I guess I'm not such hot shit either. You can leave that part in, if you like...

I've gone way over my word limit, or maybe I'm just running out of air. Maybe if I smoked less... Ha, not likely. Mary Lynn sees me struggling to find a good conclusion, so she leans over me; her mouth is wrapping around mine. I think she means to give me something. Now I have what I want, the two most important things I can leave you with: her breath tastes like cigarettes, and I am very happy.

ACKNOWLEDGMENTS

I acknowledge that I have two kids, Joey and Julie, and they are perfect.

A portion of this book first appeared in *Grain Magazine* (Zen and the Art of Chicken Maintenance). I will be forever grateful to the magazine, and especially editor at the time Adam Pottle for publishing it and offering suggestions. *Parenthetical: the zine* was also kind enough to publish a small piece, and so my thanks to Will Kemp and Nicole Brewer, too.

Important people who have made me a better writer generally must include Kathryn Mockler (plus the gang in her writer's group who offered notes for much of the novel's opening sequence of canary-related events), Bethany Gibson, who has to be be as surprised as anybody about this book, given what she has read of other things of mine, and the never surprised Ruth Zuchter, who always said the book would get published. And Angie Abdou and Anita Dolman, who had cracks at an earlier version and still managed to speak kindly on it and my behalf.

A special thank-you goes out to Amanda Earl as well, for her writerly kindnesses over the years, which includes publishing my chapbook.

Sounding board/chit-chat pals Patti Leclerc and Brigitte Granton have no idea how much I love being able to annoy them about nothing at all. And sometimes the Habs. And sometimes painting.

The canary "Doris" is named after my mother. "Austin" didn't survive the final edits. (Sorry, Dad.)

Finally, Leigh Nash is the single greatest person on the planet. Well, the book publishing, book editing part of it where *The Union of Smokers* and I got to hang out and become so much better. But probably also the rest of the planet.

INVISIBLE PUBLISHING produces fine Canadian literature for those who enjoy such things. As an independent, not-for-profit publisher, our work includes building communities that sustain and encourage engaging, literary, and current writing.

Invisible Publishing has been in operation for over a decade. We released our first fiction titles in the spring of 2007, and our catalogue has come to include works of graphic fiction and non-fiction, pop culture biographies, experimental poetry, and prose.

We are committed to publishing diverse voices and experiences. In acknowledging historical and systemic barriers, and the limits of our existing catalogue, we strongly encourage LGBTQ2SIA+, Indigenous, and writers of colour to submit their work.

Invisible Publishing is also home to the Bibliophonic series of music books and the Throwback series of CanLit reissues.

If you'd like to know more, please get in touch:
info@invisiblepublishing.com

Invisible